The Adani Chronicles

BIRTHRIGHT

Megan R Graham

For Joy! Keep smiling, and hold Keep up the great work, It's worth out for your fairy tale. It's worth every minute of struggle, all of it!

Lots of Love,
Meg

PS— Don't ever let anything out beat that sunny disposition of you. It's rare, and the world needs more of it. ♡

DEDICATION

To Mom and Dad, for never letting me give less than my best.

To Nova and Chrissie, my partners in crime.

To James, my dream.

ACKNOWLEDGMENTS

There are dozens of people without whom this novel would never have happened. Ash pushed me to write that first, whim-based chapter three years ago; Summer saw me through the first several drafts; Nova has smacked me upside the head when I needed it and Chrissie has poked and prodded when I got sick of writing. James has shown me the meaning of true partnership.

Any acknowledgment of the writing of this book, however, would be remiss without mention of those people who brought me here. My parents have been unendingly supportive, as they have been since the day I came to them, and for them I am eternally and indescribably grateful. My sister Caitie has provided motivation; my brother Travis, encouragement; and my sister Sam, perspective. I am honored to be part of the Graham clan and everything that means.

Finally, I am incredibly grateful to all those who read drafts of this beast, who stood by me when writing it got difficult, who gave me advice and corrections within the story itself. Without all of you, this would still be an unnamed file on my laptop that I'd fiddle with now and then.

I am so very grateful.

PROLOGUE

The night's dew made the grass slick; Deoryn Ai'Hael stumbled as she blocked a heavy blow aimed for her head. It was a costly error; the nagrat brute she was fighting slammed his club against her back, knocking the air from her lungs. She found herself on her hands and knees fighting for breath; vaguely heard a snarl as Kota tackled the creature, savaging it with his razor-sharp claws. Her vision cleared in time to see it fall, all shredded skin and blood.

It was almost an improvement from how it usually looked. Nagrat were gray-skinned, hairless, bulky creatures that resembled men, if a man had been disassembled, damaged beyond repair, and then mushed back together haphazardly. Their only drives were to hunt and to serve their Val'gren masters; looting, kidnapping, and attacking travelers along the small roads that crisscrossed Laendor and its surrounding countries. Ryn felt no remorse at all culling the barbarians.

She was tired. The strain of the weeks-long hunt was in her black knotted staff, exhausted arms shaking with each blow she dealt. It was in Kota's breaths, heavy as he panted in between victories. It was in her feet, sore and swollen with too many miles traveled in too short a time.

The woman grunted as she forced her legs to obey her; to lift her from the soaked ground and stand to meet her next foe.

It was a near thing; she barely got her balance before a massive, chipped battleaxe came flying at her head. Ryn rolled without thinking, came up with her back against a stunted, splintery tree, cursing.

She had definitely lost the element of surprise, she had to move fast.

Save the younglings.

It was her driving force, what kept her moving much farther north and west than she cared to travel, deep into Val'gren territory. It was the reason she and Kota had run themselves ragged, braving storm and beast and heartless terrain, and the very thing that had led them to this craggy boulder field where the nagrat had pitched camp. It was what kept her pressing forward even now, despite the pain, the big ugly brutes in her way, and odds that were not stacked in her favor.

The brother and sister.

Victims of unhappy circumstance, like so many others in these lands, but nothing more than strangers to her. Their caravan attacked and parents slaughtered on the road, and they themselves kidnapped to be delivered to the Val'gren, a sacrifice to their god, Skeðu.

Children, of an age to her own brother when he had died. She could not let them go, not without giving her fullest measure of skill, courage, and resolve to save them. It would be akin to abandoning *him*.

Ryn snarled, shook off her own ghosts, focused on the battle before her.

Nagrat prisoners were kept in the center of camps to prevent escape or rescue, so that's where she set her gaze. She found it almost immediately, a ragged shelter comprised of hide and wooden stakes—

Her heart thumped hard as she spotted one of the few remaining monsters stagger toward that little shelter, knife in its hand, death in its expression. She drew her bow and let fly her arrow toward it. Her aim was true, and barely in time. She heard the prisoners screech their terror as the monster fell half-into the shelter, her arrow buried in his temple.

Another nagrat rushed her from the left, and it took long enough to deal with him that Ryn grew frustrated.

Hurry, hurry.

The nagrat intercepted the swing she took at his head, grabbing her staff and yanking it from her grip entirely. He smiled at Ryn's growl, beady black eyes squinted with vicious mirth.

If he thought her disarmed, he was sorely mistaken.

With a scrape of steel against leather, her hunting knife was in her hand. Ryn stabbed high, into the thing's chest, aiming between the ribs. It was a wild blow; too wild, for the blade struck the monster's sternum instead and broke jaggedly.

Ryn grunted angrily as the nagrat howled in agony; she yanked the knife out and tried again, an inch lower and two to the right. This time the broken steel met its target, sinking to the hilt in the nagrat's heart.

Pain exploded on the left side of Ryn's face, and she found herself sprawled against a rock, sucking in ragged breaths and blinking hard. The brute she had stabbed was on his knees, snarling at her, the death blow having sapped the last of his waning strength. She watched him die wordlessly, trying to get her bearings. It took her a moment to realize the battle was won. The nagrat were dead.

Only now did she notice the tiny pinpricks of cold on her exposed face, the shrill howl of the wind, the unyielding rock surface she had landed on— and exactly how bad it had hurt. She groaned as she pushed herself upright and straightened. Her ribs twanged painfully on the back of her right side;

she would bruise spectacularly, she could tell already.

Kota trotted to her, his face bloodied and his stubby tail high. Her lynx was still on guard; his tufted ears twitched this way and that, alert for any sign of danger. Ryn scratched between his shoulder blades—praise for a job well done—as she cast about, locating the prisoner's shelter again. Her last skirmish had pushed her further away from it, as she was sure it had been intended to.

For all the good it had done. Now the nagrat were all dead and she had *won*.

Her lynx whined, his bloody nose pressing to her thigh in concern. Ryn shushed him; no time for triage until the mission was complete.

She stumbled to the ragged little pavilion. The flap was heavy, cold and wet from the freezing rain, and Ryn's shoulder screeched a protest as she pulled it back.

The world shrank to a pinpoint. Ryn's knees hit the hard stone.

She didn't even feel it.

I

There was a sliver of moonlight through the window, cutting a path through the inky darkness of the night and spilling across a freshly abandoned bed. Hymns of mourning weaved alongside the early morning's hush in a haunting, somber harmony. Torchlight bounced and flickered off stone walls, casting shadows as a tall figure moved noiselessly into the cold, dark catacombs under the castle.

It was too soon; much too soon for him to be visiting here—folk would talk, and now more than ever, that mattered—but he found himself unable to muster concern for others' opinions, not when the nightmare was so fresh, his reality so recently and so irrevocably changed. Not when his earlier meeting with his brother had gone exactly as he had expected it would; exactly as he had feared. He needed someone to talk to, and Gunnar had been his confidante since they were children. Old habits were difficult to abandon, he was learning.

He steadied his breathing forcibly when he reached the arched doorway that led to his destination. It was too soon; much too soon for him to be leaving on such a quest; but Gunnar had left him no choice, Uncle Eirik had left him no choice, and life hadn't *asked* him what was appropriate or what he wanted.

A single large stone sepulcher stood to the right of the door; his cousin was the first of their generation to be buried here. His father, uncle, and aunt were in the next room; his grandfather and his generation in the room beyond that, all the way to the end of the impossibly long hall, where were buried the most ancient of Laendorian Kings. The young man moved to the tomb, brushed an errant bit of dust off the hard polished surface with the backs of his fingers.

"He won't listen to me."

The words were whispered, but seemed over-loud in the silence of that place. He inhaled slowly, a beaten sound broken by a hitch of grief, and the normally-imposing man curled in on himself; a calloused hand resting on too-new, too-clean white marble.

"He refuses to be dissuaded," he forged ahead, quietly. "The road is perilous, so many things can happen, and my soul tells me all will be revealed before the end." The firelight from a nearby torch made a lone tear shine against a ruddy cheek. "Why, cousin? We had an agreement, and this was not part of it." His furrowed brow met the rounded edge of the Prince's pyre, and his shoulders shook despondently.

"It was never supposed to be like this."

~~~~~~~~~~

"I'll give ye twenty silvers for the lot, and that's th' final offer you'll git, miss." The burly tanner sniffed, looking Ryn up and down disapprovingly. She knew what he was staring at. Her darker coloring was unheard of this far north, and the knife scar that ran from her upper lip to her ear was far from subtle. The cut, given years ago, had been vicious and deep, and Ryn hadn't managed to get it properly sutured before it healed, so it was a thick, raised white mark that contrasted sharply with her bronze skin and even browner freckles. Add to that the fact that she was at least a span taller than the tanner, her travel-worn clothes peppered liberally with various blades and a wicked-looking staff, and Ryn supposed she did look a bit dangerous.

Dangerous, and probably tired. She'd started awake that morning, breathing hard and covered in a cold sweat, to the feeling of Kota purring and mewling in her face. The sun had shone in her eyes, and she blinked at the mid-morning light, cursing quietly under her breath as her companion nosed her again, his whiskers tickling her skin. She'd pushed at him, all seventy stone weight of fur and muscle.

The siblings, she knew they were why she had recently been plagued by nightmares. The little ones she had tracked so far, fought off an entire hunting party of nagrat for, the bruised ribs she still was trying to recover from nearly two weeks later. And all for nothing, for her to lift that heavy flap to find the girl on top of the boy with her arms thrown out as though to protect him; and the ugly splintered spear that impaled them both together. Hastily executed by their captors, the nagrat's twisted code of honor dictating that they kill the young hostages lest they be stolen back. It had cost her every night of sleep since then, that loss.

And here she was, arguing with a tanner whose most pressing problem was that he didn't want to pay a fair price to a foreigner. She clenched her jaw at the offer, doing her best to stifle a sigh of frustration. These were buck hides, of good cut and quality, and it had been harder than usual to acquire them this time round.

"They're worth at least forty," she protested, careful not to sound too offended.

She was nobody in particular, here—nobody everywhere, really—and many merchants didn't like buying from a wanderer who looked like she belonged in the mild tropics of Southdale more than the mountainous north of Laendor. Ryn thought that a bit unfair, as many Laendorians who traveled a lot or lived in the southern regions of their country tended to be the same color as she; for all this man knew, it was entirely possible that she had been sired by a citizen of Laendor. She hadn't, but he didn't know that. She couldn't remember why her kingdom and their southern neighbors were so at odds most of the time, and honestly she could not have possibly cared less; but the tanned skin of the Southdalers was her curse, regardless of whether it meant she was foreign or not.

"Shan't give ye more than twenty," the tanner was speaking again, accent growing thicker as he became agitated. Ryn shrugged and gathered her hides.

"Very well then, I'll just take these elsewhere. I heard old Hackett, up the road, is a tanner too."

Ryn turned to leave, hefting the hides over her shoulder and wincing at her still-sore wrist. She made it five steps before his gruff voice called, "Aye, and as cheap and paltry a tanner as ye could hope fer!"

"But he'll pay fair price for hide of this quality!" she shouted back, not stopping.

She kept walking, waited a beat.

"Lass!"

Ryn cocked an eyebrow and turned, slowly. The man sighed.

"Fine, I'll give ye forty for 'em."

"Hackett will give me forty," she rejoined coolly.

The tanner's dark eyes narrowed in his rotund face. "Forty-five then, but no more." He didn't look happy about it, but Ryn didn't need him to be happy. She just needed him to pay her.

A quarter hour later, she left the tanner's, ten hides lighter and forty-five silvers tucked into her hip pouch. Along with what she'd earned from her dried herbs and salves, it was more than enough to restock her provisions; food, what medicines she couldn't make herself, new boots, and repair on a bowstring. All were wares readily found in a town this size, and she spent the rest of the morning doing just that. The vendors were slightly more willing to *sell* to her—coin was coin, after all, regardless of where one was from—than they were to buy, so it was an easy few hours. When her business was concluded, Ryn stopped to eat a midday meal, her first of the day, in the town square.

The fight with the nagrat hunters had left her worn and sore. Ryn had almost been certain her right wrist was broken, though the swelling had gone down so much the first night she suspected it had only been a sprain after all. By now, it was mostly healed. She might be able to draw her bow well enough to hunt for her dinner tonight, she observed. Her ribs still pained her slightly, and she sported several lacerations and quite a few bruises that had already gone yellow. More troublesome than the injuries, though, was the exhaustion. Her head ached almost constantly and her eyes burned; she *needed* a good night's sleep. Resting her head on her palm as she awaited the lunch she had requested, Ryn looked about the small town square.

Dreyfen was a smallish village on the eastern fringes of Sannfold, near the banks of the River Rena. Nearer, Ryn thought, to the volatile, rushing body of water than any sane person would set up a homestead; but the townsfolk didn't seem to mind the river, thriving on the moist, verdant shores. Many of the wood huts that passed for buildings stood on thick wood posts that were driven beneath the sand and soft dirt, into the bedrock below. The posts were treated with tar before being used as elevated foundations, to help prevent the water from softening and destroying them over time. The huts themselves were of light wood and thatched roofs, thin to match the mild seasons and easy to rebuild should one be destroyed by the flooding.

The entire effect was rather ridiculous, in Ryn's opinion, surrounded by huts on stilts that put her in mind of storks more than man-made structures.

Still, there was a certain hardy stubbornness to the folk of Dreyfen that appealed to her. Certainly they were a grumpy, suspicious lot, and they didn't much like anything out of the ordinary, but then all of that was to be expected. Usually, in places like this, 'out of the ordinary' meant dangerous, or at least troublesome. This wasn't a large city, with nobles and armies and games and shows, always something new and exciting. Folk led simple lives in these little huts, and simple lives meant simple habits, with simple pleasures enjoyed sparingly. Probably the most exciting thing to happen in Dreyfen's living memory was the bi-annual flooding of the Rena, which meant a bi-annual migration out of the river valley and into the townsfolk's temporary dwelling further west. And yet, they refused to take the easier path and simply relocate, instead forcing the land to work for them as much as it worked against them, accepting their hardships and transforming them into boons.

This, Ryn could appreciate.

In addition, they knew how to season their crayfish. Ryn thanked the serving girl who brought her platter and allowed herself a moment to savor the dance of flavors on her tongue, buttery and boldly spiced. A lifestyle as economical as hers—even less indulgent than the citizens of Dreyfen's— left little room for luxuries like spices, so she enjoyed them every opportunity she got.

As delicious as the local fare was, however, Ryn did not linger over it. She suppressed the now-natural urge to reach down and bury her fingers in Kota's thick pelt, missing her friend. They had discovered quickly after she found the cub four years prior—or he'd found her, as it were—that people did not generally take kindly to a wild cat in their inns and stables. After the second time she'd had to save the rowdy, snarling bundle of fur from an angry proprietor, she'd started leaving him outside the towns she visited. They hated the arrangement, both of them; but much of her life had consisted of making the most of arrangements she hated, so she was used to it. Kota was undoubtedly hunkered down in the woods outside Dreyfen, awaiting her return patiently, or perhaps hunting down a hare to eat.

She placed her mug and her money on the table and slipped out. If she hurried, she and Kota could still make Woodhall by dark. She'd not leave him again so soon, but there was a certain copse of trees just outside the town that would house them nicely for the night.

2

The men were hidden in the thick undergrowth several leagues north of the road, arguing quietly. Not twenty paces in front of them, a mountain troll snored loudly in the glade, tainting the sweet-smelling air with his musk and smashing the delicate wildflowers beneath his tough, leathery bulk. Brandt Signyson, the elder of the two, was attempting to talk some sense into his younger brother, though admittedly without much success.

This struck him as not unusual.

"It's not worth it! Let's just move on," he whispered urgently, adjusting his leather pack as he shifted his weight on the balls of his feet, ready to leave. They had a mission, after all, that in no way included plundering troll hoards.

"Come, Brandt!" The younger was grinning, gold eyes twinkling with anticipation. "Where is your sense of adventure? Mountain trolls always have the best loot!"

Brandt looked to the heavens, knowing full well the motion would incense Evin. "Yes, and they guard it fiercely! Do you relish the idea of being turned into a midday meal?"

As expected, Evin narrowed his eyes in irritation. "You speak as though the two of us together are no match for a simple troll. As though we could not sneak the brute's plunder out from under his nose without so much as waking him!"

"Perhaps we could, perhaps we could not," Brandt countered, blue eyes hard. "But I am saying that it would be foolish to try."

"Ach!" came the exasperated response. "As are many things, and yet we try them anyway!"

"Hush, not so loud! Evin, we have a quest. We cannot simply—"

The younger man held up a finger to forestall Brandt, who paused, but looked to continue the argument. Evin spoke up before he had the chance.

"Aye, brother. But we can." And with that, he broke cover, leaving his older brother cursing in the bushes.

The idiot had left his bow and quiver resting against a nearby shrub.

"Evin!" Brandt hissed, poking his golden head over the tops of the underbrush, holding the bow above his head with one hand and pointing at it with the other.

Left your weapon behind. Again.

Evin, the lout, was already picking his way carefully toward the sleeping troll, utilizing every hunter's skill he possessed to make his steps silent. At Brandt's whispered shout, he turned and shushed him silently but fiercely, with exaggerated movements that suggested very clearly the younger's plans for the elder if he woke the creature with his mothering. Brandt could read his brother's thoughts as clearly as if he'd shouted them.

I've got my sword, muttonhead.

Brandt had half a mind to shout at him, just to be contrary; but as annoying as Evin was, he really didn't want him smashed beyond recognition by a mountain troll. The indignity would be more than even his idiot brother deserved.

Not to mention, Mother would kill him.

So he gestured back furiously, making it clear to Evin in no uncertain terms that he was responsible for this mess, when it became a mess; because it would and he knew it because he was the eldest and *how come younger brothers never listen, anyway?*

Evin grinned at him, the numbskull, and turned back to his sneaking, managing to make it past the slumbering, slobbering monstrosity without so much as a sound. The troll snored on, a rumbling, wet din that would cause any civilized human being to cringe in disgust. The mucus that blocked the thing's nose and caused such an unholy racket covered the entire lower half of its face. Its mouth lolled open, revealing a thick gray tongue which vibrated in time with its snores.

Brandt made a face and turned his attention back to Evin, who promptly tripped over a collection of swords standing precariously against the stone ledge the troll was using as a makeshift shelter. The clatter was loud enough to wake the dead, and certainly loud enough to rouse a living creature that was viciously protective of its loot.

He closed his eyes, pinched the bridge of his nose, and didn't bother silencing the groan that rose in his throat. Mother was going to outright *murder* him. They would find pieces of him strewn across the fields. The farmers would be traumatized. He didn't see the troll wake completely, but he sure heard it. The thing came alive with a monstrous roar of rage that it was not alone anymore.

Ah, damn.

He did, however, see his brother skid to a stop beside him, reaching for

Elizaveta

nking hard. Evin was holding a slightly curved dagger in one
ndt had never seen before—the entirety of their spoils from
an.

this was a bad idea!" he shouted as he stumbled to his feet,
smashing random trees and boulders in the background, a fit
at being wakened so rudely.

Evin's expression was pure mischief. "Congratulations, brother, on your
continued talent at always being right! Would you like a reward? Or a title,
perhaps?"

"Oh, shut it," Brandt growled.

Evin opened his mouth to continue needling, but let out a shout of
surprise instead when a massive oak club—the troll's crude weapon—
struck the ground to his right with a resounding thud.

Brandt yelped too: he'd felt that in his bones, and it hadn't even hit him.
"Run!" he shouted, thrusting Evin in front of him with nary a thought and
chasing the younger man away from the creature that had evidently just
figured out who was responsible for its aborted nap.

They ran, years of playing in the woods outside their estate working in
their favor now. Tree roots, pebbles, underbrush; all of it was a potential
fall, yet they managed to keep their footing as they slowly began to outstrip
the monster in pursuit. Mountain trolls were massive and not very
coordinated, so it was honestly a bit like watching a fully-grown man chase
a baby rabbit or a mouse; the troll had size and speed, but lacked the
dexterity to manage catching them. Too, it had to use its club to clear a
path, since it was far too large to fit between the trees in the thick forest.

Evin glanced back, saw the lead they had gained, and grinned again.
"How about Sir Brandt the Neverwrong?"

Brandt gritted his teeth. "Evin, I swear by Aeos—"

"Sir Brandt Mostwisest."

"I'm going to take your head for a trophy in a moment!" he threatened,
growling when the younger laughed, put on a burst of speed, and
disappeared into the brush ahead of him.

Blasted younger brothers.

~~~~~~~~~~

Ryn secured her bedroll onto the bottom of her pack with more force
than was strictly necessary. Another night of nightmares, another morning
waking in a cold sweat, another day of searching for the parasite who was
abusing the memory of her sweet brother.

After refreshing a bit in the freezing river and tossing a strip of dried
meat to Kota, Ryn sat down under a tree to eat a small breakfast and take
stock of herself. Her trip to Dreyfen had been exactly what she needed to

refit her gear, but since then she had been doing little more than wandering. The anniversary of her family's deaths always made for a depressing week this time of year, and combined with the little ones she'd just failed, she was having a harder time than usual this time around.

Ryn sighed, made a face at the carras fruit in her hand, and tossed it under a tree for the birds to finish. She was no longer hungry, and it was time to get moving anyway. Her fingers drifted to her pocket, the shape and weight of the wooden toy coin inside refocusing her like little else could. The trail was growing cold and she wasn't sure where to look next. But yesterday had borne her a very thin lead that the seller might be in Easton, one of the last towns along the Great Road before the Sands.

"Looks like we're headed east, *kisa*," she muttered to her companion, managing a small smile at the silly endearment. The old women called their housecats 'kisa', and Kota was so far from a mild housecat that it just made the nickname ridiculous. Not that he cared, she thought as her lynx rolled around in the fragrant grass, purring, but it made her grin. She took amusement, like spiced food, where she could find it.

Kota froze, then shot to his feet, ears rotating and every sense alert as he regarded the surrounding woods with intelligent eyes—far more intelligent than his simple wild cat heritage warranted, or so Ryn always thought. Or maybe that was just a product of being raised by a human, even one as solitary and odd as she.

Kota's stubby tail bristled and he bared his teeth, but stayed silent. Having learned long ago the lynx could sense things she could neither see nor hear, Ryn shouldered her pack and bow. She dropped into a defensive stance with her long staff and faced the same direction as Kota, watching and listening. Distantly, she heard shouts, and a loud cracking noise thundered through the air. Then another, and another, and an ear-splitting roar cut through the air, freezing the blood in her veins. Kota hopped back, growling.

"Kota, let's go," she murmured tightly, backing up, preparing to run. The lynx snarled his agreement and turned at the same moment Ryn did, off like a shot, powerful hind legs sending him into the trees before she even got up good speed. She followed, only to feel something slam into her left side as soon as she hit the tree line. She tumbled to the ground, registered a low shout of alarm before her assailant landed atop her in a heap of leather and short dark curls. Ryn yelped and shoved, surprised to find herself assisted by another, a burly, puffing man; he was pulling at the one that had run into her, shouting at him.

"Come on, you idiot, we have to go *now!*"

The dark-haired one stumbled upright, and she registered the split-second impression of honey-gold eyes and smirking lips before he tossed her a wink as he answered. "Couldn't help it. Saw a pretty girl."

14

"By the astra—" the second man muttered, shoving him forward—*run, for Aeos' sake!*—and reaching down, fingers closing around Ryn's arm. "Come on!"

A snarl sounded a split-second warning as Ryn yanked her arm away. Shock widened the man's blue eyes when Kota pounced, landing between him and the lass on the ground, but the sound of trees crashing behind them broke the moment.

The man gave her an almost pleading look, still breathing hard. "Please, come!"

Ryn was on her feet before he even finished his request, and they were running, side by side, catching up with the dark-haired one quickly. He looked back, mischief written all over his face, and grinned.

"Bit slow in your old age, brother-mine!"

"Shut it and run, you idiot! If it weren't for your stupid plan, we'd not be running at all!"

Ryn wondered at these two, sprinting through the woods by her side with...*something*...tearing up a wide swathe of forest behind them. It was big, whatever it was.

"We could've got the loot if you hadn't been so bloody loud!"

"You're the one who tripped over the swords and woke it up!"

"You sneezed and I nearly shat myself—"

"You're off your head! I sneezed after you roused the blasted thing—"

The...thing roared again, louder this time, and Ryn realized Kota was out of sight a split second before she heard him scream. It was a flesh-raising sound of distress, one she didn't hear often, and it froze the blood in her veins. She pulled up short, trying to hone in on the sound, her staff ready in her hand. She heard the men shouting at her to hurry, confused about her delay, and then the creature howled its victory and Kota yowled. Ryn moved.

A quick sprint back the way she came, a jaunt to the left, and she was there. The brute—a mountain troll, she could see now—had demolished the trees in a wide circle around Kota, who was crouched in the middle, ears flat, claws out, snarling and ready to fight. The ugly, squinty-eyed monster was baring large dirty teeth at him. The club raised, and Ryn knew her staff was no good here. The troll was just too big; everything vital was far above her head, and there was no *time*. She dropped the echowood rod, unshouldered her bow, let an arrow fly with a prayer.

Aeos was with her this day—either her aim was that good, or the troll moved just the right direction and speed, but her arrow buried itself to the feathers in the creature's right eye, black blood spurting from the deadly wound in pulsing streams. Kota pounced, climbing the screeching creature, locking powerful jaws around a thick neck and riding the monster down as it fell, tearing without mercy. It was overkill, Ryn knew; the troll was dead, its tiny brain pierced by her arrow. She whistled, calling Kota to her, and he came after a moment, teeth bared red now.

"Calm, *kisa*," she soothed, dropping to her knees and holding her hands out, palms up. Kota could be dangerous, even to her, right after a kill, so she had learned to be careful with him when he was wound up.

It didn't look like today would be a hard recovery though, as the lynx dropped his snarl almost immediately and mewled at her. She smiled at him, clicked her tongue, rubbed her fingers together in gentle invitation. Kota nosed her fingers, and she grinned, pulling out a scrap of linen to wipe the blood from his muzzle. "That's my boy," she crooned softly. "You sure showed that monster, didn't you?"

Their moment was shattered when the rustle of underbrush announced the arrival of the two strange brothers who had led her along on this most odd chase.

"By the astra!" the shorter, blond one panted, blue eyes wide and angry. "What were you *thinking*?!"

She said nothing—she did not answer to these, or any other—only stood to face them, a faint smile on her face. She always found it oddly amusing when folks were confused about her or her behavior. Kota growled low in his throat, and she placed a single hand on his head. A murmured command quieted him instantly.

"Are you well, Lady?" the other, the one who had bowled her over, asked. He was taller, of slimmer build and paler coloring, and looked nothing like his brother; save perhaps for the nearly identical way they both were looking her over in obvious concern. "I am so very sorry for—um, rather literally—dragging you into this. Please, let us do something to help you."

Ryn raised a single brow, uncertain whether she wanted to smile or frown. In the end, she settled for neither. "That is not necessary," she assured him, fingers tangling in Kota's fur. "It is barely an inconvenience. Good day." She turned to go, but a restraining hand landed on her forearm.

"Wait!" the tall man blurted, but that was as far as he got before Kota lunged. He barely managed to get his hand out of the way quickly enough, snapping jaws closing on air instead of flesh. The lynx landed, whirled to face his backpedaling opponent, and snarled a challenge. The blond man growled as well, yanking his brother back and drawing a thick, wicked-sharp axe—one of two he carried across his back—that he very clearly knew how to wield properly.

Ryn clicked her tongue, amused, and Kota backed up instantly, teeth still bared. She stared pointedly at the tall man, who had stepped forward again, tossing a glare at his brother. So the blond was eldest, then. She recognized the wordless exchange; the instinctive protectiveness exhibited by the elder, and the long-suffering annoyance felt by the younger. It made her want to smile and rage at the beauty and injustice of it.

"I am Evin." The younger one twisted his hand over his heart in a gesture of polite greeting, supplemented by a small bow and a dangerous wink. "And this...oaf...is my brother, Br—"

"We are grateful for your assistance," the other said coldly, those blue eyes just as icy as his voice. He still held his naked blade in a defensive posture. "Good day."

Ryn narrowed her eyes, assessing. The younger—Evin—was rolling his eyes and attempting to cover for his brother's rudeness, but she cared nothing for his flirtatious smile or his fine words. She locked gazes with the elder, warrior to warrior, and bowed her head, once, before turning to leave again.

Evin called out once more—though he kept his hands to himself this time—and she turned round, ready to tell him off. "Please," he said, motioning for her to stay put. "Are you familiar with these lands?"

Ryn paused, tilted her head to one side. "You are lost?"

"No," the elder replied, tossing a glare at his brother. Ryn gave them half a shrug, but Evin stepped forward again.

"No, not lost. But we need a guide to get where we're going."

Ryn squinted suspiciously. "And where exactly are you going?"

"Retwood." The blond one eyed his brother, but Evin paid him no mind. "We need to get to Retwood, but we must avoid the road."

One eyebrow arched of its own accord, and Ryn fixed the elder with a glare—he seemed slightly less flighty and slightly more dependable than his brother, and she wanted the truth. "And why, pray tell, would you need to avoid the road? Are you running from someone?"

The elder brother cocked an eyebrow of his own as he answered her. "We are neither bandits nor fugitives, if that is what you are asking."

"We come from noble stock!" Evin added with a laugh, as though nobles couldn't possibly break laws. "We simply wish to avoid drawing attention to ourselves, is all."

Ryn, against her better judgment, found herself considering. They were headed the same direction as she—Retwood was a little further north than her original route would take her, but it wasn't far from Easton—and despite her suspicions, their nobility was fairly obvious. It was in everything from their well-made clothing to their regal bearing to how they spoke. She did not doubt their blood.

Also, the elder was as suspicious as she, which made her believe they may not mean her harm. Predators looking to ensnare a woman were more likely to act like this young Evin than his older brother—more interested in drawing her in than pushing her away. Besides, she and Kota were a nigh unbeatable team; even if they did mean her harm, they'd find her a difficult target.

"What's in it for me?" she finally asked. This time the blond answered. "Gold," he said.

But Ryn shook her head. "I can acquire all the gold I need on my own. Don't have much use for anything extra on the road."

He looked a little confused at that. "You cannot store it at home, or in a vault?"

"The open road is my home, and I certainly have no need of a vault."

The brothers stared at her like she had grown an extra head, which made Ryn's lips quirk into a short, reluctant smile. After a moment, Evin asked, "Then what may we offer to secure your services?"

She shrugged. "There are many things worth more than gold out here. Information, assistance, weapons. I happen to have a vested interest in the first."

Both men paused. "What kind of information?" the blond asked suspiciously, after a moment.

"None you two would be able to give personally," Ryn snorted. "All I ask in return is use of the royal archives."

Evin glanced at his brother, eyebrows reaching for his hairline. The older man's face hardened, almost imperceptibly. "Not possible."

"Then I imagine you'll find your way to Retwood on your own." And she turned to leave. She made it five steps before...

"Done," the eldest called. "You will see us safely to Retwood in exchange for one day in the royal archives. *Supervised.*"

Ryn paused, then turned and walked back to the young men. Evin still looked a little shocked at her nerve, eyes wide and lips slightly parted. She gave both a respectable bow and a single nod. "I accept. This is Kota," she motioned to the massive red lynx, "And you may call me Ryn."

"I am Brandt," the eldest answered, coolly.

~~~~~~~~~~

Brandt would have preferred to hire someone more thoroughly vetted, but he was willing to admit the lass was smart and tough; if she knew the way to Retwood without taking roads, well, all the better.

He'd been considering a guide since they started this venture. Uncle had recommended they find one after they left the city, for no one was to know of their journey. Once they left Sannfold, he'd begun looking, but very few traveled from the King's City to Retwood—it was, after all, leagues from most anything—and those who did stuck to the road; for there was no safer way to travel the wild lands just south of Val'gren territory.

This lass though; there was exactly one reason Brandt hadn't pulled Evin away by his ear and reproved him soundly for inviting along some random archer who happened to kill a mountain troll for the sake of her pet cat.

They were not so isolated in their home that they had not heard tell of *Leyna*, the Guardian of Roads; the lone figure in black who kept company with a large cat—the legends often varied on what kind, but apparently it was a lynx—and protected folks on the roads from bandits, Val'gren, nagrat, and other sundry threats. A lone woman with a lynx was rare enough that he was all but certain Ryn was this *Leyna*, in which case they were in more than capable hands.

And he knew it had crossed Evin's mind, too. His brother, while impetuous and sometimes brash, was not stupid. He wouldn't have imperiled the success of their mission for the sake of someone he didn't trust.

So that was that, and now they had a guide. And a lynx. Which had to be worth something when it came to protection, as well. Not that he and Evin weren't perfectly capable of looking out for themselves, but on a trek through the wilds, one couldn't have too much assistance.

Although, he realized as he watched Evin try to talk to the girl—she answered him only as much as was absolutely necessary, with one word whenever possible, her remarks getting shorter and more irritated the longer he tried—it should be amusing as all seven hells to watch his younger brother try to charm this one. Evin was something of a hit with the ladies at home, with that flattering tongue and those big golden eyes and that clear complexion, so unlike the rest of his people, who tended to be freckled, with red or brown hues of hair, and generally standing less on flattery and more on feats of strength to garner the attentions of women. But this one wasn't having any of Evin's charm; she seemed entirely impervious to his appeal, and the younger man was clearly confused at it.

Brandt took the opportunity to study the lass from where he walked behind her. She was almost of a height with his brother, which made her tall for a woman, and clad all in black, as the legends said. Her skin was darker than any Laendorian he'd ever seen—though there was no true guarantee she was Laendorian at all—but she was as freckled as anyone back in Sannfold. The marks dusted her cheeks, marred by a thick scar over her lips, across her cheek all the way to her right ear. He wondered where a mark like that could have come from; an animal attack, perhaps. It did seem deep like a laceration from a claw might have been. Startling green eyes focused on his brother, slightly narrowed in irritation, and she murmured a response to one of his questions that managed to somehow put the lad back on his heels. Evin's steps faltered slightly, though she kept moving, and thus he fell behind, found himself walking beside his brother instead.

"What was that all about?" Brandt asked, curious what could put that particular expression on happy-go-lucky Evin's face. His brother looked stricken.

"I asked of her people," Evin answered quietly, "as she looks nothing like ours. I think the question offended her."

"What did she say?"

"That she is of Kota's people, for they are the only ones who've never mocked and derided her." Evin looked to Brandt, all little brother for the moment, pleading with his older sibling for answers. As was often the case as they grew older, Brandt held none that would satisfy. So he let Evin see his visible wince, to let the younger man know he understood his response—the idea of being without a home, a family, a heritage, was one that was not to be considered—and gave him a simple shrug.

"Perhaps she will someday find a place," he answered, doubting the words even as they left his mouth. There was clearly something wrong with the lass, despite the legend surrounding her; no respectable lady would be living as a nomadic hermit. She doubtless had some flaw in her personality that prevented her finding a proper standing in society.

Regardless, it was a thing he would soon discover, he was sure. Traveling with someone was one of the best ways to know them at their truest.

3

They made camp in a tiny grove of feathered aspens well before sunset that evening. Brandt wanted to continue until nightfall, but Ryn refused, arguing that it was better to cross the nearby wraith-hills in broad daylight, rather than at twilight. The possibility of getting stuck within those eerie mazes of burial mounds in the dark was too great, and Ryn had done that exactly once before, when she'd first struck out on her own.

Never again.

The brothers, to their credit, heeded her advice—she would have doubted they could manage a guide/traveler relationship if the men had begun arguing against her so soon—and within an hour there was a roaring fire, bedrolls laid out nearby. The men had brought small collapsible canvas shelters, she could see, but Evin had a good eye and predicted there would be no moisture tonight. Sleeping under the stars was easier and would make for a less rushed morning. She preferred it anyhow; there was something inherently peaceful about falling asleep beneath a blanket of twinkling lights.

This particular evening was shaping up to be a pleasantly quiet one, the kind of night that made folk say that quests were lovely, agreeable things. Obviously, such reasoning was hopelessly faulty, given what living on the road really entailed; but even Ryn had to admit there was some joy to be had in sitting around a campfire with a comrade, doing the soothing things one did after a day of hard travel—sharpening knives, repairing gear, cooking food.

The latter, tonight, was to be stew; Kota had brought in two hares that afternoon, and the men's vegetables were still fresh enough to be used. Kota munched happily on his dinner while the stew filled the cool evening air with delicious scents, the fire providing warmth as the day began to chill. Evin was sitting across from Ryn, who was mending a strap, his golden eyes focused on an elegant dagger in his hands. The blade was as long as her forearm, slightly curved and double-edged. The hilt was some sort of dark wood, wrapped in what looked to be leather.

Curious, Ryn laid down her work for the moment. "It is a good dagger," she stated without thinking, then immediately felt awkward for saying anything at all. Evin looked up, apparently surprised. She very nearly blushed outright, feeling foreign and clumsy, and cursed herself, wishing she'd just left him alone.

"I found it in the troll hoard," he answered, with a tiny smile quirking the corners of his mouth.

Ryn tilted her head. "The troll that you led right to me?"

Brandt laughed from her left, where he sat writing something studiously in a thickly bound book. She blinked. She wasn't being funny; she was genuinely curious. But Evin was smiling, too.

"The very same, my Lady."

Putting aside for the moment the title she would not presume to bear—she'd correct him later—Ryn rubbed Kota's tufted ears thoughtfully as she asked, "What do you know of it?"

"The troll?" Evin's brow furrowed in confusion.

Ryn just stared at him.

Brandt reached over and smacked his brother on the back of the head. "The knife, you numbskull."

Evin's eyes widened, as though surprised to be asked. "Oh!" He laughed. "Not much, aside from what I can deduce on my own. The hilt looks like arancia wood, actually, wrapped in dragon hide. The curve of the blade and the hilt material suggests it's ancient Y'rai."

"Y'rai?" Brandt questioned, though he didn't look up from his writing. "Thought they were just legends."

"They are, now. But once, they were real." Evin shrugged, looking back down at the blade he was wiping with an oiled rag. "This comes from the Dragonbacks, at least. Arancia wood isn't available anywhere else, and true dragons, while rare, usually only live in the far northern peaks. Would you like to see it?" he asked Ryn.

She nodded and took it when he handed it to her, hilt first. The blade was lighter than she expected, well-balanced, and the dragonhide leather provided a nice grip. "Could be Eloni," she remarked. She'd never seen one of the wood-elves in person, but she knew their weaponry as well as anyone.

But Evin dismissed the idea. "It is a good guess, but there are slight differences. The only curved blades Eloni use are single, not double-edged, and the half-moon shape is generally more pronounced. Besides, Eloni don't fight dragons, they ride them. Sometimes." She could not argue, he was right about all that. The man grinned again. "But the Y'rai had double-edged blades like this one, and look at this—" he reached over, stretching around their small fire to point at tiny runes that decorated the edge of the blade near the hilt. Ryn didn't even remember to draw away from him, instead leaning over to see. "This etching, it is far more akin to the Y'rai ancient language than the elvish tongue."

Ryn had to concede the point; the runes were definitely not Eloni, though they were similar. But she said nothing. She didn't believe the legends about an entire race of folk created by Eir Windweaver, Aeos' immortal consort, to heal the hurts of the world. If such a race had existed thousands of years ago, they had failed miserably and were of no concern to her now.

But some still held to belief in the Old Tales, and she did not begrudge the man his faith.

Still. The dagger was far too sound to have been that old. Perhaps a dagger made in the style of the Y'rai, by one who still believed the Tales, in their honor. She handed the beautiful knife back to Evin.

"Keep it," he said. "I have no need of it."

"What?"

Evin rolled his eyes and smiled. "I want you to have it."

Ryn blinked, shook her head. "It's yours, and it's clearly old and very valuable—"

"And I got it doing something I oughtn't have, that nearly got us all killed." Evin laughed out loud. "Come, my Lady, accept the gift. It is a good knife, solid and sharp. It will serve you well, and I've a hope, bring you a smile when you see it." He paused. "Something to remember our adventure by."

Ryn sat back, stunned, but still holding the dagger. It had been years since she'd been given anything; she never stuck around long enough, preferring to defend travelers and leave the moment the danger passed, often before her clients even realized it was over. Ryn studied the knife more closely than before, as it was to be hers. Evin had done well, sharpening both edges and oiling the blade; it gleamed in the firelight.

"I'm no lady," she returned in answer.

Evin just grinned.

~~~~~~~~~~~

The River Rena wound from the far north, to the furthest reaches of Southdale, before it disappeared into the Amaranthine Sea. It was the largest river in Adan by far, and its many tributaries helped water the land all the way from the Western Ocean to the Dragonback Mountains, the range that divided the known world in half.

At Neth Heoran, the massive lake that hemmed in the city of

Thaliondris, the river split into two large serpentine forks that wound their way south side by side about a league apart, meeting again at the ancient ruins of Galaron. They were aptly named the West Rena and the East Rena, and it was the former of these that the travelers stood beside now, readying to cross. The West Rena was the shallower and gentler of the two, which wasn't saying much, Brandt thought as he eyed the swift current and rocks covering their path across.

"All right," Ryn said as they gathered at the water's edge. "We'll ford here. It doesn't get any shallower."

"How deep?" Brandt asked.

Ryn motioned to the middle of her thigh. "Not terribly, but the current is swift and dangerous in places. We will need to assist one another if we are to cross."

"Have you done this before?" Evin asked as they all removed their heavy boots, replacing them instead with lighter leather strapped sandals, which would keep their heavy boots dry and provide them better footing in the water.

Ryn cocked an eyebrow at Evin. "I ford rivers all the time, Master Evin," she replied.

The younger man gave her a crooked grin and pulled on his pack again, boots strapped to the outside tightly.

Brandt was following suit. "And what of your pet cat, lass?" he asked, motioning to Kota, who was sniffing at the water as he searched for a place to cross, delicately picking his way along the beach on giant padded paws.

Ryn smiled, tightening the straps holding her weapons beneath her rucksack. "He'll get across in his own way. And he's not my pet."

Brandt looked at her oddly, but she didn't give him a chance to probe further.

"Come," she ordered, holding out both arms as though to a lord in a mighty manse, waiting to escort her to a dance. Both men linked arms with her, one on each side, then with each other, so the three formed a sort of tripod. "This way, if one of us slips, the others can assist easily. If you do fall and lose grip with the others, position yourself feet forward in the water and let the river carry you til the current lets up before attempting to swim to shore. If you panic or fight the river, you will make things worse." At a nod from both men, she gave the signal and began shuffling them into the water.

Brandt bit back the urge to gasp at the frigid water swirling around his ankles. While the leather sandals provided no protection at all from the cold, he was glad of them; it would have been torturous to wait for their boots to dry while their feet were that cold. They traveled in a diagonal sort of pattern, toward the opposite shore but following the current loosely. As Ryn had told them; their best chance was to work with the river rather than against it.

They were a little past halfway before anything of note happened. Ryn slipped, on what, they never did find out; she went down swiftly and with a soft gasp of surprise. Wet, her arm slid right out of the crook of his elbow when he stumbled, and Evin shouted in surprised concern. Kota was already on the other bank, yowling and dashing forward and yon, as if they weren't reacting quickly enough for his liking. However, Ryn reappeared a moment later, carried further down by the current, but head held high and holding a thumb up. Brandt breathed a short sigh of relief; she was following the very advice she had given them, all was well.

"Keep going!" Brandt called to Evin, shuffling forward again, holding tightly to his brother. "She will do as she said and swim across further down!" Evin nodded, and they kept moving forward and downstream, working a little harder to remain balanced now that there were only two of them.

They were nearly at the other side when Evin shouted in alarm. His brain practically conditioned to respond to that sound, Brandt whirled to see what had distressed him, and his heart leapt into his throat unbidden.

A limp body was tangled in the thick leafless branches of a fallen tree trunk further down. Brandt cursed vividly.

It was Ryn, and she wasn't moving. He acted on impulse, shoving Evin the rest of the way toward the shore even as he turned to go back.

"Watch Kota!" he ordered. The lynx was screaming now, pawing ineffectually at the river. Brandt was concerned the creature might try to save his Mistress and end up in worse straits for his trouble.

"But—"

"I'm the better swimmer!" Brandt roared, then turned and dove. It was true, after all; he was the stronger swimmer, always had been, as Evin was far from comfortable in any water deeper than he could touch the bottom. He kept his stride short—the current took him far with each movement, he didn't need to try to go further—and his eyes open as he carefully navigated the distance to their guide.

When he reached her, he wedged his feet firmly against some underwater stones that seemed stable enough. He thanked Aeos that whatever had happened, she had gotten jammed into the tree branches face-up. He checked her over quickly—steady heartbeat, deep breaths, a scratch on her forehead that bled more than the mark seemed to warrant, as head wounds do. Her nose was also bleeding, but he could see bruising along that side of her cheek that led him to believe the damage was mostly external. He prayed her neck was unbroken, for he had little choice but to move her. He could not rightly leave her in the river, and besides, there were no healers for leagues in any direction.

"Ach, lass, come now. Let's get you out of here, shall we?" he murmured, more to himself than her, for Ryn did not respond. He disentangled her from the stiff wet branches with some level of difficulty—her staff and longbow held him up, tangling in the rough branches several times, too well-secured for him to pull them loose. Finally, out of desperation, he pulled his knife and sliced the straps criss-crossing Ryn's chest. The move loosened her pack and freed the bow and staff, which he threw to the shore—he'd always had a good arm—then he tossed the woman unceremoniously over his shoulder, holding her pack by the severed straps, and waded the rest of the way out with the assistance of her erstwhile prison, the felled tree.

She woke near the bank with a shout and a kick that nearly brained him. Brandt called her name to let her know he was a friend, and she went limp after a moment, making his job infinitely easier. They reached their worried party moments later. Brandt staggered onto the bank, setting Ryn gently on her feet and holding her by the shoulders to be sure she didn't sway. Ryn shoved him off gently—"I'm fine, I'm fine"—and he stumbled a step or two away, hands on his knees, breathing hard. Evin rushed to him and pulled him upright roughly, checked him over for injuries. It was a familiar custom, one he had returned plenty a time, so Brandt didn't protest.

"Are you hurt, brother?" Evin asked. Brandt responded by slapping him on the shoulder to assure him of his well-being. He was far too winded to speak just yet.

Ryn was bent over at the waist, clearly not as fine as she'd asserted, receiving a similar treatment from Kota; the lynx whined and nosed her gently in his search for injuries, licking her face and hair like a mother cat cleaning her kitten. Ryn snorted a laugh, then coughed as blood dripped onto the gravel bank from her head and nose. She moaned slightly and, failing to find something on which to lean when she searched blindly with one hand, went to her knees and leaned against Kota. Wiping shaking fingers on her leggings, she fumbled for a scrap of cloth to stem the flow of blood. She startled, garnering a low warning growl from the lynx, when Brandt thrust a torn cloth between her face and the gravel.

"Here," he muttered, ignoring Kota.

"Thanks," she murmured, sounding a bit faint yet.

Brandt eyed her worriedly. He tore his gaze away when Evin made the strangest noise in his throat, almost like a scoff. He blinked, blue eyes meeting gold, and Evin cocked an eyebrow at him, his expression straying dangerously toward teasing.

Brandt's brow lowered. "What?" he asked.

Evin just tilted his head toward the lass, who still wasn't looking at them and was shivering in the wind. It occurred to Brandt they ought to build a fire.

But that wasn't what Evin was on about, he realized with a measure of annoyance. His brother was *teasing* him, for his concern over their Guide. He stared at Evin for a minute, then rolled his eyes—he wasn't King yet, after all, the childish gesture was still allowed him.

"For the love of Aeos, Evin, can you think of aught else?"

Evin snickered outright.

4

It was the red eyes, always the red eyes, that terrified him beyond belief.

Why? He had confronted Val'gren before, many of them had red eyes.

But they never seemed quite so scarlet, never quite so familiarly shaped as these. Never quite so cruel or hateful.

There were no words in this dream, only flashes. Long, pale fingers closing round his throat. An elegant blade, etched with runes and slightly curved, plunged into his brother's heart, bleeding red as those eyes. A brutal smile that sucked all the hope from his chest. He couldn't breathe.

Brandt!

The dagger lay forgotten in the snow beside his brother's still fingers, blade sparking faintly.

Brandt gasped.

Evin bolted upright, gulping for air. It was dark, the moon white against a black sky, washing the world in odd contrast. The air on his cheeks was cool—almost cold—and he reached up to press his shaking hands to them.

They came away wet.

He suddenly felt trapped in his bedroll; it was constricting and hot, and he needed to get *out*. He stood unsteadily, knees shaking still from the punch of adrenaline the dream had delivered, and turned about to locate his brother, to assure himself it really was just a dream.

Golden braids shuffled in a soft breeze against the bedroll beside his, and he relaxed a little. The dream was far too fresh for the simple sight of his brother sleeping peacefully to settle the pounding in his chest; but it was a start. A second cursory glance revealed that Ryn was sitting watch; she was huddled in a wool blanket, leaning against a sleeping Kota as she looked out over the plains. The slight overhang they'd camped under provided shelter at their backs, so she only had two directions to watch tonight. Disentangling himself from his damp, tangled blankets, he made his shaky way over to her post and sat heavily on the fallen log beside her. The jagged horizon to the east was just beginning to lighten to a pale blue, stars fading slowly in the impending dawn. Ryn didn't startle when Evin sat, which implied he'd probably been tossing for a while before he woke.

"Can't sleep?" Her voice was low, soft. It reminded him painfully of his mother for half a moment.

He shuddered visibly, grateful she did not look at him. "Bad dreams."

The lass frowned at that and pressed a leather-clad shoulder to his in a silent gesture of solidarity. "What of?"

Evin's throat constricted at the thought of the dream, and their too-recently-deceased cousin; his and Brandt's childhood partner-in-crime, a crown prince who'd never lorded that fact over his boyhood playmates. Their brother-in-arms as they grew, training and scouting beside them.

Dead in his arms, a simple patrol gone horrifically wrong. Not six weeks ago. It was still too fresh for comfort.

It could have been Brandt. So easily, it could have been his brother in his arms that day. He knew sometimes Brandt thought it should have been. He had a way of taking on responsibility like that, even when it didn't rightly belong to him. It drove Evin spare half the time.

"Death," he answered, voice cracking.

Ryn finally looked up at him, understanding written all over her face. "Whose?"

Evin shuddered. "Brandt's. Gunnar's. Those I love."

"Gunnar is…another brother?" Her voice was quiet, gentler than he'd ever heard it.

He shook his head. "Cousin. He was killed on patrol."

"Oh." Ryn seemed to deflate beside him, looking out toward the lightening horizon. She moved slightly closer, not even a scoot, just a shift of her weight into his bicep; Evin almost laughed at the difference between her and his brother, imagining Brandt's version of after-nightmare comfort, which was to toss a muscled arm around his shoulder in a gesture of careless self-assurance. That was Brandt, all surety and strength and confidence.

Not that his brother didn't wear it well; Brandt was the most incredible warrior Evin knew, and he knew a lot of warriors, had trained with some of the most skilled in the realm. His older brother sometimes seemed invincible; and though Evin was old enough to know better than to engage in such boyish awe toward someone who was, after all, only human, the fact was that Brandt still engendered a measure of hero worship in the younger man. Evin couldn't seem to help but to look up to him, even as an adult.

Look up to him, and recently, long to protect him. This ache was new, likely a result of both coming of age and Gunnar's recent death—more specifically, his inability to save his cousin, and his subsequent vow never to lose Brandt in the same way—and Evin wasn't quite sure what to do with it yet. He was a formidable warrior himself, quick and lethal with his sword and deadly with a bow; but recently he'd wanted nothing more than to work harder, be faster, stronger, better.

Not for his own benefit; but because the nightmares had begun after Gunnar's death, and he was determined to be good enough to protect Brandt, whatever came.

"You and your brother are very close," Ryn remarked, startling him back into the moment.

He realized she was studying him, something in her eyes he could not name, and he nodded belatedly. "Too close, some say."

Ryn's answering gaze was sharp, fierce. "Impossible."

He tilted his head. "Is it?" Their guide shifted and turned away again, but Evin moved with her, keeping their shoulders pressed together. "Do you have a brother, Lady Ryn?"

"I am not a lady."

He let her have the rejoinder, waiting for her response to his question.

She did not pull away, though her lips thinned and her face appeared even paler in the gray morning light. He waited her out, was patient and let her come to him. After a while, she nodded, once. "I had a brother. He is dead."

Evin tried not to gasp audibly, but the sound of dismay that stuck in his throat sounded instead choked and horrified. The thought of losing Brandt was enough to gut him entirely, a possibility not to be borne, and here he was beside a lass who had endured it?

"Tell me?" he croaked. It might have been the wrong thing to say—it probably was the wrong thing to say, but all Evin could think was that if Brandt were dead, he would want him honored in every way, including in Evin's own stories.

Ryn seemed to be of a similar mind, because she considered, though she didn't lean back into him. "He was a beautiful boy," she began, voice husky and soft as she stared into the horizon. "Five years my junior; I was old enough to fall in love with him the moment I met him, but young enough to be his playmate and protector." A gentle smile touched her lips. "He never left my side from the moment he could walk. We played in the woods, by the river, in the creek, in the house and the barn and the town square...always at one another's side." The smile turned a little wry, and she looked at him. "I got in such trouble for dragging him all over the place. Mother said I'd get him killed before he came of age."

"What was he like?" Evin found himself asking, suddenly desperately curious to hear about this lad who had obviously possessed so much of their guide's heart. He didn't over-analyze the feeling.

Ryn was smiling fully now. "Pure Laendorian stock, that one was. Wild and strong, adventurous and clever as an asp. He dreamt of being a warrior, you know, and I never doubted he would. Even as a small child, it was obvious he was going to be tall and sturdy. He would have been lucky in love, too," she added, glancing over at him with a grin. "He had these thick, beautiful curls and sky-blue eyes and freckles everywhere." She paused, then sighed softly.

"How did he die?" Evin asked, hushed.

Ryn tensed, but told him anyway. "Val'gren attack. Râza himself, in fact, since Mother's brother was someone of some importance in the village where I grew up."

Evin winced visibly.

Ryn didn't seem to notice. "I hid." She blinked, swallowing convulsively as if the memory made her sick, which Evin reflected, it probably did. "Mother ordered me to hide, and I did, but the house was on fire and she was inside...something fell on me and the last thing I saw was Talos running into the burning house..." she petered off. Evin could fill in the rest, and the image in his head made his chest ache. He wanted nothing more than to hold her. "When I woke he was dead. They were all dead. I was fourteen summers," she eventually finished.

Evin waited half a minute to see if she had more to say, but she just sat quietly, ramrod-straight against him. "I am sorry," was all he could think to say, though he knew it was horribly inadequate.

Ryn hummed an acknowledgment, then seemed to realize how much she'd said. He watched it happen, watched the gates slam shut and her eyes harden to unforgiving emerald green as she fixed him with a glare that could curdle new milk. She looked positively fierce, and he was reminded, in that moment, of the legend this lass had built around herself. Was reminded that Val'gren regarded her as a Phantom, a horror story to scare the younglings; and remembered how many of them had discovered, at the end, how much of her legend was true.

"It matters not," she growled. "It was long ago, and I have since forged a place for myself in the world."

"Aye," he agreed. "So you have, lass. I meant no offense."

She softened a little at that. "You have not offended me, Evin. I simply have no use for pity; yours or anyone else's. When it would have mattered, I had none. And now I no longer require it."

He wanted to ask her to elaborate further, but the sun was well and truly risen now, bathing her bronze skin in golden light.

She stirred and stood. "Come," she said. "We must make good time today. There is a storm coming."

Evin thought, as he poured some of the icy water they'd left beside the fire over Brandt's head, that perhaps she meant more than just the weather.

~~~~~~~~~~

The journey from Dreyfen to Thaliondris—through the wilderness rather than over roads—was a rather long and difficult one, and Ryn had spent much of it blatantly suspicious of her clients. But after the near-disastrous river crossing four days ago, and more recently, Evin's bad night, she had noticed a difference, both in the way she saw them and in the way they saw her. Both parties, while still dubious, spoke more easily, snapped less, and were generally more pleasant to one another. Brandt had even slapped her shoulder the other day, at something Ryn said, which had startled her so badly she stared outright for several seconds before stammering an excuse through her fierce blush. Evin found the whole thing riotously amusing, which had equal parts rankled and pleased her.

This day's sunset found them stopped in a dense forest north of the tiny village of Ramshed, sheltered in a grove of willows that Ryn had visited before. The day's travel had been quite productive, and the discussion had turned to weaponry when Evin caught her studying the dagger he'd gifted her with. She had explained her own staff, a beautifully sturdy piece of echowood she had acquired years prior deep in the Dragonbacks and had since interlaid with runes and spells against exposure and general wear and tear. Weaponry had turned to technique, and Ryn had confessed she often avoided up-close confrontations with multiple enemies due to her fighting style and lack of formal training. To her surprise, upon hearing it, Brandt had offered to spar with her. Evin had agreed enthusiastically, saying they needed to practice as much as she did.

And so it was, after their evening meal, Ryn stood with Brandt on a cleared rough circle they'd use as training grounds. Evin watched off to one side, one hand in Kota's thick fur, grinning widely. The lynx, to Ryn's surprise, allowed the contact. She wasn't sure if that made her happy or jealous; Kota, while raised by a human, was still every bit a wild animal. No one else had ever dared touch him, and Ryn had always felt they would have regretted it if they'd tried.

Somehow, all the usual rules didn't seem to apply to Evin. She got the feeling that was a common occurrence with this man. She couldn't pinpoint what it was, but there was something about him that was...disarming.

Brandt, steely as ever, told Ryn to assume a fighting stance, bringing her focus back into the moment. She placed her feet shoulder-width apart and bent her knees, holding her staff in a defensive position before her. Brandt studied her stance, circling while prodding here or poking there, making suggestions to improve her form.

Without warning, the man charged her with both battle axes lifted high. He didn't make a sound, and it disoriented Ryn for half a second. Her eyes barely had time to widen before he was on her, all ferocity and bulk; she ducked under his swing, coming up on his left and swinging about quickly, dropping to her knees to avoid the horizontal blow he had pivoted into. He granted her an opening a moment later as he raised his weapon high over his head for a vertical stroke intended, in a real battle, to cut her in half from crown to belly. Growling, Ryn decided to bring the fight closer than his longer, bladed weapons would allow; she pushed herself up nearly into his chest, and shoved her staff across his throat. In battle, she'd have turned the move into a blow intended to bruise or break his windpipe.

There was a beat, and then he smiled. "Good, lass, but that trick will only work once."

Her grin was fierce. "I only need it to work once."

He answered her with a nod of his own before attacking again.

For several minutes, she danced around, avoiding his blows but also not scoring any of her own. The fact did not bother her at first; she needed only one blow. Unfortunately, her technique worked best if an enemy was dispatched quickly, and he wasn't giving her another opening to end this.

She began to tire, her reactions slowing as the minutes passed. Sweat coursed down her face, and her ribs began to sting with the strain of breathing, but she refused to give him the satisfaction of wearing her down to forfeit. In desperation, she tried for a questionable opening as he swung toward her. Shifting his weight to his right foot at the same time he let go of one axe entirely, he turned. His free hand gripped her opposite shoulder as his foot swept the back of her knee; he turned her about as she fell, smacking her staff from a stunned grip and bringing his remaining axe to her throat as she landed on her knees.

"Dead," he intoned.

Ryn was surprised to hear Evin laugh and applaud from the sidelines. She dropped her gaze, feeling ashamed he had seen her get so thoroughly whipped, but Brandt was squeezing her shoulder and his eyes were smiling when she looked up.

"You did well," he assured her. "Evin and I would have been hard-pressed to last that long with only a stick for defense."

She did break a smile at that, gaze flicking to the man in question as he cheered loudly from next to the fire.

Brandt spent the next two hours correcting Ryn's form—her lack of formal training was evident in this portion of the lesson—and teaching her to block, rather than just dodge, her enemy's attacks. By the time he called a halt, she was shaking and sweating. Evin offered her a ladle of water from his skin as she stumbled toward the fire in the dying light. She took it gratefully.

He grinned. "I've never in my life seen a maiden fight like that!" Golden eyes sparkled. "And that was before my idiot brother worked with you for two hours! You're going to be unstoppable soon enough."

33

Ryn found herself laughing. "Well, they're skills that will certainly come in handy on the road, there's no denying that. I've always thought I was lucky to be able to avoid multiple-enemy confrontations, for the most part. Truth is, I'd probably be dead already if I hadn't."

Evin gave her a dazzling smile. "We will cure you of it yet, my friend. Pity the poor nagrat who get in your way once we're through with you."

She returned his grin as she finished her water. It felt good to smile with a friend, she realized with some level of shock.

He's not your friend, she reminded herself forcefully.

She deliberately schooled her thoughts as she readied for bed. These men were her clients, nothing more. There was a *reason* she traveled alone, lived alone, had no friends or family to speak of. She refused to put herself in that position again, especially not now, after so many years of safely guarding herself. She buried her head under the cover of her bedroll, ignoring the protest of sore muscles as she closed her eyes tightly and sought sleep.

Sleep did not come for a long time.

5

It had been twenty days since that strange situation with the mountain troll, and they were within a week of Thaliondris now. The mountains rose majestically before them as they traveled; slowly, but inexorably taking over the horizon. Ryn didn't mind; she liked the rugged beauty of the dangerous peaks, snow-capped even in high summer.

Tonight, Ryn watched with gentle amusement as Kota, in a fit of kitten-like enthusiasm, chased a moth through the field in which they stood. She was using the last light of day to gather some marjoram leaves about a quarter of a league from their camp. The leaves were generally best when they were used just before the plant flowered, so these were a little early, but they would still make a tasty addition to whatever Evin cooked up that night for dinner. He always appreciated her knowledge of herb lore, especially when it made his food taste better. Early on, when the brothers had both been extremely—and stiflingly—clingy, they had tried to stop her from leaving camp to hunt or gather or scout. She had tolerated that attitude for about ten seconds, and it had led to the first true fight within their small party; a conflict that had been only very slightly assuaged when Ryn promised to take Kota with her any time she left camp. Even they, Evin had argued, took one another when making short jaunts away. No one went anywhere alone, he had said, not even the toughest among them. Not in this wilderness.

Ryn had struggled through the most extraordinary combination of affection and annoyance at that, but had conceded. She needed that information from the archives, and thus she needed this job. So she took Kota wherever she went; which was hardly an inconvenience, he went with her everywhere anyway.

Her thoughts were interrupted when her lynx stopped short and sniffed the breeze, his hackles rising, ears twitching. She straightened, looking for danger but finding none. The long grass in the field swayed with a slight breeze, and the sun was just disappearing behind the mountains to her west. Kota was still about twenty feet away, there was no trouble in sight, and all was quiet.

Too quiet.

The birds had too suddenly ceased their song, and the only sound she could hear was the wind in the trees. Instantly, her senses sharpened, and she recognized the feeling as a punch of adrenaline—she could smell the scent of the marjoram and wildflowers around her, feel every ridge and fold of the leaves in her hand, see vividly the field they were standing in, each contrast more distinct and every detail more obvious.

"*Kisa*," she called quietly, infusing a tiny bit of urgency into her voice. Kota bounded to her in three strides. Ryn dropped the herbs and turned slowly, nocking an arrow to her bow, always strung and warmed when she left camp, alert for anything out of the ordinary. Nothing revealed itself, but *something* was out there, and she wasn't about to stand here and wait to be hunted. "Come," she ordered, and the lynx needed no more encouragement than that. He bared his teeth and pasted himself to her side as she began moving backward, back toward camp.

That was when all seven hells broke loose.

An arrow came flying, stabbing the dirt not far from where she had stood mere seconds before; she danced back at the same moment, and three leather-clad nagrat emerged from the long grass, blades held up in a ritualistic gesture that was more frightening than dangerous.

That wouldn't last but a moment, she knew.

"Kota, run!" She shouted, turning on her heel.

Only to find two more at her back, crude axes held high. Kota darted between their legs in a move that would trip up a mere bandit, but only vaguely knocked one monster momentarily off balance. Ryn wasted no time watching, dodging under the arm of the least steady one and rolling so they didn't catch her outright. Kota paused just long enough to see it, then took off at a dead run toward camp.

The lynx was faster than her by far, of course, but the thought relieved Ryn rather than upset her—Brandt and Evin would be on guard when she got there. She heard one of the nagrat behind her shout a word in their guttural language that made her hair stand on end, and she threw herself to one side as a knife the size of her thigh whizzed by her ear, missing her by inches. She shouted as she stumbled for a moment, caught her feet, and began zigzagging her way back toward reinforcements as quickly as she could.

The brutes were following; she could hear their booming voices, feel the displacement of air as their arrows and throwing knives rushed by on all sides.

And more was wrong. As she neared camp, she could hear battle sounds—Evin's challenging shout, the clang of swords, and the snarl of an attacking lynx, calling her to them. The nagrat had hit the camp at the same time they surrounded her in the field. Ryn put on a burst of speed; she *had* to reach her friends.

The knife hit her so fast she never saw it coming.

~~~~~~~~~~

Steel met bone with a sickening crunch as Evin brought his sword down in a powerful arc, severing one nagrat's arm completely and snapping the knee joint of another. Neither made a sound, only fell back and let their brethren take their place, which frankly was more eerie than if they'd screamed and dropped. Evin didn't have time to consider it as he fought off three of the fiends, two at his front and one that thought to make a bid to get between him and Brandt.

He and his brother fought back to back, as they'd been taught since they were big enough to wield tiny wooden swords. Fire and ice, their coaches had insisted, fire and ice they were; Brandt's quiet coolness and steady deadly blows a perfect complement to Evin's shouted taunts and whirling dervish attacks. Brandt was strength, an immovable rock that could easily take out two or three opponents with a single blow, and Evin was speed, laughter and menace in equal measure as he struck from all sides. Even nagrat could be defeated, and these were clearly unaccustomed to hunting prey that fought back as the Princes of Laendor did.

And glad he was that they didn't know *that* particular bit of information, else he and Brandt may have been prime targets for ransom. As it was, this group seemed to be out simply looking for a sacrifice to Skeðu.

Which meant they'd snatch the first of them to go down and then melt into their surroundings in that way they had, leaving whoever was left to lick their wounds and mourn their losses.

Evin growled at the thought, impaling another of the beasts on a long blade.

A snarl to his left alerted Evin to Kota's arrival, and he turned in time to sever one of the ragged creatures' windpipe before it could make a bid for the large spotted lynx. He spared a bare moment to search for Ryn, but did not see her before he was swept away in the rhythm of battle once more.

Turn, parry, dodge, thrust, strike.

One of the creatures appeared at Brandt's side, bellowing a victory at finding his ribs unprotected as it brought a mean-looking club around for a swing. Evin lunged, his heart in his throat as he saw the blow land. Brandt's leather armor protected him somewhat, but did little to mask the crunch of wood meeting bone, and time slowed to a crawl for Evin when he saw his brother fall. Then he was face to face with Brandt's attacker, running the creature through with his sword before the smirk had even left its twisted, ugly face. He turned to find Kota standing over Brandt, who was struggling to rise. The lynx was snarling, nimbly dodging a nearby nagrat's attempts to stab him before pouncing, jaws locking around its throat as he rode it into the ground.

Evin reached for Brandt, giving the man a hand up. Once his brother was back on his feet, he was a force of nature again, destroying anything that got in his way. Evin stayed at his back, rage coloring his blows now; he always took it personally when someone tried to kill his brother.

He had just disposed of a lumpy-faced nagrat on his left when a booming shout echoed over the remains of their camp. It was a word he did not recognize, but the meaning was clear when the nagrat left standing retreated soundlessly, disappearing into the shadows of the forest before anyone could protest. Brandt stood beside him, trembling with tension, his breathing jittery. He stood still in a defensive stance with one of his battle axes dripping blood onto the grass. The other was a few feet away, buried in a misshapen skull. A few bodies littered the clearing, one or two moaning and writhing slowly on the forest floor, but their attackers were gone entirely.

"By the Light," Evin panted, spinning to check on his brother. In the absence of a threat, Brandt's axe had dropped slightly as he curled in on himself. His face was twisted in a grimace of pain that brought the younger to his side immediately. "That...thing...landed a blow," he said breathlessly, needlessly, reaching for Brandt before pulling back, a little aborted gesture of concern. He knew if he demanded too much information too quickly, his older, too-tough brother would retreat and refuse his assistance.

Brandt lowered his weapon entirely and moved his free hand to the side that had been struck. He pressed gingerly, a grimace contorting his face, then nodded once. Evin breathed a sigh of relief; Brandt was in pain, but well. He dug dirty fingers into Kota's fur as he turned to find Ryn. "That was—"

Brandt. Kota. Him. No one else was standing.

"—was—"

No one else.

Dread punched him hard in the gut when he did not see her as he had expected to. The press of battle, the chaos of bodies and weapons and armor, he'd been sure she was nearby even though he hadn't been able to see her. But now...beside him, Kota was mewling softly, nosing the air in an apparent attempt to locate his mistress.

"Ryn?" Brandt called, even as Evin searched the few scattered corpses in the clearing and knew she was not among them. He started toward the forest, in the direction from which Kota had originally come, hoping to retrace her steps, but Brandt caught his arm and held firmly.

"Evin, no."

"But—"

"We cannot separate right now, it is too dangerous."

"She's out there—"

"She might not be," his brother argued, low and urgent. "They may have taken her. If they did not, then she will find us."

"And if she's hurt?" Evin's voice was rising, too wound up to notice how wound up he was. "If she is unconscious and cannot come to us?"

His brother's blue eyes spoke volumes, and he continued, low and calm. "We will search the area where she and Kota were, briefly, before we leave. But we cannot stay here. If they have her, we must close the gap."

Evin blinked hard as he realized what Brandt had just said.

He meant not to abandon their guide, their friend, to the nagrat's tender mercies. He did not intend to leave her behind and continue their quest as though nothing had happened.

Brandt meant to hunt.

6

The scent of wood smoke was the first thing that reached Ryn through the inky black heaviness that blanketed her consciousness. Natural and earthy, it tempted her toward wakefulness. She struggled through the gauzy layers of oblivion, registering rough voices and other everyday sounds as she cracked her eyelids open slowly. Sunlight made her eyes water and the pain in her head clawed its way to the forefront of her attention, forcing a soft moan out of her despite her disorientation. A throaty chuckle reached her from somewhere to the left. The sound brought Ryn's last memory rushing forward; her heart thumped into her stomach at the same time she forced her eyes open again, ignoring the pain.

Dashing for the camp, behind Kota, an explosion of agony in her right thigh, searing heat spreading insidiously through her veins, then...nothing.

She could feel it, as signals from her extremities began rolling into conscious realization: stiff muscles, the chafing of ropes at her ankles and wrists, biting sharp pain emanating from her leg. Now she could tell the rumbling voices she'd heard while waking up were actually the rough, throaty language of the nagrat, growling and snarling at one another as they went about their late-day business in the camp.

Well, shit.

"It is good you have awake," the voice to her left croaked in poorly-executed Common. Ryn held her breath and kept her eyes shut, her face impassive, hoping the creature would mistake her for having passed out again, but now that she was awake the nausea in her belly refused to be ignored. Two heartbeats later she was doubled as far over as her restraints would allow, heaving bile into the sparse dry grass. The spell made her eyes water again and her head felt ready to fall clear off her shoulders by the time her stomach finished spasming. She spat and sat back, willing her gut to settle, recognizing the feeling instantly—that heavy awareness of her bones, the way her skin felt too tight to contain her, the heat in her veins.

The knife had been poisoned. That was going to make escape slightly less manageable, though she was determined to arrange it anyway, just as soon as she got her bearings.

The nagrat guarding her was grinning when she finally squinted up at him. The expression revealed sharp, blood-stained teeth and smashed the brute's one puffy eye closed entirely. Gray skin covered a bulky frame, and rough-made steel armor reflected the sun, dull with filth and dented from multiple blows. Metal armor meant this one was fairly high ranking in his clan. Nagrat of lower importance only warranted leathers. He was toying with a crude knife, but rose and lumbered away when she opened her eyes fully. Ryn took stock of her surroundings while he was gone.

A camp had been set up in a small grassy field several leagues north of her last conscious location. She knew because the ever-present mountains had shifted, the double peaks of Haradhorn closer than before—and her friends further away, for their route had taken them well south of that dangerously rocky ridge. Nagrat of varying sizes, shapes, and degrees of deformity trudged here and there, erecting shelters and preparing the evening meal. Dinner was to be several bucks, Ryn could see, though she looked away immediately from the enthusiastic way the only female nagrat present was tearing into the hide of one poor animal. It was bloody, gory work, and not to be relished, with death so near.

Ryn herself was tied tightly to a thick tree near what looked to be the center of the camp. Her wrists were chafed and her back hurt enough that she suspected she'd been bound for some time, probably on the way here. She was dizzy and dry-mouthed, and her skin felt feverish; all symptoms of common snakeroot poisoning, she knew. She was unlikely to die, unless the dose she'd received had been massive, but she was definitely going to wish for death within a few hours.

The guard returned with the largest, ugliest nagrat she'd ever had the displeasure of looking upon—what she knew of their culture told her this would be the leader, the Hunt Chief. She squinted up at him, trying to muster a look of utter disdain.

She was fairly sure she managed complete dejection instead.

"Echowood," the Hunt Chief growled. His Common was much more coherent than that of her guard. Her stomach lurched again—this time it had nothing to do with the poison—as he spun her staff in his hand, looking as though he could have snapped the thing in two easily, though Ryn knew the runes carved into the black wood would prevent that. "Very rare, very hardy, near impossible to damage." He pulled back and whipped her across the ribcage with her own staff, the limber weapon singing through the air before it struck her. Starbursts exploded behind Ryn's eyes at the pain, and she gasped—a mistake, as her ribs were screaming in agony now.

The Hunt Chief went on as though nothing had happened. "Very difficult to fashion into any sort of tool. In fact, Kudrack has only ever heard of it being formed into a weapon by one particular human." She realized slowly that Kudrack must have been her tormenter, referring to himself in the third person. Charming. His smile disappeared, leaving in its place an expression that unnerved Ryn. It was equal parts eager anticipation and unadulterated hatred. "You were found in the company of a large spotted lynx."

Ryn swallowed the rapid heartbeat climbing her throat, refusing to give the monster the satisfaction of knowing she was actually frightened. She had created this legend surrounding herself, inadvertently perhaps, but never blind to its potential to get her in real trouble if her enemies managed to catch her. She cursed herself for being taken out by something so simple as a thrown knife. "I don't know what you're talking about."

The sound of wood meeting linen and flesh registered almost before the pain did; a hearty *smack!* followed by blinding agony, this time in her right shoulder. The Hunt Chief looked down on her, a satisfied smile contorting his face. "The reward for finding you will be great indeed, Little Phantom."

~~~~~~~~~~~

The wyvern hit their little camp with all the force of a hurricane.

Evin had been sitting watch, dozing, and had barely heard his brother's shout of alarm before the massive reptilian creature bowled him over, roaring its victory. He choked, trying hard to force air into spasming lungs, flat on his back beneath the wyvern's massive feet. The thing was the size of a horse, and he was certain that his ribs were going to be at least bruised after this.

If he even survived it.

The creature bared its razor-sharp teeth at him, growling as it brought its face—and fangs—closer to his exposed throat. Evin's stomach turned, in both disgust and fear, and he wriggled desperately, trying to escape or at least reach his hunting knife—

The wyvern screamed when Kota tackled it from behind, his claws raking its back mercilessly.

Then everything was a blur of fighting—Evin took a sweep of its massive tail to his already-bruised ribs, Kota took the worst of its claws, Brandt its teeth—before both Evin's long sword and Brandt's axe found their way into the creature's skull.

In the aftermath, Evin had stood, breathing hard.

Failure is all the worse when others suffer for it.

Such was the sentiment—no, self-recrimination—echoing through his head on repeat. An incessant mantra that, with every iteration, broke a little something more inside his soul.

Before him, Kota whimpered as Evin did his best to apply bandages to the lynx's thickly-furred left flank. He was no Healer of Beasts, but battle medicine seemed to be much the same across species lines; sweetroot juice to disinfect a wound, pressure bandaging to stop the bleeding. Nearby, his brother hissed as he struggled to tie off the linen bandage wrapped round his forearm. Brandt hadn't said a single word since that first warning. The bite his brother had taken had been meant for Evin himself, a fact which did nothing to quell the indictments screaming through his skull.

He tied off the last of Kota's dressing, laid a hand upon the beast's head for a moment in a gesture of attempted comfort. Kota growled low in his throat, but licked Evin's dirty fingers before lying back down, dull gold cat eyes drifting mostly shut. Evin turned to Brandt. His older brother was still fumbling with the bandage, growing more frustrated by the moment, but Evin dared not speak. Brandt was an honorable, kind man who could be cold and vicious when he was in a great deal of pain, or in the midst of a fight. It was a strength on the battlefield, and thus something their uncle and teachers had always encouraged; but off it, Evin was of the opinion such a characteristic was anything but an asset.

Finally, once again losing his grip on the end of the knot he was attempting to tie, Brandt let go of the linen entirely and placed strong fingers about his own thigh. He clenched, slow and hard, until Evin could see the blood vessels standing out on the back of his hands, and took two deep breaths; an attempt to calm himself, the younger realized. Another moment, and then Brandt was holding his injured limb toward Evin, eyes hard and glittering.

Still he said not a word.

Evin moved forward silently to assist, adding more of the cotton cloth before tying it off—Brandt had bled through the original bandages already. The younger man tried not to remember the glance he'd stolen at his brother's arm before Brandt managed to turn and hide the severity of the wound. The entirety of the muscle from wrist to elbow had been lacerated, mangled by the wyvern's double row of razor-sharp teeth. The sharp fangs had sliced clean through leather and cotton like nothing Evin had ever seen before.

It was with extra care he finished the knot. His face was unbearably hot, adrenaline now replaced by something much more insidious; guilt, gnawing at his belly, suffocating. He felt almost lightheaded with it, as though oxygen were suddenly in short supply.

Your fault.

He studied the bandage briefly, checking for thin spots or areas where any of the wound would be exposed. There were none; it was a thorough job.

Your watch. Your fault.

All set, he opened his mouth to say, but the words stuck in his throat, emerged as a choked cough instead. Brandt moved, but Evin couldn't bring himself to look up, to meet his brother's eyes. He knew he would, in a moment; he was a prince and a warrior, after all, had been raised from the cradle to take responsibility for his own actions, be they right or wrong, whether they made him proud or horrified. But if there was one person he could not stand to disappoint, it was his older brother.

Warmth and weight on his right shoulder did not really register consciously at first. He leaned into it instinctively before withdrawing, finally looking up and meeting stormy blue eyes. But Brandt didn't look angry; his face was pale and lined with what appeared to be concern, drawn and exhausted. Brandt didn't let Evin retreat, gripping his shoulder even tighter and shaking him once, as if to make sure he really had the younger's attention. Evin stared.

"Not your fault," Brandt said simply, without fanfare. Evin winced, but Brandt just curled pale fingers tighter in his shoulder, the grip almost painful now. He held on for a long moment, until Evin gave a small, jerky nod. Seeming satisfied by that, Brandt sighed as he sat back, moving his injured arm experimentally. His face contorted in pain, and Evin forced back a visible cringe of sympathy.

"How bad is it really?" he asked, taking advantage of Brandt's rare openness. Unexpectedly, his brother seemed to actually consider the question before speaking, rather than simply slam a lid on his pain and insist he was well. Brandt opened and closed his fingers experimentally, moved his arm this way and that, jaw clenched and sweat beading his forehead—though Evin couldn't prove that was pain rather than exertion.

After a moment, Brandt nodded once. "I will manage, I think. We should go." He stood slowly, sighing at the mess the wyvern had made of their hastily-erected camp. Bedrolls were torn apart, their gear strewn about. Evin's pack was ripped and spilling foodstuffs all over the bare dirt. "We have lingered here too long as is."

Evin nodded, and went to work gathering their things up as quickly as he could. He tackled the more difficult tasks quietly, not giving Brandt a chance to try to wrestle his bedroll back into shape or handle the broken leather pack. His brother was right; every moment they spent here, picking up scraps of dried meat and torn blankets, was a step further they lagged behind their guide.

Haste was essential, now more than before.

7

The Dragonback Mountains ran north and south the entire length of Adan; from the Northern Wastelands all the way to the Amaranthine Sea, where they disappeared into the water reluctantly, a line of islands the final resistance against the inevitable, for the sea swallowed them up several hundred leagues south of the shoreline. Legend said the entire range had once been an army of dragons, a battle line when the forces of Skeðu first marched against the Astra. The immortal agents of Aeos had left their blessed home in the Isle of Emai, far to the East, to confront Skeðu's army. They held the line just east of Neth Heoran. The greatest of them partnered with the Dawnmages of the Eloni to conjure such a spell as had not been seen in Adan before or since. They soul-bound an Astra by the name of Konn with the greatest elven Dawnmage in history, Tarya Darksbane. The result was the purest form of Light Magic the world had yet seen, so intense that the pair had to wear hoods or helms at all times to avoid blinding their own allies.

It was during the Vast Battle they finally revealed themselves and their full power, working their way deep into the mass of Skeðu's servants before uncovering themselves. The Light from their faces combined with their bloodcurdling war cry to create a shock wave which turned the battle quickly and permanently to their allies. Great swathes of the dark battlefront were destroyed, turned instantly to ash by the Light. Most of the ones who remained were mowed down by the thousands of Eloni knights and Astran warriors who still lived and fought.

All but the dragons. As old and nearly as powerful as the Astra themselves, the ancient beasts were slowed but not destroyed by the Light, pure as it was. Instead, Konn and Tarya turned them all to stone, trapping them where they stood, creating the Dragonbacks in the process.

Skeðu they banished to The Lorn, the empty space where is Nothing, and bound him there, to pay for his crimes and to prevent his further interference in the fate of Adan. It was said he would someday break free, at the End of Ages; that he would return to the World, break the stone surrounding his dragons, and war again against Aeos and the Astra.

But that was not for many years to come, and in the meantime, the mountain range, steeped as it was in the darkest and lightest of magics in turn, was home to bizarre creatures, dangerous terrain, and the most intense weather in all of Adan. Magic the strength of what Konn and Tarya wielded was not without cost, nor without lasting effect. The pair had died not long after the Vast Battle, untouched by sword or spear or arrow, but burned out from the magic within. In the place where they had stood, in the very midst of what had been Skeðu's line, there grew up a wood over the centuries. It was a cursed place, most said, comprised of impossibly tall, thick trees that took every sound and reflected it back tenfold. Echowoods, they were named, and they towered over the whole of the Darksbane Forest, black from root to crown. The effect of sunlight shining through such a thick black canopy would be arresting, indeed, but it was not known since none who entered that forest ever returned alive. Some who had traveled near it said the woods echoed with moans, strange cries, and the laughter of children—that, combined with the disappearances, kept all but the most stupid from braving the trees. Even the Val'gren avoided the place.

Echowood, therefore, was exceedingly costly. The strong, dark, limber wood was found deep within the Darksbane; the only way to acquire it was to pull out any branches the river happened to wash down as it flowed through the wood. A small figurine carved from true echowood would make a man rich for life, and the lucky few who had managed to come by an entire felled trunk or thick branch could feed their next three generations off the coin.

But when Ryn had stumbled across a bough as long as she was tall eight years prior, she hadn't even considered that for a moment. She'd been a bit busy with trouble, actually, fighting a gang of dirty, angry bandits who had a mind to sell her down in the barbarian city of Ongrund, far to the south. They had kicked her feet from under her—she was barely seventeen summers at the time, still young and inexperienced—and her scrabbling fingers had closed around the smooth wood, warm from the sun. Even as one of them yanked her to him by her feet and rolled her onto her back, she'd brought the makeshift staff around with all her might. The branch sang as it moved, striking the bandit full across the head as he straddled her and knocking him completely unconscious to lie in the grass at her side.

Ryn had scrambled to her feet, swinging and spinning the branch as best she knew how, calling on her small knowledge of sword craft—for she had spent many an hour as a child observing the knights and squires in her uncle's service. When she had temporarily wounded all four of the large men, she had run for it.

She never went anywhere without the rod of echowood after that. Over the years, she had smoothed the knots away, all but the twisted one at the end, large as her two fists together, letting that tangle naturally as it would and using it as a club end when she fought. She painstakingly carved various runes into the beautiful wood, spelled it to resist wear and tear and breakage, with the help of one of the Tribe during her brief time with them—not that it needed it, as echowood was nigh on indestructible—and worked on wielding the thing until she could easily kill with it. It was her most prized possession, as much an extension of her will and body as Kota was.

And they beat her with it.

Kudrack had ordered her Branded that first day after she awoke tied to a tree. The sigil had burned the tender skin of her forearm far worse than seemed warranted, but Ryn was unsurprised by this. She had heard of the Val'gren using such arcane measures in their sacrifices; spells and sigils intended to push the unfortunate victim past the limits of their mental or emotional capacity for pain, even as the physical torment ravaged their bodies. Supposedly, it made the sacrifice more powerful, the complete destruction of an entire person; body, soul, and spirit.

What was a little surprising was that nagrat were using it. The practice was generally looked down upon by the nagrat Large Clans, the ones who still held to their Old Ways, from before the Val'gren had seduced and enslaved their race. The Old Ways made killing a glorious act that directly reflected one's skill and brought honor to his clan, but torture was eschewed as undignified and pointless.

Clearly Kudrack's band did not care for the Old Ways.

For five days, it had been the same. The nagrat broke camp every dawn, bound her to the back of a smelly, filthy chimaera like a sack of potatoes, and rode north all day. As the sun neared the western horizon, when she was sore and jangled from her ride, she became the evening entertainment while they awaited their dinner; each night they started off with her hair, jostling her between them, alternately yanking out handfuls of the dark curls and sawing at them with daggers. Then they beat her, poked and prodded her with sticks and spear butts and boots, to see how much she would take. This part Ryn bore silently, refusing to give them the satisfaction, which unfortunately, seemed to make the game more fun for them. It was disheartening; the few times Ryn had been captured in her time alone—once by bandits and once by a small band of nagrat, much less experienced than these, merely a scouting band—her silence had gone far toward frustrating and distracting her enemies, enabling her escape. That trick did not work here, had not worked for nearly a week now.

After supper—at which time she received a clay cup of dirty water, her only nourishment for the day—she had the distinct non-privilege of a few hours with Kudrack. He was both cunning and ruthless with his rack and his tools, she had learned. She had a feeling the nagrat were under strict orders not to kill her—to begrudge their Val'gren Master of the honor would be death—but they were doing their very best to tiptoe right up to the line.

Tonight, Ryn's thoughts drifted as she awaited Kudrack, strapped cruelly to a makeshift table the nagrat had built from branches and stones. Random twigs and points of rock poked at her, but they were more nuisance than pain, her mind nowhere near here.

Of enemies, she had no short supply. Life on the road was hard, and she knew personally of kobolds, the little man-like creatures interested only in gold and vicious mischief; the hairless ones, re-animated bodies of the dead that sometimes wandered within swamps and other places of filth; sprites and chimaeras and wild animals that would as soon eat her as look at her. There were even regular folk who'd fallen on hard times, or just enjoyed their mean streak—pirates on the sea, bandits on land—who would rob folk before murdering them outright.

All of them Ryn had dealt with personally at least once in her past.

She was mostly sure no experience had ever been this brutal. She came back to the moment as Kudrack stomped toward her—he seemed angry tonight—and without preamble, sliced deeply into the tender skin of her belly with his short knife. He knew enough about human anatomy not to hit any organs, but the pain was incredible anyway, and Ryn whimpered. It was not the first of these small, deep punctures she had received—nor was it likely to be the last—but that in no way meant she'd grown used to the pain of them. To the contrary—the sigil made it such that the pain seemed only to grow, never lessen, under its influence. The bruises and lacerations she'd received three days ago hurt as though they were happening at this very moment, just as badly as the slice she had just been given moments before.

It was intense in a way she wasn't sure she could handle much more of.

The worst of it was, Kudrack never even asked her any questions. There was no chance to earn a respite while she blathered an aimless answer, nothing with which to distract herself from the ongoing agony. The brute was entirely devoid of commentary the whole time, and Ryn didn't like to admit how unnerving it was.

Not that she hadn't tried to remedy that part of the situation. She had tried for four days to goad Kudrack into some sort of response that she could control, even a little bit. She had remained completely silent throughout his torture, just to annoy him. She had screamed insults, threats, and curses. She had cried and even gone so far as to beg for mercy, a break, anything; but he would just smile and continue his work.

Tonight, worn weary by the unrelenting torture, she finally sobbed, hoarsely, "What is it you want from me?!"

Kudrack smiled and slid his crude blade across Ryn's exposed skin before stabbing again, just to the left of her belly button. The Hunt Chief leaned in, close enough for Ryn to smell the rotting flesh of his last meal on his breath. Her stomach churned with pain and nausea as she tried to jerk away, to no avail. Her bonds were quite snug.

The nagrat sniffed once, enjoying the scent of her fear, licked a smear of blood from her cheek. Ryn flinched, and hated herself for it.

"Kudrack wants you to suffer," he whispered, and sliced her, hard and deep and fast, from right hip to knee. Ryn screeched in agony. The abuse continued for hours more, for Kudrack was in rare form tonight. The shadows in the forest grew long, and the air grew chill. Ryn stopped shivering after a while, when her body seemed to decide she couldn't spare the energy for it. Her screaming degenerated into breathless gasps and the occasional moan.

Eventually, the monster decided she'd had enough. Still silent, he snapped his fingers, and two of his lackeys lumbered over, releasing her from the table and yanking her off of it. She shuddered as they jostled her roughly, lances of pain piercing through her bruises and cuts, old and new, but had no more energy to protest. They dragged her across the camp, letting the lower-ranking nagrat jeer and throw stones as she was paraded toward tonight's precarious-looking lean-to guarded by three massive hunters. They dropped her unceremoniously inside and trussed her up, tying her legs together and restraining her hands behind her back. She wished they'd left her hands in front; she needed to stop the bleeding from her various lacerations if she could.

Left alone with no way to stay warm, Ryn curled into the closest approximation of the fetal position that she could possibly manage, restrained as she was. Her head ended up near her knees in a futile attempt to retain heat and manage some semblance of pressure for her bleeding wounds, but it took a lot of effort to remain in that position with her hands bound behind her back. She was forced to give it up mere minutes later, swallowing a sob as her abdomen began bleeding sluggishly again. She shivered against the dirt, trying not to think about how much pain she was in, trying not to think of her matted, ripped out hair or her tormentors, sitting round a blazing fire and eating venison, something that would normally have smelled tempting, if she wasn't currently battling crippling nausea in addition to her pain.

Five days. Five *days* of this nonsense they had put her through, never asking any questions or giving any demands beyond "I want you to suffer"; stabbing, cutting, punching, kicking, all with the undercurrent of that insidious Val'gren magic that wouldn't allow her body to rest or recover.

Wait.

Ryn's eyes widened in the darkness as she realized it, kicking herself for not thinking of this days ago. The sigil! The sigil was a good portion of what made this so impossible to bear—the building pain, no break, no rest, just more and more pain til she nearly went mad with it—that was all the sigil's work! She knew basically where on her arm it was. If she could break it, she could hold out until…well, escape seemed unlikely, given the size of this group, but maybe once she could think straight she'd be able to manage it. She did not dare hope for rescue.

"Hate this," she heard one of her guards mutter, and found herself agreeing with the brute. It was a damned appalling situation all around. She gleaned a tiny bit of satisfaction that, for whatever reason, her enemies—or at least one of them—was enjoying this about as much as she. Ryn cast about in the darkness for something sharp. A rock, a stick, anything would do. She just needed the tiniest nick on the symbol itself to render it inert. "Should be on the Hunt," the raspy voice continued. A scuff followed, as though he had kicked the ground in frustration.

Ryn knew the feeling.

"Should," a second, more nasal, voice agreed. This one's voice was grating, like the scream of a vixen in heat, and made her cringe. The slight motion made her hiss in discomfort, earning a kick against the lean-to that shook the thing precariously.

"Quiet!" the first guard hissed. "'Fore we make you." They both chuckled wickedly at the threat.

Ryn resisted the urge to kick back, simply on principle. She needed them to talk to each other, to leave her be. She lay very still. A few moments later, their complaints started up again. "Want to hunt the runt princes," the nasally one whined, and if his voice had been cringe-worthy before, now it was downright painful. Ryn moved her hands slowly over the ground, praying, hoping for something that could cut her skin. Her stomach lurched as a hard object pricked her finger. A broken piece of wood, as far as she could tell, long enough to reach the blasted burn on her arm. She positioned it slowly, turning it so the point rested at her wrist.

"Gotta catch 'em while they're away from home," the growly one said. "Never be able t'snatch 'em from their stinkin' city." Ryn moved the stick's point carefully up her arm until she felt it touch the aching sigil. At the contact, agony radiated from the brand, and she almost gave up.

Think of Kota. Think of your friends.

Think of yourself.

She pressed, firmly but carefully—she needed to nick the symbol, not kill herself—and swallowed a whimper as she felt the wood sink into her flesh.

"They's s'pposed to be movin' south," the other nagrat carped. "Don' ev'n know why we stopped for this little slut." He kicked the side of her lean-to again, and Ryn jumped, hand slipping, causing her to yank the wood far harder than she'd intended across her forearm. She yelped at the pain before she could stop herself.

Deep into their grievances now, the guards ignored her entirely.

"But Râza'll be pleased t'have her, know?"

Ryn barely heard him. It had worked—the pain of her injuries from days past had lessened considerably, to a much more normal level for old cuts and bruises—but her arm was on *fire*. The ache was deeper than ever, and she could feel hot blood pouring over her fingers and the wooden shiv.

Oh no.

She felt the ice in her veins, forming thicker with every beat of her traitorous heart. Her arm hurt so badly she had trouble concentrating, and blood continued to pour even though she'd clamped her fingers over it as best she could in her position. Her head screamed with agony, her hearing was going fuzzy, like she was underwater. And through it all, cold flowed its slow but inexorable way through every fiber of her being, numbing.

I am not ready.

The thought struck her like the sky-fire on the plains. She had thought herself prepared for death, near as it often was in her line of work.

The coins are not returned to Talos. I cannot die yet.

So it was thoughts of her lost brother that were the last, before the pain and nausea finally became too much and Ryn's world went black.

~~~~~~~~~~

It was nearing sunset when Evin finally realized the truth of where they stood. It had been coming on for nearly two days, ever since they'd defeated the wyvern. Brandt had been energetic, almost sprightly, for the first hour or two after they left their ransacked camp. He had run as though they were racing along the parapet back home, turning ever so often to shout encouragement to Evin, who huffed along behind, carrying Kota as gently as possible on his shoulders, wincing as each breath pulled his own bruised ribs. But as the hours wore on, Brandt had succumbed to his wounds; the sun was high in the sky as he grew silent and pale. Later he slowed, and by midafternoon he had stopped entirely. He'd fought for breath, damaged ribs protesting every intake of oxygen, the pain of his arm making itself known.

Evin had suggested they walk for a bit.

That had been the day before. They had struck camp near sunset, in a cleft of sharp gray rock, despite Brandt's very vocal protestations. "The nagrat do not stop to rest," he had growled.

51

"The nagrat are not near falling where they stand."

Salted beef and hard bread had been their spartan dinner, for neither of them were daft enough to suggest starting a fire. Evin had changed Brandt's bandages, applied a salve he'd cobbled together from elderberry and cat's claw, checked to see if the stubborn man had done any lasting damage to his ribs, and sent his brother to bed. Exhausted beyond measure, he had crawled into his own bedroll minutes later. He'd uttered a quick prayer to the Master of Light that no enemies would find them this night, for he knew that if they did, their sad little party was unlikely to survive the encounter.

But the darkest hours had passed, uneventful, and now the sun was cresting the horizon while Kota wheezed at his feet, bandages bloody and the heat from a poison-induced fever obvious even through Evin's clothes. It was a poor sign. He hadn't mentioned it, and neither had Brandt, but they both knew that the nagrat's tracks were leading them ever closer to the northern border of Laendor—that they would soon leave friendly lands entirely and be well inside the Val'gren's own kingdom, Karokhim. There were practical considerations to be made for that—Evin couldn't imagine Brandt was blind to the fact that Uncle would bust both their heads if he found out they'd been bumbling about in enemy territory; and if they were caught, it would not go well with either of them were their identity to be discovered. He hoped beyond hope that Brandt was wrong, that the nagrat were stopping for frequent, and long, resting periods. That they would be able to somehow sneak into a heavily guarded enemy camp and rescue their friend. That they could do it without being seen, for the nagrat numbered too many to defeat with two of them and a huge lynx, even if they'd been at their peak, and they were none of them at that, certainly.

And there was Kota. Evin knew Brandt's arm was blazing with pain and hot with fever, but for some incomprehensible biological reason, the saliva of wyvern was non-lethal while its claws held the toxin that could end a life. The lynx had received more than a fair share of said poison, and it showed in his shallow breathing, painfully-fast heartbeat, and the heat that raged through his body. Frankly, Evin was surprised the lynx was still alive. That's when he realized.

They weren't going to be able to continue the hunt. How could they, in such a state?

He reached down to bury freezing fingers in Kota's damp, limp fur. The lynx growled softly at his touch—even that much contact hurt him now—and Evin drew his hand back, stung.

"He worsened overnight." Brandt's voice behind him didn't startle Evin, for he knew his brother's movements like he knew his own. Instead, he simply nodded once to confirm the elder's suspicions. Tired as he'd been, Evin had woken every hour to check on Kota, and he had watched the creature fail as the hours passed, hopelessness settling in his breast, right beside the still-festering guilt. It was a near-physical pain now, a knot the size of a small boulder inside his rib cage, squeezing the life out of his very soul.

"We cannot keep up the pursuit," Brandt continued, softly, as though he expected Evin to push back, to argue with him. The younger wanted to, *oh* how he wanted to rail and protest and fight the idea that they should leave their guide—their friend—in the hands of the nagrat; but he knew better. Kota would die; there was little anyone could do about it now. Wyvern poison was very much real, as the legends said, and very deadly. Brandt was injured and unable to fight as well as usual. Evin himself was exhausted and badly bruised. They could not take on an entire hunting party of the barbarians like this.

"Thaliondris is not far," his brother's voice was low, comforting, and Evin felt a big hand warm on his shoulder. He shivered; he hadn't realized he was cold. His answer stuck in his throat, and he had to cough before he managed to get it out, thick and quiet.

"Then let us make for the City of Healing, brother." Evin swallowed against that hard stone of guilt and grief in his chest. "Kota will be more comfortable there, and I want that arm of yours taken proper care of." He looked up at Brandt, finally, breath catching as he noticed that his brother looked much worse for wear; barely better than their lynx did, even. His eyes were sunken and dull, rimmed with red. His cheeks were bright with fever, scarlet against his gray skin. He even held himself differently, half-slumped and exhausted. The Heir needed Healers, and soon. *Immediately*.

And yet, his heart was divided still. "But...Ryn?"

Brandt sighed, tired eyes projecting the same regret Evin himself felt. "I am sorry."

~~~~~~~~~~

She was poised atop a rocky hill overlooking a valley. She did not recognize the place; green meadows and tidy farms stretched before her, far as the horizon. Neat little roads provided paths between, and as she looked she could make out marketplaces and small towns, great cities and tiny hovels. On either side, magnificent mountains rose from the flat earth, rugged and steep. To her left, the sun shone on white stone—the bones of the mountain range white as any human's. On these grew mighty forests and strips of rich grasses and wildflowers. Deer and hares and great cats roamed freely, and the birds sang happily.

But a cold wind blew upon her skin from her right, drawing her attention as her skin pimpled with gooseflesh. This mountain range was rugged and beautiful, as well, though in such a different way as to be day

53

and night. Sharp rocks and barely-balanced boulders cracked in the freezing air. Nothing grew at all, the blackened stone foundations of the right-side mountain range visible for all to see. The soil was hard and dry, and only the most twisted of plants grew there, stunted and tough, with thorns to protect them from the wild beasts that roamed. Of those, she could see several kinds—chimaeras, wyvern, a true dragon seated firmly upon one of the taller peaks. He was bigger than anything Ryn had ever seen, easily equal in size to one of the smaller mountains near the fringe of the range, and all black from head to tail tip. He did not appear to see her, roaring now and then and bathing the black mountains with his fiery breath, seemingly for the sheer pleasure of it. Oddly, the fire seemed to possess no heat.

The light faded over the valley, and night came as she watched. The dark rolled across her field of vision, seeming to come from the Black Mountains and the dragon seated upon them, consuming everything it touched. She watched in horror as the inky blackness of night reached the farmhouse nearest it; the moment it contacted the wood of the little house, the structure faded to dust, along with the echoed screams of its inhabitants. Ryn tried to cry out but found her voice silenced, her legs paralyzed, could only stand there and observe as the Dark destroyed everything it kissed, the green valley turning brown and desolate before her very eyes. Ryn resisted the urge to cover her ears at the screams echoing around her—if she did nothing to help, she could at least endure their cries. Tears stung her eyes.

A puff of air tickled her right ear and ruffled her hair, startling her. It rumbled into a low growl as she turned slowly to regard a massive silver chimaera, all black eyes, razor-sharp teeth, and curved claws. The monster stood so close Ryn could smell its putrid breath rolling over her. She stumbled back in silent shock, tripping clumsily on her own feet, as the chimaera followed her with its eyes. Upon its back sat a massive Val'gren, deliberately-patterned ritual scars standing out in sharp relief to the blue light the moon cast on his white skin. Ryn knew little of their culture, though she knew more than most, and the scars were marks of those a Val'gren had killed. This one, staring haughtily down at her, had killed hundreds.

Râza.

Now she remembered! She had heard the name of the Val'gren war chief when her mother told her of the Sons of Laendor. Râza the one responsible for the death of King Bjorn and nine of his ten sons; the eldest, Prince Hakon, had been the one to defeat him.

Defeat him.

He was defeated. Dead. Gone and doubtless a rotted carcass somewhere in the deep, dark places of the world. Nothing more than a legend now, a tale told to make naughty children mind their parents.

Then why had the guard said Râza would be pleased to have her turned over to him?

A clawing of panic stirred in her gut. The stories only said the Val'gren had been defeated, not killed. What if he was back? She thought, with a jolt of fear, about the reputation she'd been building for the last decade— *Draugr*, the Phantom, bane of Val'gren scouts and harasser of all things evil. Leyna, the Guardian of Roads. Surely, it was no large stretch, after ten years, for such rumors to have reached the war chief of the justifiably-feared Val'gren.

What had she done?

She heard a shout of her name and tore her eyes from the horrifying creature beside her to two men that seemed to be fighting the encroaching destruction. It took her a moment to recognize them, so bright were they to her eyes, beings of light and courage with flaming swords, pushing back the Dark. Evin, mischief in his eyes and honey in his words, taunted the wraith-like creatures that harried him, while steady Brandt hacked mercilessly at the slender tendrils of Black that kept trying to worm their way between the brothers. They fought back to back and side to side, one indivisible unit, unstoppable and unbearably radiant. Ryn's heart skipped painfully in her chest and she willed them to run away, even while hoping beyond wild hope they would help her.

They were joined by others, then, others she did not recognize, but that shone just as fiercely. Together, they began to make some headway against the Dark itself. Something told Ryn that safety lay with them, if she could just *get* there. With hardly a backward glance at the chimaera or its rider, Ryn sprinted toward the knot of heroes.

She tried to sprint, truly she did. As often happens in dreams, her legs felt like lead and she could barely move. Her heart pounded a wild tattoo in her chest, her breath coming in shallow, panicked spurts as she fought to free her legs from the mire. Val'gren surrounded her, slender white fingers inhumanly strong, pulling her hair, bruising her skin. Râza laughed and began riding toward her, slowly, murder in his gaze. Desperate, she screamed:

"Evin!"

Shouting a challenge, both brothers sped toward her, mowing down everything that got in their way.

Ryn bolted upright, disoriented, then immediately moaned as the movement sparked pain in every muscle of her body. Her hands were still tied behind her back, and it was throwing off her balance. The sun shone brightly through the canvas top of her little shelter, warm and pleasant on her skin. Her legs were numb, her back cramped, her shoulders *really* ached...

She stopped moving as she realized:

55

Her punctured stomach no longer hurt.

Well, unless a growl of hunger counted as pain. Astra, but she was *famished*. Ryn looked down and tried to see her skin without the use of her hands, with no luck. Her linen shirt, torn and ripped as it was, still covered what she most wanted to see. She blinked, settling back and trying to take stock of herself.

The pervasive silence struck her, out of place for a traveling camp. Ryn could see a strip of sunlight on the dirt near her thigh. Mid morning...the nagrat should have left already, come and bound her to the back of one of those cursed chimaeras and headed north again. Ryn scooted forward on her rump, not caring she would likely get kicked in the gut for this, and used her foot to push back the scrap of wool that covered the entrance to her lean-to.

Her breath caught in her throat.

They were all *dead*. Beside the fire, in the doorways of small shelters, slumped at the entrance to her own lean-to; bodies lay, white and still and stiff. Even the chimaeras were dead, their dark fur dull in the morning light.

By Aoes.

Ryn couldn't imagine a creature, or any force of nature, that could kill an entire camp of nagrat like this, swift and silent and leaving not a scratch; and she wasn't about to stick around and find out. Scooting out of the shelter entirely and maneuvering so her back was to one of the dead guards, she felt around until she'd located the utility dagger sheathed at his right hip. She drew it, the rasp over-loud in the quiet forest, and went to work on her bonds. She cringed as the pins and needles sensation began in her fingers.

It took only a moment for the sturdy ties to snap under the sharp blade, but it did take a good while for her hands to be worth anything more than decorative limbs on either side of her torso. When they did finally wake up from their rope-enforced sleep, they tingled and ached and stung most vehemently. Despite that, Ryn cut her legs loose and used protesting hands to work feeling back into her lower extremities too. In all, it was over a quarter hour before she was finally able to stand, sort of. She leaned heavily on the frame of her former prison, working out the last of the kinks and debating the benefits versus risks of looting the bodies.

She hadn't decided on a course of action yet when the clear, rich tones of a war horn sounded nearby, startling her.

8

The decision to turn toward Thaliondris had been the right one, Evin knew. But knowing it didn't quell the pit in his stomach with each step they took away from their quarry and their friend. A single word, the only descriptor he could think of, in spite of the logic behind their actions, rang in his head with every league toward the elven city.

Abandonment.

It was ridiculous; Ryn would've skinned him alive if they'd kept going when Kota's injuries were so grim and their own chance of actually helping her kept diminishing by the second. Of their party, Evin himself was the only one left relatively unharmed, so long as you didn't count the bruised ribs he was sporting and trying to hide from his brother. Brandt had problems of his own right now. Wyvern saliva may not be poisoned, but that didn't mean it didn't contain Aeos-only-knew-what filth, and despite Evin's homemade herbal concoctions, Brandt's fever persisted.

Before them, a clearing opened in the trees and they could see that the sun was just beginning to crest the ridged horizon. The pale sky was clear— it was to be a beautiful day—and the new sunlight shone in bands through the trees around them. The sound of hoof beats gave barely a second's warning before a horse thundered into the clearing, whinnying at the sight of them. Brandt turned, snatching one of his axes from its sheath with his good arm, twirling it threateningly. Evin crouched to lay Kota gently between him and his brother, assuming a defensive stance over the lynx, who moaned but lay still.

More of the beasts rushed into the clearing; ten or so, though it was difficult to count them. The travelers found themselves surrounded, the horses snuffling and pawing as their riders brought them to a halt. The wood-elves were instantly recognizable; a smattering of richly-colored faces, for the Eloni were born with skin that suited best their particular strengths and probable place in the wood elves' society. Healers tended to be shades of blue, Growers different hues of green, and Warriors like these, reds and browns. They wielded elegant bows, slung across their backs already strung, and long slender blades, which they had drawn immediately upon seeing Brandt and Evin. Clearly, they were expecting battle, the younger thought, dropping into a crouch and drawing his own sword. He had not realized they had drifted so far East while tracking the nagrat. The Eloni were allies to the Men of Laendor, but their land was sacred to them, and to trespass upon it beyond the road without express permission was death for anyone.

Brandt seemed uncertain whether to fight or talk, eyes moving rapidly as the elves surrounded them. His face was hard, but Evin saw the faint lines appear in his forehead that told him his brother was afraid; and well he should be. The fate of their kingdom and their quest—not to mention Kota's and Ryn's lives—depended heavily upon what would transpire in the next few moments. Brandt's gaze settled on a burgundy hulk of an elf wearing a swirling circlet - the group's obvious leader – but before he could utter a word, a slight she-elf lighted from her white mare and rushed to Kota's side. Her skin was light enough to be pink, and she bore the intricate tattoos of a battle healer. She skidded to her knees in the grass, paying absolutely no mind to the two large warriors standing over the creature, shouldering Evin's legs aside as she touched the lynx gently on the forehead.

Evin did not stumble, but he fell back a couple steps, aghast. "Hey!" he shouted, uncertain how to react.

Brandt got out half of a "what?"" before the leader spoke.

"Travelers," the elf stated, his voice a booming rumble. "What is your business here?"

"We are making for your fair city," Brandt answered, clearly calling on his statecraft training to make his words smooth, confident, nonthreatening. "Our guide was taken by the nagrat six days ago, and our lynx was ravaged by a wyvern night before last. I also was bitten by the same creature before we dispatched it. We were hoping you could render us some assistance, as well as allow us to rest and refit for the remainder of our journey east."

"Commander, he is badly wounded," the young woman spoke up from beside Kota, her roseate hands bright against his red-brown fur and the stained bandages. "He needs the Menders."

The elf nodded from astride his massive destrier. "And the Menders he shall have, just as soon as it is possible." He looked to Brandt and Evin. "I am Commander Jorlan Windspeaker, this—" he motioned to a lithe, burgundy-skinned warrioress on a bay mare, who nodded once, "—is my lieutenant, Nenna. We have received reports of a nagrat hunting party in the area, and ride to battle." The look on his face was fierce. "They must needs be reminded why they so seldom trespass upon our lands."

Brandt looked to his brother—a question—and Evin nodded, once. "We may be of assistance," Brandt offered. "We are both trained fighters. If any of your mounts can bear us, we would be honored to ride with you. We wish to know the fate of our guide."

"Any blow to those barbarians we can serve, we would gladly deliver,"

Evin growled behind him.

Jorlan stared at them steadily, yellow eyes assessing as he considered. "You are wounded. You are not strong enough to be of use," he said to Brandt. Evin saw the elder's face pale slightly at the affront, and felt the heat in his own face.

"My brother is strong," he protested, but Brandt held up a forestalling hand.

"The Commander is right," he confessed softly, just to Evin. "And he certainly means no insult." His brother turned back to the Eloni and lifted his chin. "I will take the lynx and make for Thaliondris on foot, with your permission, while my brother accompanies you to hunt down these nagrat brutes."

Jorlan seemed to consider. Apparently he took too long for the lady healer, who spoke up. "I will take them on to the City," she said. "My lord, the kit cannot wait."

"Very well, Calle," Jorlan agreed after a moment. "It shall be."

It took a matter of minutes to ready for departure; Jorlan gave Brandt and the Healer two horses, requiring a few of the warriors to double up. It took a couple of the stronger elves to get Kota settled in such a way that the ride would not injure him further. Evin mounted up behind the fierce-looking lieutenant—Nenna, her name had been—and waved to his brother. Brandt looked stricken for half a moment, but then they were off, like sky-fire upon graceful steeds. Evin sent up a prayer of protection for Brandt as his brother faded into the distance behind them.

Jorlan thundered ahead of them, and Evin took a moment to observe his companion. The lass was an archer, her short bow held in one hand as she rode, a quiver slung at her side. She wore leather armor, light and easy to travel in, and her wine-colored skin was a stark contrast to the white bear's paw that was tattooed over half of her face. Evin had to admit the effect was both striking and intimidating. Her white hair was straight and short, practical for a fighter, but unusual for a woman.

A human woman, he corrected himself. The Eloni were definitely not human.

Beneath their feet the ground flew by, and the wind tangled Evin's hair despite the living shield behind whom he rode. He wondered vaguely if Eloni horses were faster than Laendorian ones, for he had never ridden at such a speed in his entire life.

"How far?" he shouted after a while.

"Less than a league now!" Nenna answered, and it was then that Jorlan placed a war horn to his lips and let loose a thunderous note that vibrated in the very atmosphere. It made the hair on Evin's arms stand up, an undercurrent of powerful magic, the promise of death to those who served the Dark.

Not for nothing had the Eloni been considered allies of the staunchest sort through history. They seldom went to war or fought battles, but when they did? Legend said the earth itself would shake with the force of their magic, and all but the strongest foes would flee in terror.

Around him, warriors drew their swords, their bows, released their staves from back sheaths, readied for a fight. Evin stretched to peer over Nenna's shoulder and caught a glimpse of the camp toward which they flew—smoke drifted lazily from several smoldering fires, lean-to's and small shelters marred the field, tucked against the border of a small forest. A banner upon which was painted the elegant swirl of Skeðu drew his attention, blood-red against a black background mounted upon a war spike taller than he.

Evin drew his long sword and joined the others in a wild battle cry, the sound blasting through his veins and making him itch to fight something.

They thundered into the camp, blades held high, to be met with complete silence and not the slightest word of protest from their enemies. Slowly, they came to a canter, then a full stop. Something was wrong: they had just ridden straight into a nagrat hunting camp without being challenged once.

"Well. This is eerie," he murmured to no one in particular, glancing about and trying to see. But Nenna shook her head and pointed her bow at the feet of her mare. Evin's gaze followed.

"Oh." He couldn't help the murmur of shock that left his suddenly-numb lips. The party had gone completely silent in the wake of realization, and Evin shuddered. Around him, nagrat lay dead in every imaginable pose, as though they had just been stricken in the midst of everyday life. Pale and stiff, eyes wide and unseeing, they stared up into the morning sky.

With not a visible injury upon them.

It was honestly the most terrifying thing Evin had ever laid eyes on. Any mage—for it was clear their deaths were magically produced—powerful enough to do this to a hunting party of the massive, beastly dark creatures was something to be feared. Even the chimaera mounts were dead.

Evin felt cold despite the bright morning sun, and he looked around desperately for any sign of Ryn.

He could see none. He shivered.

"We should leave this place," Nenna murmured, shifting uncomfortably. Evin silently disagreed with her, but Jorlan appeared to be considering something. The Commander sat perfectly still, eyes closed, face twitching as if he sensed...something.

"The magic here feels old, but not evil," he finally spoke, in response to the questioning gazes upon him. "It is......unfamiliar to me." He shook his head, black hair shining in the early morning sun. "Check for living. Do not touch the dead. I will return here with the Elders. They must see this place." He turned to Nenna. "We will depart the moment we are certain none yet live." The lass nodded and signaled to the others.

Evin dismounted and moved cautiously to the front of their mount, kneeling to examine the prints in the soft dirt; Nenna was speaking softly to Jorlan. "Bring Kenelm when you return, my lord. He will know of this."

"The old one?" Jorlan questioned.

Nenna gave what was apparently an affirmative, then said, "He is eccentric, but wise in these matters."

Evin saw no human footprints, so he stood, chucked their horse under her chin gently and moved toward the midst of the camp. He studied the ground, poked and prodded at several motionless nagrat with his sword, growing more uneasy with each lifeless body he saw. None of them bore any evidence of battle, or even sickness. They were ugly, in the way nagrat were, but they were not damaged. They were simply...dead.

Finally he caught sight of several prints that were neither animal nor nagrat. There were long scuffs in the dirt, just on the very top layer of soil, punctuated by close-set prints that looked distinctly human, distinctly distressed—Ryn had been dragged. One side seemed to strike deeper than the other, which implied she was either injured or off-balance. Ignoring the chill that crept down his spine, Evin followed the tracks to the very center of the carnage, leading straight into a small lean-to with a canvas flap over the open side. He crouched and looked inside, steeling himself for what he might see.

Evin's heart jumped into his throat when he saw the blood covering the small wedge of green wood. It was very sharp on one end, but the entire thing was the ugly dark red of coagulated blood, and the grass in a good foot-diameter circle around it was stained the same color.

It was the first sign of injury he'd seen here yet. It didn't make him feel any better.

"Ryn, no, come on..." he murmured shakily. Backing out of the rough shelter on his hands and knees, he noticed the ropes.

Blood-covered ropes, sliced cleanly in half. Then others, unstained, longer than the first but also clean-cut.

"Ryn?" he murmured, looking up as though she'd be standing right in front of him. He rose, ropes still in hand, and scanned the ground around the shelter. His heart thumped in his chest when he found them, uneven and stumbling, human footprints.

Ryn.

Evin rose and began to follow the halting tracks, completely unaware of the bustling Eloni around him now.

On the very edge of the camp, he found a nagrat that had evidently stepped away from the rest—a guard, perhaps, or a scout maybe. The tracks led straight to it. The creature's eyes were closed, but when Evin nudged it with his sword, it flailed suddenly with a savage growl. He startled, jumped back even as muscle memory brought his sword down in a lethal blow. He stopped it just in time, his desperate need for information overcoming any sense of danger he felt—the nagrat was weak and struggling to breathe, clearly not in any condition to do him harm.

"What happened here?" he demanded, resting the point of his sword at the creature's neck. Muddy yellow eyes squinted up at him as the nagrat fell back, its head hitting the ground with a low thunk. Evin waited for a moment, thinking it would answer once it caught its breath, but the nagrat stared fixedly at the sky. He could see it breathing, so he knew he was being ignored. Thinking of his friend, Evin growled his rage, pressing harder against the nagrat's vulnerable neck. "Where is she?" he asked, his voice icy. "Your prisoner, what did you do with her?"

The brute looked at him then, met his eyes and gave him a weak grin. "So many questions," it croaked, voice rough as filing stones. "Your little whore is dead." Then it began to laugh, a pained, choked sound that evoked no pity in Evin.

No.

"If she is dead, then so are you." Evin was looking the nagrat in the eyes when he thrust the tip of his sword deliberately into its chest. He kept its gaze during the few seconds it took for the thing to finish bleeding out, gasping and choking as black liquid pooled in the grass. Only when it stopped moving entirely, blank eyes fixed on the sunny sky, did Evin allow his expression to twist at the nagrat's claim.

Dead? It cannot be. And yet...

The tracks ended here. There was no one left alive in the carnage of that camp. The only reason this one seemed to have survived was because it had been further away from its companions, outside the light of any campfires and well past the line of hastily-erected canvas shelters. If Ryn had been held inside the camp, in that rough, tiny lean-to, she would have been directly in the line of whatever had struck down the rest of them.

Also there was all the blood. The sliced ropes and staggering tracks leading away from the lean-to made it seem she had survived, at least temporarily; but there was a *lot* of blood. Evin's heart clenched and his stomach twisted at the thought.

He liked Ryn. She was fierce, and smart, and refused to fit any mold she was shoved into. She'd taken what was obviously a painful childhood and turned it into a downright heroic adulthood, and Evin couldn't have admired her more for it. He bowed his head, allowing the grief to wash over him slowly, knowing it would be all the worse when Kota eventually realized—

"What did you do?" Nenna growled angrily from his left. Evin looked up at her; she looked down at his sword impaled deep in the dead nagrat's chest.

"It was dying," he supplied, his voice sounding distracted even to his own ears.

Nenna studied him for a moment. "You should have called one of us over. It might have had information—"

Nenna petered off, staring past him, and Evin startled a little when he heard a gasp to his right. Whirling to meet whatever danger lay there, he nearly fell over entirely when his eyes registered what he was seeing.

Their guide was standing before him. She was bloody, dirty, pale, and her hair was a hopeless tattered mess, but it was definitely her.

"You," he murmured.

~~~~~~~~~~~

"You," Ryn breathed, and her knees shook. Had he been here the whole time? Had he been a prisoner too? She looked him up and down. He was filthy and gray, looked tired and his face was slightly pinched with some pain, but he didn't seem to find it overwhelming. He looked far too well to have been a...*guest* of the nagrat. "What in the name of all that's sacred are you doing here?" Her gaze skipped between Evin and the warlike party of wood elves at his back, trying to process the shock. Now that she was more certain she wasn't in danger of dying in the next five minutes, her legs seemed to have decided they'd had just about enough supporting her. Her vision swam.

Oh I might need to sit down.

"He said you were dead," Evin answered faintly, gesturing vaguely to the motionless nagrat at his feet. Ryn saw his long sword impaling the brute's chest, and couldn't muster even a little pity for it. Not after the last several days of captivity. She bit back a wild desire to laugh.

"He was obviously misinformed."

Evin blinked, then barked a choked-off chuckle, but the sound was more stunned than amused.

Ryn tried to smile, but couldn't quite manage it all of a sudden. Darkness encroached on the edges of her vision; she was not keen on the idea of fainting right here and now, and certainly not in front of everyone. Evin stepped closer to her, hands out in a conciliatory gesture, as if he was afraid she might bolt.

She almost laughed at the thought. Running was the furthest thing from her mind, even if the Eloni around her were quite alarming, all strange colors and unfamiliar armor and stern faces. They had a lot of weapons, but she had no strength to run. She was barely on her feet.

And then suddenly, somehow, she wasn't. She was on her rump in the dewy grass, swaying dangerously close to being flat on her back; when she blinked again, Evin and a fierce-looking Elon were at her side trying to keep her upright. Ryn squirmed against the intrusion and struggled to sit up on her own.

"'M fine," she whispered, stomach churning.

"Yes, we can see that," Evin replied agreeably, getting an arm around her and pulling her gently but firmly to lean back against his solid bulk. That, more than anything, gave Ryn the strength to move, and she rolled to her hands and knees before struggling upright once again. Her body protested the treatment, exhausted and wanting nothing more than to accept her friend's offer of comfort and strength, but she stood nonetheless.

She couldn't need his help.

Evin blinked, confused, and moved once more to assist her. She flinched, and hated herself for it, but he got the picture and retreated. By now, they'd caught the attention of the leader of the Eloni, and Ryn looked up as he moved forward to meet her. He was terrifying, looming and large and well-armed, but his eyes were kind. He stood before her and opened his mouth.

"Don't touch me," she said, before she had a chance to think about it.

He tilted his head, nodded. "Very well. I am Jorlan. Who are you?" She shook her head, and the wood elf smiled wryly. "No? Then I shall call you Miriae, 'nameless one', in our tongue. Can you tell me what happened here?"

Ryn took a steadying breath, swallowing her first impression of terror—*you have nothing to fear, here, they are allies*—and answered. "I was their prisoner. When I woke this morning, they were all dead."

Jorlan nodded, then looked her over and narrowed his eyes just slightly. "They did not harm you?"

"No, they did," she answered, shuddering, struck again by the confusion of what happened. "All my wounds were...were *healed*. I don't know how." She paused a moment to gather her wits before looking around, then to Evin. "You are alone." Her voice was small, disappointed and fearful even to her own ears.

His tired eyes held a strange look, but he smiled. "They are alive, fear not. They've been sent on to the city with all speed to have their wounds treated. We tracked you as long as we could."

She shuddered at the confession—Kota had been hurt, and Brandt too!—before several realizations hit her at once. The first was an intense feeling of relief and joy, both at the news Kota was alive, and at seeing a familiar face. The second was the sudden remembrance at just how out of sorts she was at the moment, panicked and broken and dirty beyond belief. The third was a crushing physical exhaustion, brought on by six days of travel, torture, complete lack of sustenance, and now shock. Healed, her wounds may have been, but she still suffered physical ailments in response to the treatment of the past days. These conflicting feelings were all so powerful, and so intense, she didn't have any clue how to respond to any of them; so for a long moment everyone just stared at each other.

Ryn sucked in a breath that was equal parts desperate and painful. Evin moved closer again—close enough to murmur, but not so close as to spook her. "What do you need, lass?"

Her hand going to her tattered hair instinctively, she barely registered the heartbroken look he gave her. "A cloak?" she croaked. "With a hood, please? And...food?"

9

Thaliondris was everything Brandt had been told it was. It mere hours after he and the lass Calle began their desperate ride, before the Heir of Laendor could hear water ahead; she led them out of a narrow crevasse between steep, dangerous peaks and into a clearing overlooking a beautiful valley. The city rose white and elegant before them. Mountains surrounded it on three sides, snow-tipped and rugged, cradling the city in a massive hollow of verdant life. The west side of the valley was enclosed by a sparkling lake so large it was impossible to see the other side from where they stood. The mountains and lake made invasion near-impossible, so the city walls were less threatening, less for protection, than any Brandt had seen in his lifetime. Some kind of light wood coiled in natural patterns depicting leaves and flowers to create a gate, of sorts, which they moved toward after a moment. The road was dark, rich earth packed down by many a weary traveler; for all the Eloni were rather isolated, they were also excellent—if slightly aloof—hosts to those they called friends, the humans of Laendor among them.

"Drath Feóran." Calle spoke for the first time since they'd started their desperate ride. She adjusted her grip on Kota carefully. "Or so it is in our tongue. 'The Greenest of Valleys.'"

Brandt nodded and murmured, almost to himself, "As everyone else knows it, Thaliondris. By the Astra, it's beautiful."

The warrior-healer nodded an acknowledgment and led him down the well-kept path into the valley. They made it into the courtyard without incident, and were met by a team of Healers who handled the lynx gently off the white mare while Calle gave a report of her patients' conditions. The Master Healer was a wizened, sapphire-skinned old man, long hair and beard white as the snow blossoms on the ubiquitous trees. Everyone seemed to take the presence of a full-grown wild cat in stride, which the prince found a little surprising, but was relieved. The old man ran wrinkled fingers over fur in practiced gestures, obviously classifying injuries and speaking in a low voice to the two younger Healers accompanying him. Brandt couldn't understand him; he used the Eloni's strange language, elegant and flowery. It made his tongue itch just listening to it.

Brandt found himself receiving similar treatment from another Healer; this one a bit younger but still old enough to be his mother, and obviously no less competent than the old man. Her tattoos were many and varied—which his statecraft lessons had told him denoted someone of great experience—dark blue against her pale lichen-hued skin. Slanted gray eyes regarded him carefully, studying his reactions to her questions, making him feel as though she were taking in his answers with more than just her pointed ears. Her movements were sure and precise as she removed the bandage Evin had helped him apply over the wyvern bite; Brandt was careful not to make any sound as the rough material came loose from the deep lacerations reluctantly, tearing a bit.

The lady clicked her tongue in sympathy when she got a good look at the bite. "Aye, youngling, you'll need our care for this." She poked a little at the redness surrounding the cuts, and Brandt sucked in a pained breath in spite of himself. "It is becoming infected already; it is fortunate that Jorlan found you."

Nearby, the Healers had Kota ready for transport and began to walk quickly toward what the Prince only could guess were the Healing Houses. He stood quickly and made to follow, though his Healer protested. He looked back at her stern, questioning gaze.

"I cannot leave his side," was the answer he gave, and after a moment of thought, the lady stood too.

"Well then, hurry up," she urged, following close behind him.

They accompanied Kota and the Master Healer through vaulted halls and into a large room, open and bright, where the team of Eloni set to work on the lynx. They spoke soft words in their language, assessing with gentle hands, cleaning the blood from mottled fur and wrapping the smaller wounds with plain cotton gauze. The Master placed himself at the cat's heart, magic flowing from his withered fingers into Kota's chest.

Brandt watched the whole thing, paying little attention to his own arm, which was reopened—that bit hurt more than he wanted to admit—disinfected, stitched, dressed in herbs to stymie the infection, and wrapped. When at last the Master was finished, Brandt sighed in relief and moved closer to the lynx, settling beside the bed upon which Kota now rested peacefully. He placed a hand on the creature's flank, stroking his soft, thick fur.

Soon enough, the Healers left him be, with promises to come back with food, and orders that he was to bathe and rest within the next few hours. Brandt caught a glimpse of the city up close through the tall open arch near his back.

Seclusion had been kind to the citizens of Thaliondris, peaceable and elegant folk that they were. It was rare to see one of them outside their own borders; save for their scouting parties, who, assisted by the unforgiving

67

terrain around them, kept out any unwelcome visitors. Brandt remembered learning that the Eloni had not been to war in centuries—hadn't needed to—but were unashamedly brilliant at the design and construction of near-impenetrable mail armor. Rumor had it their legendary skill was rooted in the use of magic in their metalcraft.

Brandt didn't think he believed in such nonsense, but Evin was of the opinion that there was something more at work in Eloni armor and weaponry. He'd seen it firsthand, he said, and it was nothing like what they smithed at home. Brandt had seen it too, but he was far more inclined to attribute the wood elves' success in forging to skill than magic.

Nevertheless, he would very much have liked to see their craftsmen at work; doubtless could have asked and perhaps been granted such permission, were he and Evin to reveal their identities while they were here. But their Uncle Eirik had been clear in his instructions: secrecy was paramount, no one must know of their identity or mission. Maintaining the element of surprise was their only real advantage over the Beast when they confronted him, and they could not afford even whispered rumors of their absence from Sannfold.

So he would have to wait to see the legendary armor makers of Thaliondris at work. Perhaps on a diplomatic visit someday, when he was King and his brother General. For now, he turned back to the lynx and got comfortable on the floor, leaning against the wall and readying himself to sit vigil until Evin returned, hopefully with Ryn in tow.

~~~~~~~~~~

Ryn found herself mashed up against Evin's back on the ride to Thaliondris. It was a position that would have been uncomfortable on the best of days; given her recent experiences, the vulnerability she usually despised feeling warred with the mad desire to just hang on tight to someone strong and safe and never let go. She didn't bother looking up from her companion's shoulder blades even when they entered the city, in spite of her previous wish to see Thaliondris.

Now all she wanted was Kota.

Luckily, Evin seemed to understand, and rode the mare he'd been given straight to the Healing Houses without a word. He helped her down, his strong grip keeping her upright as she dismounted. They walked quickly through vaulted halls and past large breezy rooms furnished with plush beds, washrooms, fireplaces. It struck Ryn suddenly how tired she was. She felt as though she hadn't slept in weeks.

When at last they reached the right place, she saw her Friend lying still and quiet on a pallet in the center of the sickroom. White bandages contrasted sharply with his summer fur, and he seemed to be sleeping, but he lifted his head and let out a whimper when he caught her scent. The sound tore at Ryn's heart, but so did utter relief at seeing him. She let out a shuddering breath she didn't know she'd been holding inside.

He was alive, and her heart could beat again. She stumbled to him and pressed her face into the unmarred fur at his neck.

"Kota, I'm sorry," her voice cracked. "I'm so sorry, my *kisa*."

The lynx nuzzled her weakly and licked her forehead before closing his eyes again. He began to purr, the sound rumbling through her sore head. Ryn stayed where she was for a moment, allowing a couple of sobs to escape before attempting to work her breathing into something resembling normal. After a long moment she sat back, swiping impatiently at her eyes and gathering herself before standing to face the brothers.

Brandt looked primarily relieved; a sentiment she found she shared. She hadn't realized just how worried she'd been about these two, as well as Kota, while she was captive. But Evin was looking between her and her lynx, and his smile could've lit much darker places than this one. Before she had a chance to move, he threw his arms around her and squeezed, then let go so quickly she wasn't even sure it had actually happened.

"I was so worried," he said quickly, still grinning. "But all is well now; we're all together again, and I'm so grateful."

Ryn tried her best to return his smile, but it had been a long day. Stifling the sudden and unexpected urge to bury her face in Evin's shoulder and just not move, she nodded. "The same is true for me. I had no indication whether you lot were alive or dead, and it was..."

Startlingly worrisome, is what it had been, but she wasn't about to admit as much to them aloud.

"...It was difficult," she finished hesitantly.

"What did they *do* to you?" Brandt asked, and she realized he was looking at her with that infuriating mix of concern and protective instinct.

Forcibly shoving back memories of torture, Ryn shrugged. "I've been through worse."

That, for some reason, didn't seem to relieve either of them. Evin stared wide-eyed, while Brandt regarded her with an expression of perfect skepticism.

She stared back as hard as she could manage. They didn't budge, and she sighed. "There was...you know, starving, beating and slicing and hair yanking—" she motioned to her tattered locks, "—but I'm fine. Look at me, I'm fine!" To punctuate her point, she spread her arms and tried to crack a smile.

Judging by their expressions, she managed something closer to a grimace. The sympathy in their eyes was edging uncomfortably close to pity; Ryn fought down a rush of irritation.

"You look...tired. Half-dead, in fact," Evin pointed out, tilting his head, "but you actually *don't* look like you were beaten."

Ryn flushed, heat crawling up her neck and making her ears burn. She tugged a lock of her ruined hair, holding it up for inspection. "Do you think I did this to myself?" It came out more sharply than she perhaps intended; she was very quickly nearing a breaking point and she needed to be alone.

Now.

Brandt's face was darkening at her aggressive tone, but for once, Evin seemed to be the wise one. He gripped Brandt's arm tightly and drew him out of the room. "Of course not. It has been a tremendously hard day for everyone. We'll be back later. Rest well, Ryn."

And with that, they were gone. Ryn nearly collapsed on the floor beside Kota's pallet, head in her hands, and didn't move for hours.

When at last she came back to herself—*had she slept?*—a cool breeze was ruffling her hair, raising bumps on the skin of her arms and the nape of her neck. The sun had apparently gone down hours ago, and it was chilly. She thought perhaps that was deliberate; lynxes were naturally built to endure colder weather, and thrived at a lower temperature than was comfortable for most humans. She didn't mind. A soft, fur-edged blanket had been draped around her shoulders at some point, but she couldn't recall by whom.

The Master Healer had visited once, she remembered that much; he'd checked on Kota and given Ryn the run-down of his condition, but other than that she had been left mercifully alone. Despite her rest, she struggled to keep her eyes open now, caught in that strange limbo between bone-deep exhaustion and fear of falling asleep again.

Kota was hurt. He'd nearly died. The Master said he'd likely pull through, but the damage the wyvern had done had been extensive.

How could she have been so foolish as to bring him out here, to take this job? She had tackled the Great Wilds once before, but that had been before she met Kota, and she'd been lucky. It was actually, she thought, on the backside of that trip that fate had smiled upon her in the oddest possible way.

If she hadn't sprained her ankle, it likely would never have happened. It had been raining profusely in the hills a few hours southeast of Sarelton; Ryn had slipped on a wet rock, wedged her foot between it and a downed tree, and then fallen over, twisting her foot into a highly unnatural position. By the time she'd managed to work it free, the rain had become a deluge; she was cold, wet, and in pain when she had limped into a cave nearby. It was a little thing, perhaps large enough to shelter a family—and a family it did turn out to house. A litter of lynx kits and their mother rested inside, she discovered as she fumbled toward the back of the cave in an attempt to determine how deep it was.

Curses had been many and varied when she realized she'd stumbled into a wild cat den, but the little ones had just sat calmly, tilting their fuzzy heads in curiosity while the mother moved to face her, teeth bared and claws showing. Ryn had backed up slowly while the larger lynx had studied her for what seemed like several full minutes. She cooed quietly to the mama, sweating and hurting and dripping all over the unfinished stone, afraid to spook the animals and wind up the family's dinner.

Finally, the lynx had chattered at her, began to purr, and turned her attention back to her tiny balls of fluff. Ryn had breathed a sigh of relief and begun to back up slowly again when she noticed the mother's odd behavior. Mama lynx was snuffling her babies, pushing them toward Ryn, and one by one they'd regarded the tall human in their midst. One by one, the little ones had eyed her—*inspected her?*—before turning back to their ma; until the tiniest kitten had taken one look at her and yowled, in its strange, lynx way. The mama mewled back, and the kit ran to her, propping himself on two legs against her wet boot, begging for attention. Awed, Ryn had acquiesced, kneeling to scratch him behind the ears.

She'd spent two more hours in that den, being thoroughly ignored by the entire lynx family save for the little spotted brownie, waiting for the rain to stop; and when she left, the kit had followed. She'd tried to send him back to his family, but he wouldn't go. He kept following her for three days, until she accepted it, some part of her glad of a companion. She had called him Kotani, after the massive companion of the Great Hunter, Rorik. Legend said Rorik and Kotani had hunted the Forest Wyrm Gorshod, who had held the Northern Wood in terror for centuries in service to Skeðu himself. The battle had been fierce and long, but the pair had prevailed, at last ending the Wyrm's tyrannical reign and opening the way for the Eloni to build Thaliondris. She had wanted Kota to have a strong name; it would protect him on their travels.

He'd been by her side since. And now he was lying here severely injured because of it. This wasn't the first time one or the other of them had been hurt—it happened all the time; slips, falls, sprains, heat sickness, lacerations and bruises from the skirmishes they tended to start, all of these were fairly regular occurrences. But this was the first time she'd nearly lost him, and after she'd sent him ahead, so she wasn't even nearby to help when he'd been injured. Ryn swallowed the hard lump in her throat, refusing herself the release of tears.

She startled a little when the door opened—it was silent, well-oiled, but the brightness grew as torchlight from the hall spilled in. She looked up, squinting a little despite the gentle orange glow, to see the figure of a man in the doorway. A tall man, with curly hair and a smile, holding a bowl of something that smelled truly tantalizing.

"Evin," she greeted, a little more shortly than she intended. She was pleased to see him, but also wanted nothing more than for him to go away.

It was very confusing. His smile did not falter, though; he simply took her recognition as an invitation and came to sit down.

Ryn did not feel like socializing. She was exhausted, achy, and had just nearly lost her best friend. She stifled a sigh.

"I brought you food!" Evin said cheerfully, plopping down on the floor cushion beside her. Ryn scooted away slightly but reached for the food. She had forgotten she was famished. Evin's smile widened as she took the bowl and spoon, and she sort of wanted to smack him for it.

"Thank you," she grunted, by way of politeness.

The man took it as permission to stay, apparently. "You're welcome," he nodded, the low light playing with the shadows of his face. Ryn turned away. "I expected you hadn't stepped out to eat or rest, so I thought I could help with at least one of those."

"Mmm."

"My brother said you probably wouldn't want to be bothered, but he's kind of an idiot when it comes to the personal touch, so I didn't listen to him."

You probably should have, she thought, then scolded herself. Her friend was trying to be kind; she could at least be courteous. She spooned a little of the thick stew into her mouth, careful not to eat too fast. It was rich and salty and *delicious*.

"I'm sorry about earlier," Evin said after a moment, and Ryn sighed quietly, turning to face him. He looked contrite. "I was more curious than doubtful, about...the, uh—."

"I know," she murmured back, feeling a little sick. "I have no answers for you. I don't know what happened." She turned back to her meal, eating stiffly, appetite gone. Evin said nothing, but sat by her side until she finished, and then for another hour, without speaking.

When the distant bells chimed midnight, he rose quietly with her bowl. He stretched, sauntered to the door, stopped on the threshold. The light framed his silhouette, blocked his smile, but she saw it anyway.

"We're at the Wildtree Inn, if you want a warm bed to sleep in. Goodnight, Ryn."

~~~~~~~~~~

The moon cast its weak white light on the wrecked nagrat camp, filtered through the same clouds that blotted out the stars entirely. Scavenging animals paused in their bloody meals, turned tail and ran, for they could sense the darkness encroaching, sharper and more sinister than any mere night could conjure. Black and empty, the Dark coalesced in the midst of the dead camp, a mist that began to gain form quickly. A den of rabbits screamed nearby as their hearts all gave out at once; their small sound was the only audible one, though a wide assortment of beasts in the vicinity suffered the same instantaneous fate. White fire leeched from hundreds of small bodies, burrowers and scavengers and birds alike, lent itself to the black mist, dancing and whirling until a corporeal form finally stood in its place.

It was a Man, or at least a close approximation to one. He was impossibly tall, an effect only heightened by his black, fitted clothing. He looked almost regal in velvet leggings, a black leather vest over a linen shirt, inlaid with gemstones of exact equal color and cut—rubies all, blood-red. His leather riding boots were black, too, as was the doeskin cloak fastened by a heavy silver brooch at his white throat. His face was hooded, but the deep shadows highlighted sharp, pure features marred artfully by twisting ritual scars that wound over every inch of visible pale skin. Scarlet eyes peered out over the carnage, handsome mouth curling into a dangerous glower.

Huffing a low growl, the tall man turned, white palm opening to reveal a single bloodstone that glowed dimly. He whispered a sibilant word to it, and black fire swept through the remains of the camp, rolling over every rotting corpse in the clearing. Over most, it simply paused, then moved on; but over a few bodies, the black fire sparked bright red, some brighter than others. The brightest of these was a twisted, gray corpse near the edge of the settlement that garnered a small geyser of the red sparks. The man smiled, pleased, as he picked his way toward it, black steel staff leaving small impressions in the rich earth. His smile disappeared when he noticed; the air here, so close to the wood elves' domain, was full of vibrant life magic—his own lackeys' very-dead bodies excepted, of course. The force of it, white and pure, made him vaguely nauseous, though that was not unexpected. He was far closer to Thaliondris than he generally preferred to venture, but news of what had happened here had prompted him to come see it for himself. He had a feeling he would not regret it.

But all this excessive *life*, this radiant magic, it was distracting.

Growling, the man knelt, pressed his bloodstone into the dewy grass, and whispered another word. Green mist this time, bright and vivid, wove its way through the soil, choking, poisoning. The luminous, glittering force that gave the plants their life sputtered and dimmed before fading entirely, leaving the camp and several hundred feet around it dead and dark. The dry grass crackled under his knee and he watched a thatch of wildflowers in front of him wither instantly. The man nodded once in satisfaction before rising to continue his primary mission.

When he reached the dead nagrat guard, he stopped. His sharp features twisted into an expression of disgust—horrid, ugly creatures they were, though useful—and drove the end of his staff into the creature's barrel chest. The tip punctured leather armor and bone easily, settling deep inside the thing's still, bloody heart. The man murmured a series of the hissing words and brought the brightly-glowing bloodstone in one hand to touch the carven head of his staff in the other. The point of contact between the foci of his magic sparked blinding heat for a moment before settling and darkening to a point of black light. The man smiled briefly, then removed the stone from the staff, scooping up the small dark orb and holding it so the wan moonlight caught it. The sphere wriggled, then seemed to hop off his hand, flattening and lengthening until it floated before him like a small black stage. Upon it flashed faces, impressions, feelings.

Resentment at having to pull two night watch shifts—the nagrat had gotten in a scuffle with a superior earlier in the day and been punished with an extra turn that night—then boredom. There were no dangers here. Sleepiness—no predators meant no need for a night watch, perhaps he could catch a few hours' rest in spite of his punishment. Black unconsciousness, restful and deep. Awakening, to the strangest prickling sensation. Confusion. Instant agony, but no visible wounding—it was simply pain, grinding and sparking on every nerve without explanation. Exhaustion, the feeling that the very life was being sucked from his body. A merciful cease of the onslaught, though the creature knew it would die, and soon. Anger at defeat from an unseen foe, the despair of knowledge that it would die an honorless death, that its spirit would find no place in the Eternal Hunt. The man cared nothing for such things, but the creature was devastated by it. Blackness again.

The sorcerer frowned; he knew this magic, though he had not seen it used thus in centuries. A most interesting development, but not one he was happy with.

Then, blinding light, immediate shadowing by a nearby face; a woman...a young human who looked both out of her mind with fright and fiercely determined. She startled at the sight of the nagrat's open eyes, staggered back slightly, recovered, reached for it. The man watched, slightly surprised at her nerve, as she snatched the nagrat's knife and leather carrying pack. She was looting. He would have guessed her to be the prisoner he'd gotten word this group had taken, the one they called The Phantom; except that she was uninjured and not even a little bit threatening. Nothing but a passerby who'd happened upon the bodies, he reasoned.

But no, he felt the dying nagrat's fury at being looted by a mere prisoner, a slip of a girl that he didn't even understand the importance of; she was clearly only a small threat, and they had bigger game to hunt. Had they not stopped for this little shrew, they may have been the hunters to bring the Princes to Râza, a prize that would have given them much honor.

Ah, the sorcerer thought. So this *was* the Phantom. Slipped through his fingers this time, but he would remember her face. Her time was coming.

The nagrat's world went black again, for what felt like a few moments. When it opened them again after a vicious nudge, it was a snarl and the weak realization that the end of its life was nearer now. Its vision was tinted, blackness gathering around the edges, but there was a man standing over it this time. Like the girl, the man startled, having clearly expected it to be dead already; but he recovered quickly enough and lowered the point of his sword to the nagrat's thick neck, moving further into its field of vision. A scowling face swam into view, with high cheekbones and a long, straight nose, eyes gold like the wheat fields in autumn.

The sorcerer paused the image with a word, and it froze where it was. He moved closer, studied the young face, honed in on the sword the lad was using. It was folded steel, a single sapphire set in the hilt, honed to a razor-sharp edge. The sorcerer moved in just a little closer...there, just where the blade met the hilt; the royal crest. He smiled; he'd been right, it had been worth every second of trouble coming here.

"There you are, Prince Evin."

10

The days moved more slowly in Thaliondris, Ryn would think later. The wood elves were a peaceable folk, settled within their city and seemingly oblivious to many of the machinations in the rest of the world; it gave their home a heavy, steady aura that created weighted moments and wrung every possibility from them before letting them go. Minutes felt like hours, but far from bored, Ryn felt instead refreshed. It made a good night's sleep feel like a week's rest and, she was convinced, promoted healing within its citizens and guests. A mere two days after she reunited with Kota, they both were showing marked improvement and she was released from the Menders' care. Her wounds had been healed the morning of her rescue, true, but she was still exhausted and famished enough that Master Áedán—she had learned that was the name of the stern old Master Healer who oversaw the Menders—felt the need to observe her recovery carefully for a short time, especially since they didn't know exactly what had caused her original healing. Reluctantly, Ryn had agreed, her desire to be left alone warring against the ingrained impulse to follow Menders' directions.

She found herself the fair morning of her release exploring the Healing House's gardens. The early breeze tousled the scarf she'd been given for her head, and she shivered a little in the thin cotton breeches and shirt she wore—also borrowed. She would see about acquiring proper leather armor and underclothes in the next few days. Thaliondris was bound to play host to vendors who could help her.

A rather small lad approached her by the creek, where she sat enjoying the cheery sound of water rushing over stone. "Are you...the Lady with the Lynx?" he asked, deep-set lavender eyes standing out against skin so dark it was almost black. A small white feather was tattooed carefully in the very center of his forehead, but she could see no other marks; this one was very young and had little experience at his craft yet. He shifted his weight, gaze flicking between her and the rest of the courtyard, as though he expected to see Kota nearby.

Amused by his obvious fascination, Ryn smiled. "I am. Kota has not yet been dismissed by the Menders."

The youngling stared, then remembered himself and bowed. "Right.

Yes. My name is Faelar. I have instructions to see you to your room, miss."

Ryn nodded. "Well then. Lead on, Master Faelar." The boy smiled and trotted off, leading Ryn out the arched gate of the garden and into the city proper.

Well-traveled as she was, Ryn still struggled not to stare open-mouthed at her surroundings. She had never seen anything quite like this city; its beauty was legendary, but the tales paled in comparison to reality. White arches stood side by side to her right and left as they walked down the broad street; there were small shops everywhere selling spices, leather goods, armor, food, fabrics, trinkets, and some things Ryn had never even heard of. What structures weren't made of alabaster stone seemed to be grown from the ubiquitous trees themselves; awnings and homes, balconies and bridges. As they approached what appeared to be the City Square, Ryn couldn't suppress a gasp, which made Faelar turn back and grin proudly. In the midst of the large open courtyard there stood a magnificent tree, the largest Ryn had ever seen. The trunk was wide enough to live in, its thick boughs worn smooth by time. The wood was white as the stone the city was built upon, and the leaves were a rich blue-green that reminded Ryn of the single time she'd seen the sea as a child. Shade from the tree covered the entire square, turning the stone a dappled verdigris, and the laughs of children echoed as they played and climbed among the massive boughs, shouting challenges to climb the highest, or jump from branch to branch. Ryn's eyes widened at the sight; the village she had lived in as a child would never have allowed such reckless behavior to take place in a public area, in broad daylight.

"The Lelaenis," Faelar supplied helpfully, though he needn't have. Ryn was no stranger to the legends of the Tree that had helped protect Thaliondris for generations. Rumor said it had been created by the greatest magic weavers ever to live, in the Age of Champions a thousand years ago, and planted in the midst of the valley. The Eloni City had grown around it in the centuries since. Ryn stared, awestruck, just letting herself take in the sight.

A pink-skinned Eloni lass caught her eye, waving wildly to her friends from fifty feet above ground. They cheered and began to chant something Ryn could not understand, but the intent became clear a moment later when the youngling grinned and launched herself into the air. She was aiming for the bough upon which her friends stood, it was obvious, but Ryn knew in an instant she wouldn't make it—the jump hadn't held enough power behind it, though it was definitely better than any human could have done. She threw herself forward, intending to position herself below where the child would inevitably fall, but with an impossible twist in midair, the little one managed to grab a bough much lower than she perhaps intended, but high enough off the ground to prevent hurting herself seriously. Her palms slammed into the smooth wood and held tight, somehow managing to grip despite the velocity of her fall, and the girl pulled herself up onto the lower branch to the raucous applause of her companions. Ryn shuddered out a relieved breath as the lass laughed and bowed at the attention.

"My lady?" Faelar was at her side almost instantly, clearly confused as to her reaction. "Are you well? Perhaps the Menders released you too soon?"

"No," she interrupted him, puzzled. "I—that girl almost fell out of the tree, did you not see? I thought to help her, but—"

Faelar laughed, showing white teeth. "She would not have fallen. We seldom do."

Ryn tried not to stare. "Your parents do not protest?"

The young Elon tilted his head, expression suddenly serious. "Would you protest your child learning to walk, my lady?"

Ryn had no answer to that, so she ceded the point with a nod. "I understand, I think."

The boy smiled again and gestured her on. They moved north now, along a smaller road than the last, framed by branches and flowers. Faelar led her to an inn that was small but elegant, dark wood framing royal blue doors and shutters. Ryn breathed a sigh of relief; she had not walked this much in days and she was beginning to feel tired.

"Your companions chose this inn when you arrived," Faelar explained. "Lady Naleti has seen to their every comfort." He led her inside, waving to a matronly brown wood elf who was tending to the breakfast fire behind a long counter in the main room. Few inn patrons remained, breakfast was well and truly over by now, but two or three humans and a cheerful, hairy dwarf sipped rainbrush tea in the corner, laughing together. Faelar did not stop, but led Ryn to a room at the end of a sunny hall, brightly decorated with fresh blooms that scented the air. He bowed as he held open the door for her, standing aside as she went in. It was as lovely as her room in the Healing Wards had been, and more open—a balcony and large windows facing the south, high arches and soft drapes surrounding a feather bed, a small table, and comfortable-looking chairs near the fireplace. She smiled at Faelar, about to thank him once more, when her gaze landed on a thin dark shaft of hard wood leaning against one of the chairs, and she froze.

She bent beside it, going to her knees in the mossy carpet as she ran shaking fingers over the twisty, knotted head of her staff. An unfamiliar long bow of Blue Nutwood was there too, oiled and polished, accompanied by her leather quiver. Even the Y'rai knife Evin had given her had found its way back to her, tucked into its ill-fitting simple sheath. She had intended to make a specific one for it as soon as she had access to the leather. Ryn looked up at the young wood elf, who was grinning unabashedly at her reaction, boyish enthusiasm shining through as he explained, "Aed, the

Lord of our City and brother to Mender Áedán, sent a group out to search for your gear when you first arrived, after you told him the nagrat had stolen it. They didn't find your pack, and your bow was shattered, but the staff and quiver were being kept with the Hunt Chief, who's dead now, and they repaired them for you and everything!"

Ryn laughed breathlessly as he chattered on, lifting her staff carefully, its weight and grip familiar in her hand. The things in her pack—clothes and salves and food and gold—that could all be replaced; but this....her echowood staff was one of a kind, and it was the only thing she carried to which she felt any real attachment.

She would never be able to repay Lord Áed this kindness.

She looked up at Faelar, who had fallen silent, watching her carefully with a big innocent smile. Laughing, she stood and bowed low to the lad. "Master Faelar, would you find out if it is possible for me to go thank Lord Áed personally? This gift is far too great to pass my gratitude through a messenger."

Faelar nodded eagerly. "I shall! Meanwhile, is there anything else you require?"

Ryn shook her head. "No, thank you. I am well."

Faelar bowed, visibly calming himself and restoring the tranquil dignity employed by his race as he walked out the door.

Ryn smiled at his efforts and turned her attention back to her weapons. "I can't believe they got them back," she murmured.

A few hours later, Ryn found herself standing at the elegant door that led to her clients' rooms at the inn, holding a pair of shears she had borrowed from the Menders and shifting from foot to foot nervously. She reached up to knock but instead found her fingers working their way through the tattered mess of waves that had not long ago been a thick, beautiful head of hair.

Ryn wasn't vain; she hadn't time to be, living as she did. But Laendorians treasured their hair, even the men, wearing it long and loose whenever possible. There were traditions surrounding the cutting of hair, the disposal of it, and much of who a person was could be ascertained by their hair—rich or poor, tradesman or merchant, single or Promised or married, all written in the weave and style on one's head. More to the point for Ryn, though; Mama had always said that a woman's glory was her hair, and both she and Ryn had had the same dark loose curls. Of her many pleasant childhood memories, Ryn's favorite was one very vivid one when Mama had let her braid her dark tresses, and then had given her one exactly the same, unsightly lumps and all. She had never felt closer to her Mother than she did at that moment, and to this day, she treasured the sense memory of thick, long waves running through tiny fumbling fingers.

When she'd lost everything and run, Ryn's hair was the one piece of

Mama she'd still had. She cared for it meticulously, even on the road, even though her line of work dictated it be braided and tucked away most of the time.

And those monsters had taken it from her, ripped out of her very skin the thing that kept Mama close.

She'd been unwilling to admit it even to herself until she was safely wrapped in bed in Thaliondris, but the destruction of her hair had been, emotionally at least, the worst of the torture inflicted by the nagrat. Her hand shook as she forced it to knock. She wanted to run, she realized; she did not want to ask her new friends to do this, to let them see how it affected her...but it had to be done, and there was no one here she trusted—

"Ryn! You're up! To what do we owe the pleasure?"

Evin's cheer greeted her as he threw the door open, obviously pleased to see her. She managed an answering smile, but it was a tiny one. Brandt appeared on the other side of the room, entering from the small garden outside, and Evin waved her in. She stepped inside and looked at them each in turn, trying to gather her courage. Evin's brow furrowed a little in concern.

"It's my hair," she began before he could ask, hands clenched tightly at her sides. "It needs to be cut. I can't, and Kota is...well, wholly unequipped...to help me in this. Obviously, I cannot let one of the Eloni do it." She tightened her jaw, then forced herself to loosen it. "Will you help me?"

"Why ask us?" Brandt asked from beside his brother. His gaze was expectant, not suspicious or angry, and Ryn suddenly understood that he didn't know she'd been raised in Laendor. Given her complexion, that was...unsurprising. She took a deep breath, fingers curling reflexively at her side. She missed Kota.

"You're men of Laendor, are you not?"

"We are."

"I think what my brother means to ask," Evin cut in, "is why you are opposed to the Eloni handling your hair. Surely there is a shearer here more qualified to handle it than we are, and we know that Southdalers do not hold their hair in the same esteem as Laendorians—"

"I lived north of Sannfold until I was fourteen," Ryn said quickly. It was more information than she liked to give about herself, but if she wanted them to cut her hair, she needed to convince them of what it meant. "I was raised Laendorian."

There was silence for a moment, and then Evin smiled. "Good enough for me," he responded, reaching for the shears. Ryn handed them over and turned to face the wide mirror above the chest of drawers.

Evin began combing through the ragged strands slowly, murmuring the rites as he sought out the shortest pieces. Ryn knew he would only cut what he absolutely had to. Brandt stood and assisted where necessary. For the next half hour, Evin snipped and brushed, gently removing the uneven, destroyed pieces of her hair and placing them on the night table nearby for proper disposal. Thankfully, the spots the nagrat had pulled out to the roots were few and small, Ryn had noticed in the mirror that morning; nothing a couple of well-placed braids wouldn't cover up nicely. Ryn stood as still as she could, convinced after a while her legs might fold from shaking so much. Eventually, mercifully, Evin declared the work done and gave Ryn a small smile. She looked at herself critically in the mirror: the style fell a little past her jaw, curls framing her face. 'Twas short, for a woman of Laendor, but she was an unconventional one anyhow. After a few moments, she nodded her approval and turned.

"Thank you," she murmured earnestly, looking both brothers in the eye, "I could not have done that myself."

Evin smiled, and Brandt squeezed her arm. "It's actually rather becoming on you," he said kindly.

She shifted uncomfortably and nodded. "Thank you, again. I should…go." She fled before either of them could think of a reason she ought to stay, feeling far too vulnerable.

She wandered the inn's garden for most of the afternoon feeling sorry for herself. Eventually she grew tired of ranting about the unfairness of it all inside her head and forced herself to go eat with her friends. The food was delicious, and the brothers seemed in good spirits, which helped sweeten her sour mood. Relating the story of her salvaged weaponry to them resulted in the proper amount of awe and pleased exclamation, as well. "The Lord Áed is rather famous for his generosity and kindness," Brandt said with a smile. "It makes him a most welcome ally and royal visitor—or so I have heard." The man looked almost annoyed at how freely he had spoken, and Ryn stifled a grin.

They thought they were very clever, these two, but she knew how to put puzzle pieces together, and she was beginning to be really glad the nagrat had snatched her rather than either one of her clients. For it was clear that while they may not have been the royal princes Râza was looking for, they were very definitely more important than they let on, and she would've been unsurprised to learn they were close to the Royal Family. And while she had no particular home in Laendor and was an invisible, unknown wanderer, she had been raised with a healthy respect for the country of her birth and would happily do any good she could for it.

She supposed saving the Royal Family's especial friends from torture at the hands of the barbaric nagrat should count for something. Grinning a little at the thought, Ryn studied the outdoor eatery in which they sat. The table and chairs surrounding them looked, as she'd noticed all Eloni furniture did, as though it had been *grown* rather than built. That is, each appeared to be one solid piece of young wood, in every shade of brown she'd ever seen; but there were no planks, no fasteners, nothing to imply a crafter's touch had even been required. They just looked to have grown into the shape of oaken chairs and tables, and in other places, birch beds and maple stools and chestnut cubbies in which to place one's belongings. It was really quite stunning, and she wondered endlessly about the process behind such crafting.

But her thoughts were interrupted when her gaze unexpectedly met another's. An old man, tanned and leathery—definitely not a wood elf—watched her from across the clearing. She supposed he thought himself surreptitious, for he held before him a tattered scroll and was pretending to read; but she felt his eyes on her the moment she looked away.

Not so odd, really, seeing a man in an Eloni city; she supposed he could be a fellow traveler. At any rate, he was likely little threat; the man looked as though he'd have a hard time wrestling a hare, much less her and two full-grown men, so she put him out of her mind and suggested a walk.

They spent the next couple of days visiting Kota in the Healing Wards and exploring Thaliondris together. The city offered many wonders to behold: the Hall of Heroes with its great marble walls and delicate etchings, the greatest champions of Adan carved out of smooth black fire-glass, their eyes inset with sapphires; Aleth Falls on the north end of the valley, a stunning waterfall that offered a breathtaking vista from the peak of its cliff; and the caverns beneath, dripping with natural crystals that caught the light of strategically placed torches, reflecting it to and fro and coloring the rough stone every hue of the rainbow. The old man didn't enter Ryn's thoughts again.

~~~~~~~~~~

"Evin, help me!"

The shout cut through the noise of battle around him and caused him to spin round madly, looking for its source, clothes and skin catching painfully on the needled plants around him.

"Uncle? Uncle, where are you?"

He could see little through the thick black fog that covered this entire blighted landscape. Nothing was familiar here; it was all brown and dead and nubs of foreign plants that possessed more thorns than seemed strictly necessary. He could hear fighting all around him, but could identify nothing, save that one voice.

"Over here, lad, hurry!" he heard from his left. He turned, and the mist cleared so he could see Eirik beset upon by six of the tallest Val'gren he had ever seen. They were terrifying, all; possessed of the deadly elegance intrinsic to their people, masters with slender blades they took great care to poison. Evin darted toward Eirik quickly, but

stopped when a cry drew his gaze away; a voice he knew better than even his own.

His gaze landed on a golden head not far from where he had skidded to a halt; Brandt was battling the chiefest of the Val'gren himself, an impossibly large robed figure with spiraled scars winding elegantly over every inch of exposed skin.

Something was seriously wrong; his brother wasn't using one of his axes, his left arm dangling uselessly at his side as he dodged the Val'gren's blows sluggishly. Blood streamed from a head wound that was clearly making the young heir dizzy and fracturing his concentration, and with a bloodcurdling war cry, the monster kicked his brother in the chest, sending him toppling and skidding backward.

Evin bellowed a challenge as he changed direction, his only focus being Brandt. Again, Uncle's thunderous voice cut through his rage:

"Evin! I need you!"

He didn't hesitate—there was no time—but he did look up to see one of the Val'gren drive its sword deep into his uncle's chest. The young prince choked, and his legs gave out beneath him, sending him sprawling in the dirt.

No.

No. It could not be. The raw scream that stung his throat drove it home: the King was dying, dead, and it was his fault.

Forcibly, he tore his gaze from his uncle to focus on Brandt again; he had to reach his brother before he went to meet Uncle in the afterworld before his time. A gasping whimper escaped Evin's throat as he stumbled to his feet, equal parts grief and desperation. The chief Val'gren was closing in on Brandt, who seemed to be having trouble staying conscious and was scooting backward as fast as his clearly-broken arm would allow. A smile crossed the monster's terrifyingly familiar face, and he lifted his bloodstained sword high over his head, ready to run Brandt through.

Evin wasn't close enough, he'd never make it.

He put on a burst of speed, but his legs were mired in bloody mud that had come from nowhere. He couldn't move.

The Val'gren Chief looked up, locked his gaze on Evin's, and the younger brother's heart stopped short in his chest. It was his own face, eyes blood-red instead of their normal brandy-gold, but his face nonetheless. Not-Evin smiled at him and brought the blade down; the Prince saw Brandt's feeble attempt to block it, saw....

"No!" he shouted as he woke with a start, sitting up in bed and not remembering how he got there, trembling and sweating.

Brandt stirred slightly nearby, lifting his head heavily from the pillow. "All's well, brother," the elder murmured, words slurred with drowsiness. "'Twas just a dream. Go back to sleep." Then he flopped back, instantly unconscious again.

Evin stared at him, trying to catch his breath; he studied the lines of Brandt's face, listened to his brother's steady breathing an arm's length away, hoping it would lull him back into sleep as it normally did when the nightmares intruded.

This morning, it did not.

After a few moments, Evin sighed and gently disentangled himself from the soft blankets. Despite his unease, he couldn't help but grin a little at the sight a sleeping Brandt made; expression soft, mouth open slightly as he snored a bit, hair completely askew. It tumbled over the pillow and his normally-stern face, a piece of it rising and falling with his deep breaths.

Ferocious warrior, indeed.

Evin reached over and pushed the hair from his brother's face more gently than he would have had the man been awake, then dressed as silently as possible and left the room. Perhaps some fresh air would do him good.

It was early; just before dawn. The gray light of morning would soon give way to gold and pink. The birds were already singing cheerfully, and a few folks were up and about, some smiling and calling greetings as he walked by. He responded with a smile for each one, enjoying the morning and the burgeoning energy as the city slowly awoke.

His reverie was interrupted when he suddenly recognized the figure just ahead of him.

Ryn was walking briskly, Kota trotting beside her; the lynx moved smoothly, almost as if he'd never been injured. It was quite a feat, to go from death's door to such good health in the eight days they'd been here, and Evin credited the Eloni Menders as much as he did the lynx's refusal to go quietly. It was a trait the Cat shared with his mistress, Evin figured, thinking of the torture Ryn had endured not so long ago herself. This morning, their guide had her new bow and quiver slung over her cape, and carried her staff with easy familiarity. Armed as she was, he couldn't help but notice how relaxed she seemed—it appeared a week in Thaliondris had been good to her as well as her companion. He cocked his head, wondering what she was doing out here this early, headed for the city gates.

He briefly considered just following her and staying out of sight, until he remembered the very thorough lashing he'd received during a survival game with her and Brandt the day before. The game had involved two teams—Brandt and him versus Ryn and Kota, an arrangement which they both had protested until she insisted—each one with a scrap of cloth, a pennant, to protect. The goal of the game was to acquire the other team's standard and bring it back to your own side—but also not to lose your own at the same time. While Brandt had tried to overcome the lynx, who'd been left to protect his team pennant and somehow understood at least that aspect of the game, Ryn had taken a different tack with Evin's flag. She had sneaked around, staying out of sight in the trees. Even though he'd been watching for her, he hadn't expected the knife that landed point down in the dirt at his feet—not nearly close enough to hurt him, just close enough to bait him. Scowling, he'd charged into the undergrowth to confront her, remembering that hand-to-hand combat was not a strength of hers; but by the time he reached where the knife had come from, she was gone.

Or so he had thought.

She dropped from a branch overhead and had him trussed up faster than he imagined possible, and that's how Evin had learned the hard way to look up into the trees as well as around the ground, when hunting one such as Ryn. With him out of commission and Brandt distracted by a fierce and intelligent animal, Ryn had stolen their pennant and made her way back to her own, thus winning the game. The day had gone to Ryn and Kota; a fate made worse by the fact that even his dear brother couldn't help but laugh when they all trooped over to untie Evin.

Traitor.

Regardless, Evin decided that sneaking up on anyone who could so easily dispatch him if she desired was probably not an effective way to retain all his body parts, not to mention his dignity, so he called out loudly, "Going somewhere?"

The lass turned and regarded him with a coy smile that made something in his chest hitch pleasantly. "Perhaps."

Intrigued, he followed her out a quiet wooden gate and into the valley. She looked at the sky, then broke into a gentle trot, bearing a bit west, headed up the ridge, massive lynx at her heels. Once they reached about three-quarters of the way to the top, she picked a rocky outcropping and sat down facing east, pulling her bow and quiver over her head and setting them at her side with the staff. When he caught up, she patted the spot of rock next to her, motioning for him to join her. He sat as well, finally figuring out what she was doing up here. Kota bounded off, chasing a moth.

The sun had not yet risen over the mountains, but the light said it was only just below them now. The clouds, as he expected, had exploded in a riot of color—gold and pink and purple splashed across a jewel-blue sky, reflecting off the snow-capped peaks and turning the mountains a magnificent cobalt. The birdsong and cool morning air only added to the effect, and Evin had to smile; early morning was his favorite time of day.

Ryn pulled a sealed mug from her satchel and passed it to him after taking a sip. There was rainbrush tea inside, strong and sweet, the smell adding to the perfection of the moment. Reflecting his own sentiments, she leaned back on her elbows and sighed. "Dawn is beautiful," she confided quietly, as if afraid speaking would shatter the euphoria.

Evin grinned, letting the beauty of the sky soothe away what remained of his nightmare. "You hate mornings."

Ryn stared at him for a moment, then conceded with a small smile of her own. "But the dawn is still beautiful."

They watched in silence then, as the light grew stronger and the first bright rays of the sun peeked over the mountains, blinding and warm. Evin closed his eyes and let the heat bathe his face, relishing this moment, lazily basking in how peaceful it all felt.

"Ryn?" he asked suddenly, opening his eyes to find her staring quietly at the epic vista around them. Her face glowed in the early morning light, ruddy and freckled. Her features seemed smoother somehow, the tension she normally carried around her eyes and mouth nowhere to be found. It was a tranquil expression, one he hadn't seen her wear before; it struck him, in that moment, how much he wanted to not only see it more, but maybe be the reason for it.

"Yes?"

"You said you were from a town north of Sannfold. When did you leave?"

She paused, picking at a short stem of grass, then gave him a deliberately careless shrug. "Twelve years ago. After Talos and Ma died."

He waited for her to elaborate, but she sat quietly, squinting against the bright morning light as she watched a nearby bird hop from tree to tree. Evin wondered if this was the right time to ask, if she would answer him or stonewall him as before, if he would damage all the progress he'd made with her thus far, but he asked anyway after a moment's consideration.

"You've been on the road since then?"

Ryn met his eyes, looking very serious. "Yes."

Evin was unsurprised by the answer, though he found himself oddly concerned by it. "That does not bother you?"

"Does what not bother me?"

Evin wiped his sweaty palms on his thighs, trying to ask this without chasing her away. "Not...*belonging* anywhere."

Ryn's eyebrows popped up in sudden understanding. She appeared to consider the question before answering slowly, "No, I don't think so. It's not as bad as it sounds; I have made a role for myself, in spite of everything, and I am quite happy with it. Besides," her expression turned almost teasing, playful. "It's a decent life; I can go where I please and never have to deal with rude neighbors sticking their nose in my business." She held his gaze seriously, finishing with conviction. "It's not a bad life, Evin."

He wasn't quite convinced. "Forgive me, but isn't it rather....lonely?"

"Sometimes," she answered quietly. She tossed the blade of grass away. "There are worse things than loneliness."

"Yes," he acknowledged.

Something in how he said it got her attention. She stared at him, baffled. "What would you know of loneliness?"

It was asked without malice or bitterness; simply a question based upon the false assumption that because he was wealthy and powerful, his life was easy. Evin kicked himself for letting the conversation take this turn. It wasn't what he'd intended to talk about. "Let's just say Brandt has always been the more...acceptable of our mother's sons. In nearly every way."

Ryn looked completely bewildered. "What?"

He sighed. "You know, he's the consummate pr—erm, Laendorian warrior; excels in melees with blades, is exceptionally good in the forge, loves metal and stone and earth, has that very impressive golden beard."

Ryn looked mystified. "And you're...not? The 'consummate Laendorian warrior', I mean?"

He averted his gaze. "Not by any means," he replied. "I'm good with a sword but better with a bow, at hunting, tracking. I love being outside, am useless in the forge—I'm much better with detail work; leather working, etching, carving—and couldn't grow a proper beard if I wanted to. Not that I would want to, it'd just get in the way when I shoot." He snorted. "More Eloni than Laendorian, it's been said." Actually, worse had been said, whispered behind his back, though it hadn't prevented him hearing it too many times to count.

More Val'gren than Laendorian. Monster mutt.

He shrugged when she just stared at him, disbelieving. "Believe me; I've had plenty of time to accept it."

Ryn looked distinctly uncomfortable; sympathy obviously warring with something less generous—anger, perhaps? "Such folk as say that kind of nonsense clearly don't know you."

She turned back to the dawn, and they sat there until the sun shone fully on the valley.

II

There was a garden near the outer wall of the city that seemed to be less frequented than some of the others. Ryn wasn't sure why, as it was probably one of the most lovely gardens she'd seen yet, which was saying something in a city full of them. She sat on a stone bench fiddling with her wooden coin. The warmth of the shining sun, combined with the dull buzz of bees feeding on the ubiquitous flowers, gave the garden a muted, isolated feeling, the perfect setting for a good think.

Ryn thought of several things; her captivity, her new friends, the conversation she'd had with Evin the day before while they watched the sun come up. She wondered at him, trying to imagine his life back at home, where he was doubtless wealthy and—she had thought—well-favored. His words concerned her: *"More Eloni than Laendorian, it's been said."*

Ryn certainly hoped it wasn't his family who put that thought in his head.

"Let's just say Brandt has always been the more...acceptable of our mother's sons."

She had thought that particular experience was hers alone. It was interesting to her, that instead of feeling a kinship with him over a shared circumstance, she was far more angry that anyone would think such of her friend. He was a good man who did not deserve such to be dismissed and scorned. She scowled at her coin, rubbing a bit of dirt off it with her thumb, harder than necessary.

Beside her, Kota raised his head, bringing her attention back to the garden. She shook her head to clear it and looked about to see what was the matter. Nothing seemed out of the ordinary, as far as she could tell. Still the bees buzzed, still the butterflies flitted, lending their patterns and colors to the already-colorful setting. The birds sang cheerily, and unlike so few weeks ago in the wild meadow, nothing felt out of place or wrong.

Then she heard it.

Someone was coming, and they made no attempt to disguise their presence. On the contrary, they were whistling a cheery tune unapologetically. The shrill sound was unwelcome, not so much because of the sound itself, but because it signaled the end of her cherished time alone. Ryn hadn't been truly alone since she took this job, and as much as she liked her clients, dealing with other people constantly wore on her nerves after a time.

The whistling set her teeth on edge, and Ryn stood, facing the direction from whence it was coming. Beside her, Kota, normally so attuned to her own moods, sniffed the air and tilted his head in an expression of curiosity—very much not what she was feeling at the moment. Ryn didn't have time to wonder much about it before the old man she'd caught a glimpse of several days before came sauntering into their isolated clearing, all careless grace and flowing robes. He was shorter than she, and much older, though not quite grandfatherly; wrinkles and white hair told of his years, but he moved with the smooth gait of a much younger man. Bright purple eyes sparkled in his leathered face, and he stopped whistling to grin at her. Kota moved closer hesitantly, sniffing the air, his stubby tail held high. Ryn held him back with a murmured word, and the man's gaze sharpened for a moment before relaxing back into friendly greeting.

"Good morning!" he said cheerfully, and Ryn had to grit her teeth. He was worse than Evin, who was shamelessly buoyant first thing in the morning every day, and it drove Ryn batty while Brandt just dealt with it resignedly, apparently used to his brother's ridiculous effervescence.

She nodded once in answer. "It is."

The man appeared not at all put off by her curt attitude, turning his attention to Kota and clicking his tongue in invitation. The lynx chirped inquisitively and trotted to him, nosing at the man's palm while Ryn stared in shock.

"He's not very sociable," she insisted, raising a single brow at her Friend, who trilled apologetically but didn't leave his investigation, still sniffing at the stranger's hand.

"It's not personal," the man laughed. "He is intelligent, for a lynx. He knows I mean no harm to either of you."

"Is that why you were sneaking around like a thief in the shadows the other day?" Ryn challenged.

To her surprise, the man took no offense at her words, instead leveling her with a sunny smile. "You saw me!" he sounded delighted. "How wonderful!"

"Who are you? What do you want?" Ryn had little patience for this seemingly-pointless meeting. "I'm really desperately busy."

"Are you now?" the man challenged back with a grin on his face, though his eyes were piercing. "Busy wandering the gardens while you wait for your Companion to heal up?"

Ryn gritted her teeth, ignoring the man's question. "Why did you not approach before?"

"You mean when you were with your overprotective bulky warrior friends?" the man gestured to himself, his slender build, weaponless, armorless, and Ryn had to suppress a smirk. "I have no desire to confront either of them in battle."

It was the nonchalant tone, more than the words themselves, which threw Ryn off. She stumbled a bit over her response. "If you mean no harm, why do you fear my warlike...friends?" She wasn't sure what to call Brandt and Evin.

"Well," the man answered, "they seem the type to kill first, ask questions after, if you know what I mean. And what I am about to do can be, at first glance, considered questionable behavior."

"Questionable...?" But Ryn never got to finish. Throughout their short conversation, the old man had been moving closer by steps, so he was within arm's reach when he enclosed Ryn's wrist in a vice grip. In a flash, he'd drawn a knife and sliced her forearm open; a thin, shallow laceration that welled blood instantly. It barely hurt, but Ryn's other fist flew almost without conscious command from her brain, connecting with the old man's cheek in a satisfying crunch and sending him sprawling. Ryn closed a hand around her injured arm.

"What in the name of Aeos was that?" she loomed over the man, who sat on the ground looking rather dazed. "You said you meant no harm!" Beside her, Kota's hackles were up, but he hadn't attacked the man yet, which was bizarre enough to pique Ryn's anger. "And what have you done to my lynx!?"

Grasping, the old man rolled to his knees and pulled Ryn's arm forcefully toward his face. She tried to yank away, but his grip was like iron. What was that all about, anyway? She had *definitely* hit him hard enough that he should be sprawled senseless on the grass. He stared hard at her freckled skin for a moment before his face split into a grin that made Ryn want to punch him again. "No harm is done," he cried. "I knew it! I knew it!"

"What are you talking about, you crazy lardsack? You sliced my arm open!"

"But I did not hurt you. Look, my lady!" The old man chuckled as he tried to get his legs back under him. Ryn glanced down at her forearm. Where moments before had been a thin cut, not very deep even, there was now clean, unbroken skin. A little blood was still smeared over it, but she no longer bore any evidence of the man's knife.

"What?" she muttered stupidly. The old man had finally managed to stand again, and he took her forearm into wrinkled hands again, more gently this time. Too shocked to protest, Ryn looked up into his face. His smile was uncomplicated joy now, no trace of his earlier teasing.

"It is because of our bloodlines. I am Kenelm, of the Skyshifters. And you, my dear, are of the ancient line of Healers, the Y'rai."

"The..." Ryn petered off, not recognizing the old man's clan at all, so she focused on what he said of her. "But the Y'rai are legends. Children's tales."

Kenelm smiled indulgently. "I am afraid you are mistaken about that. Their origins can be debated—most say they were created by Aeos at the behest of his beloved, Eir, Keeper and Healer of Souls—but what is certainly true is that they existed. And they did indeed wield healing magic, as the Men of Laendor wield swords and the Val'gren wield dark sorcery."

"No," she answered, confused. "There must be some mistake. My mother was of the Clan Ragnar, cloth-masters and tailors of Bren Valley in Laendor. My father was from Southdale...a hunter and woodsman."

But Kenelm was shaking his head. "It matters not. Official lineage is passed down through fathers, yes, but this is a matter of blood, not legality. Intermarriage between clans—indeed, between nations, though that is often looked down upon—is not unheard of. Thousands of years ago, the ancient Y'rai lived and worked among the people they healed; and after the destruction of their society, they stayed. Married wives and husbands. Birthed and fathered children." He sat on the stone bench she had occupied minutes before, and Ryn buried a hand in Kota's fur, her fingers cold and numb as she tried to process what she was hearing. The lynx leaned into her knee, snuffling gently as though he sensed her distress. Kenelm continued. "Eventually they died off, but their blood lives on in many of Adan's population, however diluted."

Questions exploded in rapid succession in Ryn's mind, the effect dizzying and not at all to her liking. She knew who she was, good and bad and inside out, had made sure she did, for she was the only thing in her life of which she could always be completely sure. To hear she had latent untapped power given to her through the line of her parents—one, or perhaps both of them—was disorienting. Ryn sat too.

"I don't understand," she murmured faintly, staring down at her now-uninjured arm. Blood stained her fingers, and she resisted the urge to wipe it off on her pants. Instead, she studied it, trying to comprehend what she was being told; trying to see if, perhaps, her own life's blood looked any different, would provide any answers. She was vaguely aware when Kenelm slid over to sit beside her—not too close—fiddling with a thin leather thong, tying it this way and that as he wove it between sure, wrinkled fingers. "Why me? I've never healed anything a day in my life...well, not by arcane means."

Kenelm glanced over keenly, his fingers still working the leather. His gaze was penetrating. "Have you not? They tell me you were a prisoner of the nagrat. I have seen the camp where you were held, my lady."

Ryn swallowed, dropped her eyes. "That was death, not healing, and it wasn't me." Kenelm raised a single brow, and Ryn shuddered at the memory of the place, suddenly feeling defensive. "I don't know what

91

happened there, but it wasn't me. You've got it all wrong. I fell asleep that night expecting not to wake, but when I did I was healed and they were dead. It wasn't me at all."

"It was," the elder smiled kindly. "The Y'rai were Master Healers, youngling. That ability extended also to their own bodies; when they came near death, the instinct to heal themselves was profoundly compelling, an impulse near impossible to resist. It was a dangerous thing to be near a dying Y'ra, for unless they were killed instantly, they would suck the life out of everything around them until their bodies could survive. Most learned to control it, after years of study. Those who did not, well. There was a reason the Y'rai did not allow a healer near a battle until they were old enough to have mastered the discipline."

Ryn shuddered at the implications of that. "So I *was* dying," she confirmed, carefully refusing to think about what would have happened if she'd been near Kota or her new friends at the time.

Kenelm sighed. "I am afraid so."

Ryn looked down at her fingers again. Her blood was beginning to dry, darkening to a red-brown and settling into the grooves of her fingerprints. She'd have to wash it off now. The thought was chased by a dozen memories jogged loose by Kenelm's words: the time she'd accidentally eaten lifesbane berries when she was very young, how horrified mother had been seeing the blue-black juice staining her three-year-old's face, how Ryn had somehow managed to survive ingesting the most poisonous food known to her people, merely becoming ill for a few days. Or the time she'd fallen from a tree while playing in the woods, landing hard enough on her ankle to hear the bone crack. She'd lost consciousness from the pain, that time, and when she eventually limped home the next day, her repeated defense that she had broken her ankle hadn't held water when Mother had lifted her pant leg and seen nothing but a lot of bruising and swelling. She'd been punished both for staying out and for lying, that time.

Still, it was sheer luck, fighting skill…and whatever ability she had to heal faster than the average person…that had kept her from dancing too close to death over the years. There was small chance she'd always be so lucky.

"Will it happen again?" She had to know if she would wake up from a skirmish one morning to a dead Kota, or dead friends. The thought terrified her.

"Has it happened before?"

Ryn thought, reflecting on all the dangers in which she had found herself since leaving home, all the horrible situations, all the freezing nights, all the times when food and sometimes water were perilously low. "No," she had to admit. "Nothing like that has ever happened before."

"You've never been that close to death before. Once in, what, sixteen years?" Kenelm smiled at Ryn's look of mock outrage. "I would not worry over much, my dear."

"I have seen twenty-six winters, sir, and you'd do well to remember it," Ryn found herself trying not to smile in relief.

"However," Kenelm held up a finger. "The fact that it happened at all, that there's enough Y'rai blood in your veins to exhibit their traits and their magic…" He shook his head. "You need to learn to control it, lest your fear become reality. You live a dangerous life, child, you cannot afford to be carrying around such unpredictable potential with no mastery of it." Ryn's chest suddenly felt very tight, her palms cold and sweaty at the idea of unintentionally killing someone by her own demise.

"Let me help you," the old man continued, taking her clammy hands in his own. "I should very much like to teach you what I do know, if you are willing. Anyone with enough power to do what you did in that camp could be very useful in our world, and in whatever way she chooses to be."

"You are…Y'rai…too?" Ryn stumbled over the word, struggled to remember the name of his clan. It had been unfamiliar to her, and thus meant little. But Kenelm was shaking his head.

"Ah, no." He stood and shook off his long robe, leaning his walking stick against the tree under which they took shade. "I am a Skyshifter. Our once-powerful nations were fast allies. This is my magic." And with that, he tilted his face to the sky and opened his mouth. What came out was probably best described as a single, unearthly note, unwavering. It made Ryn's skin pimple with chills and her eyes water, but she didn't dare blink because she was fairly certain she had never seen anything like this in her entire life. Kenelm's whole body began to glow as if from within. The light grew brighter, the note louder, until there was a flash of blue so vivid it hurt her head, and Ryn gasped aloud.

Where moments before had stood an old man, there stood instead a magnificent griffin, its curved beak—as long as her forearm—preening ruffled feathers at its chest. Golden tawny fur covered the body of a lion, ending in deadly claws and a tufted tail. But the thing that caught and kept Ryn's attention, open-mouthed for nearly fifteen entire seconds, was the pair of glorious wings that Kenelm was shaking out, as though to stretch them after long disuse. They were the same dusky gold as his fur, and speckled and striped with darker browns, large feathers gleaming in the afternoon light.

"Oh," she found herself murmuring. Beside her, Kota was standing with his head tilted in an endearing way that communicated absolute confusion.

Kenelm trilled a sound that was a completely unfamiliar mix of feline and avian, but that Ryn took to be affirmative, then uttered that wailing note again. Moments later, the old man stood before them again, in his less discomfiting figure. He leaned on his walking stick, panting slightly.

"By the Light, that takes more energy than I remember," he muttered softly.

Ryn couldn't speak yet, so said nothing.

After several moments, Kenelm seemed to catch his breath. "Long ago, even before I was born, there was a Pact. Hamat, Chief-Son of the Skyshifters, and Falathir, Prince of the Y'rai were, according to the legend, as brothers. They traversed and left boyhood in one another's company, and when the time came for each of them to step into their respective positions as leader of their people, they made an agreement never to harm one another and always to come to the other's aid. They backed their Pact with blood-magic, tempered it with the Light, and bequeathed it to every future generation of Y'rai and Skyshifter." Kenelm sat, smiling. "It is why I cannot—*would not*—hurt you. If you needed any further proof of your heritage, your...birthright, you have it."

Ryn nodded, sitting heavily as the enormity of this all descended upon her shoulders. She, a descendant of the Master Healers of Old? A possessor of magic? A homeless wanderer still, but one with an undeniable gift of power that she could use as a force for good, or evil, should she choose.

Or perhaps, a slave to her newfound magic. Already, she felt it: the instinctive urge to accept Kenelm's proposal, not because she wanted the power, but for the threat of the power overcoming her own will. If she did not control it, it would control her. This she could sense, and it made her angry. It was servitude of the type she'd spent her whole adult life fleeing, only wrapped in a slightly different parcel.

She stood, abruptly. Kenelm's gaze followed her, serene and guileless. She clenched and unclenched her fists, a gesture of helpless agitation, cursing the roiling of her suddenly rebellious stomach.

"I—" she began, but choked on the words. "I need to think. Please excuse me." She turned, and Kota on her heels, practically ran from the garden.

To her surprise, Kenelm did not call out.

~~~~~~~~~~

Evin swiped at the sweat that beaded his brow as he set the final stitches on his worn leather pack. He would need to commission another after this trip, but the one he had ought to hold up well enough if he patched it, so he resisted the urge to buy a new one while they were in Thaliondris. As his uncle had always said, the man who could not exercise wisdom in small transactions could not be trusted to do so in large ones. And Evin would be given his fair share of large transactions to execute, when he was appointed a position in a few years. 'Twas traditional for second-born princes to fill a role close to the King: Advisor, General, High Priest, Chief Scholar, or the like. Originally, Gunnar had wanted Brandt as his Head Advisor; Brandt had made it rather clear to the Crown Prince that he thought Evin's strength to be in strategy and warfare, so the younger had trained to that end, put all his energies toward shadowing the current General, Almar the Shorn. Now, though...

With Gunnar gone and Brandt in line for the throne, he supposed there was a chance his brother would expect him to fill the position of Advisor rather than General. Eager as he was to help in whatever way he could, he secretly hoped this was not the case. Gunnar had been schooled deliberately for a diplomatic position, Brandt right beside him, since they were small children. Evin, nigh on six years their junior, had still been outside playing with sticks and mud by the time his older brother and cousin were writing courtly letters and charming the ladies with their recitations. It had made him a little jealous, he remembered with a small smile, how like brothers Gunnar and Brandt had been; thick as thieves and twice as awe-inspiring, to a child of his age and temperament. Not that they had ever shunned him. There were many, many stories told over cups and at banquets by courtiers and servants alike, of the three hellions who'd grown up in those castle halls; boyish scuffles and wild chases as much as respectful conversations and knightly courtesy.

Still, of the three of them, Evin had proven to have the least diplomatic talent. He was too impulsive, too quick to laugh, far too plain-spoken. Certainly he could hide his intentions and meanings behind layers of cordiality, but Evin had always half-despised that particular ability, even in his brother. He would much rather say what he meant, as kindly—or not—as possible. Much less room for misinterpretation that way.

All that to say, he'd make a terrible Advisor to the King of Laendor. He was better off in charge of the Crown's Army, he was sure of it.

He hummed a nameless tune as he cut the thick thread he'd been using and shook out the pack, eyeing it critically. He nodded once; it would do. He had just picked up a sheath and begun to inspect it for damage when the door to his room opened loudly. Brandt had returned, it seemed.

"Bit early, brother?" he asked distractedly, still studying the sheath. "How was the market?"

At the same moment that a wet nose snuffled its way into his line of sight, a clearly-female voice answered, only a little bit snippily, "I'm not him." With a small blurt of surprise, Evin grinned and gave Kota the attention he was asking for; rubbing the great cat's neck and flank, then growling playfully at him as he pulled his fur gently, trying to incite the kit to play. It worked; Kota bared his teeth and swiped at Evin with his claws sheathed, enough force behind it to push the prince off the bench and flat onto his back. Evin laughed breathlessly, wriggling to get free while he mimicked Kota's play-warning growls. The lynx let him get a couple of feet away before pouncing again, and the game was on.

After several minutes, he sat up, hair askew and face flushed, to see Ryn sitting in his spot on the wooden bench, several sticks in her hands that looked to have been whittled and sanded straight. A kerchief lay next to her, sharp arrowheads piled on top, and a group of fletching feathers rested beside that. Despite the normalcy of what she was doing, Evin could tell something wasn't quite right. Every line of Ryn's body radiated tension, from the way her back was ramrod-straight to the obvious clench of her jaw. He tilted his head.

"What is wrong?"

Ryn glanced up at him, shifting uncomfortably, before looking back down and beginning to wrap a thin leather thong around the junction between arrowhead and shaft. She was silent for a few minutes, but Evin didn't ask again, knowing she would answer when she was ready, or not at all.

Kota huffed a bellowy sigh and lay down next to him, lowering his big head to rest on Evin's thigh. The prince scratched behind the lynx's ears and the creature started to purr, throat vibrating against Evin's legs.

When Ryn did answer, it wasn't what Evin expected. "You believe the Y'rai are more than legend, yeah?"

When she finished the question, he couldn't decide what was in her face—desperation, or fear, or grief—but he nodded. "I do."

Ryn sighed, letting her hands fall into her lap, still holding the half-finished arrow. She let the weapon rest in her hand, pulling at her protective leather work glove nervously.

Evin felt his eyes narrow in confusion; in the time he'd known Ryn, she'd been chased down by a troll, nearly gotten a concussion in a river, and been tortured by nagrat, and through all of it, he'd never seen her so discomfited. It was a serious thing indeed that could render his confident, self-assured guide-turned-friend this jittery.

Ryn kept her eyes firmly upon her fiddling fingers as she spoke again. "I met a Skyshifter today."

Evin sat up a little straighter. A Skyshifter? They were almost extinct, the stuff of legends now, though he had heard of a few who lived here and there—one, indeed, in Thaliondris. He would love to meet the man. "That is incredible!" he exclaimed, letting himself smile.

But Ryn looked anything but pleased, her green eyes rising to meet his, more fear in them than joy. "He said I am a Y'ra."

Evin actually sat back at that piece of news, shock making its lightning way through his features. He blinked, words refusing to form on his lips. A Y'ra? It was feasible, certainly, for many people to be descended of the Healers of Old; but for their magic to manifest enough to be called by their name, to become heir to their secrets? That seemed...unlikely. "Is he certain?" he asked carefully after several moments.

Ryn flashed him a desperate smile, clearly having thought of the same question. "He is. I am not, although..." she petered off, then seemed to gather her courage in a breath. "Although the evidence seems to support his claim more than my own."

Evin tilted his head. "Evidence?"

Ryn nodded, pulling at her glove again. "The nagrat camp, for one," she said quietly. "And there are other things. Things I've always attributed to luck, but...how I've survived this long on my own, gotten out of scrapes I shouldn't have, responded so differently to poison than others, my knack for medicines and herbs..." She swallowed. "I think Kenelm—the Skyshifter—might be right."

"Oh." Evin took a moment to absorb the enormity of it, and found a smile creeping over his face. A Y'ra! What a wonderful thing to discover about oneself, the ability to become a powerful healer and mage, save lives, help people! It was a noble calling, full of honor, and he...he squinted. Why wasn't she happier about this? Instead of looking as though she'd been given the key to the world, Ryn looked like someone had destroyed her life.

"You...wish it otherwise?" he asked.

Ryn ran shaking fingers down the grain of one of the feathers she was using to fletch her arrows, clearly agitated. She took so long to answer this time Evin thought she might not at all, preferring to shut him down or change the subject in that way she had. Kota shifted, no longer purring, perhaps sensing his mistress' apprehension. After a few minutes she sighed, clearly agitated with herself. "Who am I to decide who lives and dies?" she finally blurted, and Evin understood in an instant.

She *feared* the power she possessed.

His second thought was that such an attitude was perhaps wise. He knew that some of the legend surrounding the ancient and proud Y'rai, this many years hence, would be just that: *legend*. There was no knowing exactly what Ryn was capable of, if anything. Nevertheless, there was no denying the Healers of Old had been formidable indeed, both on the battlefield and off it, and such power never came without the very real danger of getting lost in it. He had a difficult time imagining Ryn as a tyrannical mage, but the truth was, no one ever *expected* to become mad or ruthless.

That said, potential untapped was another evil altogether.

"Don't you already?" he asked, deliberately blunt. He knew Ryn well enough to know she didn't take kindly to pity or sympathy. A logical approach would reach her more quickly, and she tended to appreciate his candidness more than the lords and ladies at court did. It was both part of the reason they got on so well, and part of the reason she'd taken so long to warm to him. This was a contradiction in her he found fascinating.

Now, however, she seemed slightly less appreciative, though he clearly had her attention. She stopped fidgeting, looked up at him in confusion. "Don't I already what?"

"Decide who lives and dies," he clarified. He went on quickly, preferring to explain before she jumped toward conclusions he did not intend. "You already do that, every day. You decide the nagrat die, the travelers live. It's how you make a living." There was dawning comprehension on her face, morphing into something like anger. He pressed on. "We all do it; fight to kill the evil ones and save the good, the innocent ones."

"That's...different."

"Is it?" he challenged. "Is not magic simply another weapon in your arsenal, another means to complete your mission to save lives?"

Ryn blinked. She still looked doubtful, but Evin could see he had made his point, so he didn't push further. Instead, he reached down and stroked Kota's velvet-soft ears, turning his full attention to the lynx and letting Ryn process his words. The big cat nudged up into his hand, whuffing softly and beginning to purr once more, enjoying the ministrations of his fingers. Evin held back a laugh, not wanting to interrupt whatever was going on inside his guide's pretty head.

"So...so you think I should go to Kenelm?" Ryn asked a few minutes later. Evin looked up at her and was struck by her expression. It was equal parts curiosity, fear, and desperation, and it occurred to him that she legitimately *cared* what he thought about the matter. She hadn't been just asking out of a need to verbalize her doubt or a desire to hear what he had to say; his opinion—his advice—actually meant something to her. He let himself wonder for a moment when exactly that had happened, letting the question hang in the air, crafting his response carefully.

"I think you should do whatever you want," he eventually answered. "Treat your magic like a staff, bow, or any other weapon. Choose how you'll fight, then become a master at it." He locked his gaze with hers, gold on green. "But do not avoid it out of fear."

~~~~~~~~~~

Supper was a quiet affair that night. Brandt had returned to the inn to find Evin lolling on the floor with Kota like he was a cat himself, and Ryn sitting on their bench fletching arrows. She had just finished when he arrived, so after he roundly mocked his brother for acting like a lazy child, they had all cheerfully dug into the roast venison and warm tellas bread he'd picked up from the market. At first, Ryn had seemed off, more like the woman he'd first met all those weeks ago; quiet, reserved, maybe even a little cold. He'd wondered at it; but Evin was in high spirits, and as was usually the case, his cheerful demeanor went far toward relaxing both their taciturn guide and Brandt himself.

During dinner, Ryn had told him about her meeting with the Skyshifter. Brandt thought it all completely crazy, but then he hadn't seen the nagrat camp himself. Evin had told him of it, and it had certainly sounded strange enough, but Y'rai *magic*? Even if one believed in the Healers of Old, they had intermarried and died off hundreds of years ago; what were the chances Ryn would possess enough of their blood to manifest their power? He said little, though, since Ryn was clearly nervous about the entire thing, simply giving her a smile and encouraging her to do what she thought best. If she really was the only living heir of the Y'rai, far be it from him to stand in her way. If she was not, attempting to learn the use of magic she did not possess would clear all this up quickly enough.

Now, a good few hours after the last of the venison had been tossed to Kota as a treat, and long after the sun had set in a riot of gold and red, all three of them were gathered on the velvety rug like a group of younglings at a sleepover. Brandt was leaning against the bedpost, Evin beside him. His brother was slumped so low he was practically lying down. His bare feet dug into the mossy carpet at irregular intervals, as though he was enjoying the sensation of grass between his toes, but it seemed an entirely unconscious gesture, which amused Brandt to no end.

Quietly, of course.

Kota was sleeping heavily next to Ryn, who lay with her head against his big soft flank, now fully healed and barely even scarred. Brandt was grateful; he found he'd come to almost like the beast at some point on the road. Ryn herself seemed entirely at ease now, grinning as she looked over at them.

"Your turn, Evin."

Evin smiled back, his bright eyes lighting up. He loved tale-telling, and he was damned good at it. Better than Brandt would ever be, for certain. He was half-sure, if he'd kept record, he could look back at the nights spent on this quest and find that Evin was asked to provide the evening's stories more often than he and Ryn put together, but he wasn't keeping score, and even if he was, who could blame them? The man knew how to tell a story.

His younger brother pulled himself into a sitting position, folding his legs under him and tapping his chin thoughtfully. "Let us see, with which tale of daring adventure should I regale you this night?"

Brandt smiled; he loved seeing Evin like this, in his element, unashamedly himself in all his unique ways, and being appreciated for it. Ryn's wide eyes were fixed on his brother, awaiting the story.

"Ah, yes, now I have it," Evin's grin turned mischievous. He cleared his throat and began, folding his hands over his torso theatrically. "On this beautiful night of the diamond-skies, I tell you a tale of danger, of peril unmatched, and of daring prowess that will take your breath away!" He gestured wildly, and Ryn laughed. Brandt tried not to snort aloud. "Tonight!" Evin continued, "I tell you of the Brandt the Gentle, and how he once saved the lives of an entire herd of deer!"

Brandt realized with a start which tale Evin was about to tell, and his heart sank into his stomach. He moaned, rolling his eyes so hard he gave himself a headache. Or perhaps that was the ridiculous day he'd had.

"As you love me, brother," he cried. "Any tale save that one!"

"Shhhh," Ryn shushed him, her face lit up with amusement, and Brandt couldn't even be upset. She was almost pretty this way, the firelight playing on her scarred face, smile softening hard features.

"The lady speaks true," Evin said, all gravitas. "It is a man of no courtesy who interrupts a tale in the telling."

Brandt let his head *thunk* against the bedpost dramatically.

Evin smirked and continued."Twas a glorious morning in the month of Blossomfall, ages and ages past, for our hero is an old man now..."

Twas a freezing, dark morning, actually, and not so long ago, Brandt remembered, half amused and half annoyed at Evin's exaggeration.

"Brandt the Gentle was awoken kindly by his dashing brother Evin, the Greatest Huntsman in All the Land, in preparation for his first hunt."

Brandt began reassessing his previous thoughts about Evin's storytelling abilities. There were more factual errors in that one sentence than any tale ought to be allowed: Evin had smothered him with a pillow to wake him, cackling madly the entire time; his younger brother was most certainly not the 'Greatest Huntsman in All the Land', though he could probably compete for the title, not that Brandt would ever tell him so; and it had not been Brandt's first hunt. He cocked an eyebrow, but Evin didn't even notice. He simply continued, ridiculous embellishments and flamboyant hand gestures and all.

"The brothers left their shining home amidst a cheering crowd of admirers, waving politely and kissing babies as they went. They reached a spot where the Greatest Huntsman in All the Land knew the deer came to graze and water in the early mornings, and The Magnificent Huntsman showed his Gentle brother where to lie in wait for them. 'Await our prey here', he instructed quietly, 'and when they arrive, wait until they begin to drink to shoot. When they drink, you know they feel safe.'

"The Noble Huntsman positioned himself nearby, in a location where he could both see and remain comfortable throughout the proceedings; for the ritual stated that his brother must perform the entire operation himself—shooting, cleaning, and transport back home."

That, at least, was true. Brandt sighed. This was where things went downhill.

"There they both sat, in a small clearing with a sparkling stream, for nigh on one full hour. Soon the sun began to rise in the distance, a thin strip of gold in a lightening blue sky. The Exalted Huntsman watched eagerly as the herd of deer entered the verdant glade cautiously. They looked about for several minutes before crossing to the ice-cold stream and beginning to drink. 'Now,' thought the Greatest Huntsman in All the Land. 'Now is your chance, Gentle Brother!'

"But nothing happened. For another full hour, the deer remained in that dell, refreshing themselves and readying to move on, and still no arrows came from Brandt's yew bow." Evin paused for effect, and Ryn's brow was furrowed in genuine confusion. She was visibly biting her cheek to avoid interrupting with a question, and it made his younger brother grin.

"Perhaps you wonder why such an oddity occurred," he continued, and Brandt groaned quietly. Couldn't he just get on with it without all the theatrics? "I assure you, sweet lady, the Great Hunter wondered exactly the same thing. He was unable to assist Gentle Brandt in any way, so said the ritual, so he waited to see what would happen. The herd of deer moved on, and yet no response was forthcoming; the Famed Archer began to be afraid for his brother's safety. He slipped from his hiding place and went to Brandt, only to find him limp and quiet. Concerned, he knelt beside him to assess his condition, only to be startled half out of his wits by a loud snore!"

Brandt saw the moment Ryn understood fully the end of the story. Her round eyes crinkled at the edges, her slack mouth closing as she bit her lip in an attempt not to laugh at him outright. Evin leaned forward to finish the tale, lowering his voice to a conspiratorial tone.

"Gentle Brandt had fallen fast asleep awaiting the herd, and thus saved the lives of every deer in that glade, there on that glorious morning in the month of Blossomfall."

Ryn lost what composure she'd managed to hang onto. She laughed so hard she woke Kota, who huffed imperiously and moved out from under her head, causing it to thump onto the carpet, which just made her laugh harder. Evin snorted his amusement at the sight, and Brandt found himself laughing right along with both of them. They all laughed far longer than he felt the story warranted, including him, but in the wake of their amusement, he noticed the air felt a little lighter.

Perhaps a good laugh was something they had all needed badly.

Ryn swiped at the corners of her eyes, wiping away the small tears that had gathered there in her amusement. "I can't believe you fell asleep on a hunt," she said, dissolving into quiet giggles again.

"Yes well," Brandt offered by way of explanation, "I hadn't slept in three days."

"Through no fault of anyone's but your own," Evin interjected, still laughing. "You had just come of age and were celebrating in the most uppity, ridiculous way possible!"

"I will have you know my friends found my drunken antics hilarious," Brandt defended himself, sending his brother and their friend into yet another fit of mirth. He grinned a little, too.

"So how did you bring home the required venison?" Ryn finally asked, once they'd all calmed. Kota had given up sleeping and sat by the fire, studying them all with an expression of judgmental disgust.

"We just waited for dusk," Evin replied. "The same herd came back in the evening and Brandt shot one then. He's not a bad hunter, not really." His younger brother smirked at him. "But it makes such a great story, his failure."

Brandt tackled him.

12

Finding her destination the next morning was far easier than Ryn felt it ought to have been. Lady Naleti was able to give her very succinct, descriptive directions to the massive oak near the edge of the city, tucked away behind a grove of smaller aspens and tiny shops. News that there was an heir of the Y'rai inside the city had spread quickly, and everyone had been more than happy to help her find her way. It made her jumpy and annoyed, to be so noticed. Ryn picked her way carefully through the close-grown white trunks, Kota hard on her heels; her jaw dropped when she broke through into a bright clearing.

Before her, the old oak stood proudly, its trunk twice as thick as she was tall, and covered in moss. Huge boughs started low, reaching for the sky and then arching down nearly to touch the ground, stretching out to tangle with the white aspens at the edge of the clearing. Bright green leaves covered everything so thickly Ryn could barely see the two wood pillars, close to the trunk, that framed the first of a set of stairs that appeared to circumnavigate the tree, disappearing up into the foliage. She stepped closer and couldn't hold back an awed, 'ohhh.'

The steps circled the trunk three times, before ending at a red door forty spans above her head. The door was set in a large tree house, built atop the trunk where it split into several large boughs that grew out and up. The house was of rough dark wood, and had several windows that Ryn could see cut into the walls. It was thatched above to keep off rain and snow, and smoke wafted gently from a small chimney at the southernmost corner of the place. The rich, heady smell of wood and greenery, ubiquitous in all of Thaliondris, seemed even stronger here. It radiated cheer, and Ryn found herself drawn up the stairs, wonder-struck. She climbed slowly, and studied the red door before she knocked. It wasn't painted red, as she'd suspected below; rather, it was made of a very red wood, with a darker grain that was the same color as the rest of the walls. She had never seen the like. There was no handle or knob on the door, which flummoxed Ryn for a moment, but before she could knock, the door swung in, revealing a head of wild white hair and piercing amethyst eyes.

"You came!" Kenelm exclaimed, smiling widely.

Ryn swallowed. There was a pit in her stomach the size and weight of a wheatstone. What was she *doing* here? A complete stranger's home in a strange city, inhabited by a crazy old man-griffin-creature who swore he could teach her magic? She must be going mad. Still, at least she had Kota and her staff, and both Evin and Brandt knew where to find her. Embarrassing this may be, but dangerous, not so much. She nodded once.

Kenelm stepped back, inviting them in, scratching Kota casually behind the ears as they passed. The lynx nipped at the old man's fingers playfully, and he laughed. "Please," he gestured to the main room, "be comfortable."

The den was small, but in a cozy way. Two padded chairs faced one another beside a small fireplace, a low table between. There was a cooking area nearby, open to the main room, and a door Ryn suspected led to a bedroom on the other side. Windows let in dappled light, whose shadows played along every available surface. Ryn sat gingerly in the chair she thought was not Kenelm's—a book rested upon the other one, titled in a language she could not read—and Kota settled beside her, sniffing at the air.

Kenelm bustled back in, bringing a kettle full of water and hanging it over the small fire. He whisked about for a few minutes, doing this and that, before finally moving his book to the short table and sitting across from Ryn. He was still wearing that overjoyed smile.

"I am admittedly surprised to see you," he began, gaze sharpening as he looked her over. "You seemed troubled by my insight the other day."

Ryn answered it for the question it was. "I was. I still am." She shrugged. "But a lot of things worth knowing are troublesome."

Kenelm chuckled at that. "You are not wrong, Y'ra." He reached for Ryn's staff. "May I?"

Reluctantly, Ryn turned over the weapon. The old man studied it with a critical gaze, weathered fingers running over the smooth wood and moving to the knotted head. "Hm. Yes, this'll do." Ryn raised her eyebrows, and he handed it back to her. "It knows you. That staff should see you through most anything."

"It has," she confirmed, feeling her fingers settle into the familiar grooves worn in over the past ten years. "It was a little big at first, but it's saved my hide many a time."

Kenelm nodded. "First things first. You need one of these." He stood, gesturing her over to a small table under a nearby window, upon which rested an assortment of stones, ranging from the size of a large coin to Ryn's own clenched fist. There seemed to be no order to the selection; there were plain gray rocks, smooth flat river stones, and several faceted gems. Ryn's eyes widened at the latter, though Kenelm didn't seem to notice. "I unpacked these in case you did decide to come to me. Stone is, of course, the best focus for your magic, by far. Some Y'rai could use wooden or glass amulets, but they were very advanced and their foci very old, and all those that I know of have been lost to the ravages of time. These," he gestured to the motley array of rocks, "I gathered years ago when I traveled to Galaron itself. I cannot use them as you can, but I can sense their arcane abilities."

Mute, Ryn nodded. Kenelm smiled. "Choose one, girl, and think not for the monetary value, for it is of little use to you here. Use your instincts."

Ryn moved closer to the table, understanding now why Kenelm had asked her to bring her staff and already thinking of ways to carve the head into a shape that could accommodate one of these stones. The man meant for her to wield both a stone and a staff at once—it was a practical approach she could appreciate, for a stone held in one hand could be easily knocked aside and leave her unable to use her magic.

A stone built into her weapon, however, would be difficult to pry even from her cold, dead fingers.

She immediately dismissed both the smallest and largest stones—too small, and it could fall out; too large, and it wouldn't fit within the knot of her staff. Acting on impulse, she picked up a few of the appropriately-sized rocks, weighing them in her hands and allowing her intuition to guide her. The pretty blue river stone she put back almost immediately; it felt slippery, but not physically. In her *mind*.

As if that wasn't freakish enough, the next one she handled—a jagged gray rock, not unlike something one might kick to the side of the road— thundered through her veins, heavy and ruthless. She dropped it rather quickly, shaking out the numbness in her hand.

Ignoring Kenelm's chuckle and Kota's whine—he always could sense when something hurt her, and now she wondered if that was all companionable bonding like she'd thought, or if it had something to do with all this nonsense—Ryn let her fingers wander. She put back both a large sparkling ruby that screeched in her ears and made them ring, and a dull white crystal that nearly forced her to sit with dizziness.

Shaking her head and growing slightly irritated, she picked up a speckled gray one, roughly oval and completely nondescript. The rush was immediate and powerful, though not as severe as the last few had been. It made her fingers tingle and her hair stand on end, gooseflesh chasing itself up her arms and down her spine. The sound of wind in the trees flew through her mind, and she blinked hard.

"This one," she turned to Kenelm, who looked like all his dreams had been granted at once.

"How perfect," he murmured hoarsely, then laughed. It was not a mocking sound, but one of sheer, unadulterated joy. Ryn raised an eyebrow in question, though she couldn't seem to make her mouth work properly.

The power singing through her blood made her itch to *run*, for nothing but the uncomplicated joy of it.

"It is a shieldenstone," Kenelm explained kindly. "On the outside, it appears as any other rock—bumpy and unobtrusive and most often unnoticed—but inside? Inside it is coated with crystal gems that have never yet seen the light of day." He took the stone gently, and Ryn winced a little at the loss. "It is tricky to use properly, but my dear, this is the purest focus you could have chosen. It is well done."

He spoke foreign words then, holding a hand over Ryn's shieldenstone, bright white light spilling from his palm to surround the lumpy gray rock. After a few moments, the magic disappeared and he handed the stone back to her. Ryn sucked in a breath at the rush that returned to her veins with it. She turned the focus over in tingling fingers, studying it, as though it would give up new secrets having been chosen as hers. The mottled surface, however, remained stonily silent, though the power pulsing in Ryn's chest was warm and vibrant still. "What did you do to it?" Ryn asked as Kota approached warily, perhaps knowing what Ryn was feeling, in that way he had, and sniffed the air. She lowered the stone so he could inspect it.

"I told it that it belongs to you," Kenelm answered, as though it were the most obvious thing in the world.

Ryn was stymied by that, but soon distracted by Kota: as soon as his wet nose touched the shieldenstone, the lynx startled, jumping back and huffing a sneeze that made her laugh aloud and turned the Skyshifter's attention to him.

"Best leave the magic to your mistress, youngling," he said companionably. Kota responded with another step back and a smaller sneeze, then a growl.

Ryn was still chuckling when Kenelm clapped his hands, then rubbed them together excitedly. "Now then, my young student," he said, grinning somewhat madly. "No better time to start than today. Place your staff in the corner; we will use it after you've fitted the shieldenstone into the head. For now you'll just hold the stone in your hand. 'Twill be easier to access the magic that way anyhow." Ryn did as he bid, then returned to Kota's side. Kenelm led them both out the door and down his stairs, out into the clearing, and sat himself cross-legged in the velvet green grass. Ryn followed suit and looked at him expectantly. Kota prowled the perimeter, keeping guard.

The old man said nothing for a long time, staring off at some fixed point beyond Ryn's left shoulder. She looked back, wondering what he was staring at, but there were only aspen trees and blue sky. Nothing could be seen of the city through the small forest, and even the sounds of bustle and trade were muted and faraway. Ryn turned back around, uncertain. Should she be saying or doing something? Or was this a test to see if she was patient enough to study such magic?

She did not know what was expected of her, so she followed her instincts and sat quietly. Waited.

Kenelm kept her waiting a long time.

When finally he stirred, sparkling purple eyes focusing on her face again, he smiled. "I have it."

"You have...what?"

Kenelm laughed. "I have lived many more years than you would imagine, young one. Galaron was sacked a thousand years ago, and the Y'rai have been entirely extinct for over five hundred of those years. I needed to call forth my memory of your people in order to teach you anything."

Ryn blinked. "Oh."

He nodded. "The first thing young Y'rai were taught was how to See. Today, that is what you will learn."

"I...sorry, what?" Ryn was hopelessly lost. "I see already."

Kenelm grinned. "What do you see, child?"

Ryn bit back her first, cheeky answer and considered the question truly. "I see trees, green grass, my lynx, you—" But Kenelm was shaking his head.

"You see only half of what is really there." He gestured around them. "You see what all folk see. Light reflecting off objects, creating color, sending signals through your eyes into your brain...it is not enough!" He placed a finger at her temple, tapped it once, twice. "You must see *here*."

Ryn tried not to be dismissive. He sounded crazy, but then...so did the idea of magic in her veins. She felt it still, pulsing in time with her heart, definitely real; she was well past the point of disbelief now.

"How?" Ryn asked. Kenelm pointed to the shieldenstone, still resting loosely in her palm.

"This will help you. Soon you will be able to See without it, but for now it will assist. Can you still feel the stone's effect upon you?"

Ryn nodded, savoring the coalescence of warmth inside her breast.

"Focus on it," Kenelm said, his voice low and soothing, a little slower than she'd heard it before. "Bring it to the fore of your mind and let it guide you. Your physical eyes can see and interpret light. Let the stone show your mental eyes how to See and Interpret *life*."

Ryn closed her eyes and focused on the Warm, bringing it within arm's reach and focusing all her attention upon it. At first nothing happened. The Warm pulsed through her veins, gathered in her chest, tingled in her extremities; but nothing happened. Ryn resisted the urge to open her eyes. After several minutes, something began to glow against the back of her eyelids. It wasn't light, precisely; it was heavier, more solid than that. Bright and hot, it flashed into being seemingly instantly, and she sucked in a gasp against the shock of it. A blinding bright core framed by curling white tendrils, wrapping themselves in everything she Was, bleeding out from her body to touch the world around her. Ryn Saw it, there where she held the Warm, and she suddenly realized she was seeing her magic for the first time.

Surprised, Ryn opened her eyes, expecting the magic to disappear, but instead her eyes widened further. All around her, she could see it. Tendrils of magic, woven through everything in the clearing. Since it wasn't light, it was difficult to process what she was seeing, but after a moment she could identify differences in the tendrils, differences that might have been perceived as color. The blades of grass below her feet were a richer, deeper green than her physical eyes could see, and the magic that coursed through them was short-lived and vibrant. The oak tree's brown was a heartbreaking burnished terra-cotta, the magic old and impossibly heavy. It impressed upon her the many years it had lived, the things it had seen, and it was overwhelming. Ryn had to look away, blinking back tears.

Kenelm was smiling at her, though she could barely see his face. His aura was a swirling mass of impossible blue-purple and blinding silver. It coalesced around his chest, shining into his face with such intensity that she could not make out his physical features; but she could See his joy in the pulsing dance of his life-magic, leaking out into the grass and filling it with the same joy, though the grass hardly knew why. She turned her head a little further and felt the corners of her lips curl up in a genuine smile, seeing her own scarlet aura shift with joy at the sight of Kota, who had trotted back to her and sat within arm's reach.

Her lynx was deep black, the black of a warm, starless night; the black of ebony, depthless and sure; the black of shadows she could hide in, comforting and protecting. Red tendrils sparked and sung throughout his aura, bespeaking curiosity and fear. Her lynx wasn't sure what she was doing, but it felt strange to him and he was frightened. She reached out for him and gasped when she caught sight of her own arm.

She was a glowing crimson all over, except the veins of deepest black that whirled through her, moving toward her fingertips as she reached for Kota. He leaned toward her, and the scarlet tendrils in him reached too, meeting the black in her and glowing overwhelmingly bright in her mind. This magic, when she touched him, was joy and friendship and hope and love and everything they had been through together, all clamoring in her head at once, overloading her emotions' ability to withstand the assault. Ryn retreated almost without thinking, throwing herself out of the magic with a gasp.

"Ryn? Ryn!" she heard Kenelm's voice, concern coloring its edges, as she popped open her eyes. Thankfully, there were no tendrils or auras waiting for her. The colors seemed muted, and she blinked, surprised at the feeling of loss. Her teacher was shaking her, her lynx yowling his apprehension in her ear. She stroked his tufted ears until he sat back, satisfied that she was indeed alive and whole. Kenelm seemed to require more explanation. "Are you well, child? You seemed distressed."

"It...I..." Ryn stammered, trying to come up with words, any words, which could possibly describe what she'd just experienced. "It...was just a...*lot*," she finally managed, and Kenelm smiled kindly.

"It can be," he agreed. "I am sorry for that. But you have done well for your first attempt. Go back to your inn and rest, I will see you tomorrow."

Ryn nodded, mouth dry. She scratched Kota under his chin and stood slowly, muscles protesting. "How long was I out?" she asked, stretching.

"Two hours," Kenelm answered. Ryn's eyes widened in shock. It had felt like mere moments! Her teacher laughed. "It is to be expected, youngling. You were accessing a part of your soul you have not had any experience with before today. You could not be expected to succeed in minutes." He waved a hand at her. "Now go get some rest."

Exhausted, Ryn did not protest.

~~~~~~~~~~

Brown pears, red pears, green pears; Kesi swore if she never saw another pear again, it'd be too soon. She hated these trips her parents always insisted she tag along on. Road food was bland and tasteless, road clothes ugly and dirty, road horses smelly and grouchy. She was smelly, dirty, and grouchy herself. She always was, on these trips. At least they'd reach Thaliondris soon; that place was simply beautiful; clean and elegant and magical. It was the one part of traveling Kesi actually enjoyed—the destination.

But they were still a few leagues out, and meanwhile, all she had to do was ride. Follow the horse ahead of her and just sit there, bored out of her head.

Kesi *hated* it.

Her thoughts were rudely interrupted by a dull *thunk!* from somewhere up ahead. She looked up from her horse's coarse mane to see her father's man, Borys, slouching in his saddle. *Queer*, she thought, for Borys was an excellent horseman, but everything slotted into place half a second later when someone screamed and Borys fell, a black arrow lodged between his eyes.

The man hadn't even had a chance. The thought made Kesi irrationally angry for a split second, before all seven hells broke loose. She heard her father shout her name, but before she could find him, another of the arrows barely missed her leg, burying itself to the feathers in her horse's flank. The animal screamed and bucked, and the next thing Kesi knew, she was sitting in the dirt looking up at a truly fearsome sight.

A man stood over her, clad entirely in black and half again as tall as she. He wore dark leather breeches and a vest under a fine jacket and short cloak. Leather riding boots covered his legs to the knee, and he wore a circlet of some dark metal she didn't recognize. He was deathly pale, but with fine sharp features and gold-orange eyes, the color of a sunset. The wild thought crossed her mind that he was the most beautiful man she'd ever laid eyes on.

He smiled and spoke a single word. Kesi did not recognize it, but it would hardly have mattered if she did, for a moment later, her world was lit up in fire blasts of agony. She couldn't even scream, for she had no breath. The pain went on for eternity, it felt like, until it was all she knew and all she had ever known.

"Stop!" a familiar voice reached her ringing ears, and Kesi whimpered when the pain released her. "Please, stop! I'll do anything you ask!" It was her father, and Kesi wished fleetingly he wouldn't promise such things to the Val'gren, of all people. Like as not, they'd ask him to do the torturing for them.

A sinister laugh came then, and she squinted up at another Val'gren, this one even taller and more beautiful than the one who had tortured her. His eyes were scarlet. He gestured widely to her, curled up on the needle-strewn forest floor, struggling to sit up. "What would you do, fruit man, to save this pathetic little waif of a girl?"

"A—anything," her father stammered. "Anything at all. Name your price."

"I need information," the red-eyed man said coolly. "Will you get it for me?"

Her father must have hesitated, for Kesi choked on a scream when the younger one whipped her with the flat of his sword a moment later. The force of the blow knocked her backward and she found herself staring up at a cheery blue sky.

Odd, that.

"I will!" Father's voice cracked, but he spoke loudly. "I will tell you anything I know!"

There was laughter from the assembled Val'gren, and Kesi turned her head to see the leader smile. She hated him for smiling.

"The Eloni in Thaliondris have something I want," he said. "They are harboring the two remaining Princes of Laendor inside their city, likely in the Healing Wards. Find out their plans for departure and report back to me. Meanwhile, your wife and child will remain here, as my...guests." Kesi wanted to balk at that—she didn't at all like the way he said the word 'guest'—but Father was agreeing, reluctantly, and Mother was giving her a look that said she was good as dead if she made a fuss, so she stayed quiet.

Stayed quiet, and prayed to the Astra for the best..

13

The sun beat hot upon Jorlan's back as he stared hard at the thick thatch of trees before him. His elk leather vest soaked up the heat, trapping it against his skin despite the sweat dripping liberally down his spine.

It was a minor irritation, he allowed himself to admit. Jorlan sniffed the air.

There was so much heat; the bees and flies should have been out, buzzing lazily and pestering their mounts. There should have been birds and small creatures scurrying about. He should have been able to see more than only shadow inside that quiet forest just within Eloni borders.

But he could not. It was too dark, too quiet, and the air stank of decay.

They were near.

Jorlan allowed the rush of the hunt to bloom in his chest; his team had been tracking this group for two days, ever since they had attacked a young princess and her entourage arriving from Southdale for an official visit to Lord Áed's court.

He turned to Nenna and motioned for his team to dismount. They would proceed on foot from here.

Pallyn Bowsinger was the youngest of their group. Barely an adult, the scarlet-skinned archer was Jorlan's own nephew—though that had done him no favors earning a spot in the Commander's Six. He was the most talented bowman Thaliondris had seen in an age, lethal with his arancia longbow and phoenix-fletched arrows. Twins Rowen and Jalen Brightblade were only slightly older than his nephew. Identical in both appearance and temperament, they could not have been more different in fighting style. Yet their respective strengths and weaknesses were a perfect match, transforming the two of them into an incredible fighting unit worthy of a place among the Eloni warrior elite. Other than Nenna, there was only one other female on his team; Shaia Cloudsong, of an age to him and yet so much wiser. Music was her weapon, her voice keener than any blade, able to call forth the magic of the very earth around them. Where Pallyn, Nenna, and the twins were quick to act and full of aggression, Jorlan depended heavily on Shaia for wisdom and caution. She was his dearest friend and most loyal confidante.

All together, they numbered Six.

Young Pallyn sent the horses to graze safely half a league away, and they were ready.

They moved silently toward the dark shadowed trees, weapons at the ready. Just at the tree line, the stench of death peaked, and Jorlan looked down to see a large family of rabbits, half-decomposed already but not stripped. Two adults and a litter of ten babies, simply dead. Left to rot.

Nenna saw them too. Anger twisted her face into an ugly grimace, and she spat upon the ground. "Barbarians."

Jorlan nodded his agreement. It was a grievous crime to kill without purpose here.

He would see them answer for it. That, in addition to the quickly-growing docket of crimes Râza and his ilk were already amassing on Eloni lands.

His lip curled in disgust, he moved forward, into the forest.

They found the Val'gren party several hundred feet inside, awaiting them. Jorlan counted seven, and was pleased to see that four of them were already sporting Eloni arrows in varying parts of their anatomy. One lay quietly—dead, or very nearly—on the edge of the small clearing. The rest were clearly exhausted, worn down from two days of running from the Elven hunters.

He smiled.

The Val'gren closest to him, a youngster with no hair and eyes the color of burnt scarletweed, snarled a spell. A blast of livid green exploded from white fingertips toward his warriors, but Jorlan waved a hand and it dispersed before it even reached them.

"It is not my intent to kill you," he said to the Val'gren. "Come with me peaceably and no harm will befall you or your brethren."

Several of the Val'gren growled challenge in response, and more magic flew their way—purple lightning, black mist, green fire. Jorlan blocked them as well as he could, but some of the spells found their targets. He heard Nenna roar her rage behind him as Pallyn fell hard and did not rise. The Val'gren responsible for the lightning that had struck him *laughed*, and Jorlan felt his patience evaporate.

"Capture one," he growled to his remaining four. "Kill the rest."

Weakened and injured as they were, the Val'gren were still formidable foes, even for Jorlan's hunters. Arrows and blades were treated with poison created from the darkest of magics, lethal to humans and severely damaging to the wood elves. Spells flashed across the clearing, flashing every hue of the spectrum. Secure behind Jorlan and Nenna, Shaia began singing quietly, summoning the nature magic that was her specialty. Her song took mere moments to begin working before one of the Val'gren was crushed, screaming, by the living roots of the trees around them. A swarm of crows pecked and scratched at another until he ran howling, only to fall several hundred feet away, pierced through the heart by Nenna's white arrow. Two other Val'gren met the same fate, courtesy of his second-in-command, before they mounted a real counter attack.

Insidious brown mist formed around the Val'gren mage, the bald one with dark eyes who had attacked them at first, and a sweetly cloying scent filled the air. Jorlan felt his stomach clench; he knew this spell, had seen it work before.

"Nenna!" he cried.

"I smell it," she answered tightly. She let fly three arrows in quick succession as Jorlan turned and threw Pallyn over his own broad shoulder, calling for his hunters to fall back. Nenna's last arrow found its mark, right between the Val'gren's red eyes, but the mist did not disperse.

"A death spell!" Nenna yelped, backing away quickly.

"Leave him!" Jorlan barked at Rowen and Jalen, who were dragging along a struggling and injured Val'gren. "He'll slow us! Shaia, come on!"

"I can trap…it…" the songmage ground out, sweat beading her upper lip as she tried to compress the air around the mist into a hard globe that would keep it from reaching them. It was nearly working, but Jorlan knew it couldn't last. Even if she could manage to cast a spell that strong, she could not hold it forever. There was little to be done with inkmist once it was created, little except get out of its way. The poisoned vapor would destroy all it touched—plant, animal, Val'gren, and Eloni alike—until it faded away.

They needed to run. *Now.*

"Come!" he dragged Shaia to her feet when the mist was mere inches from her face, and fled.

~~~~~~~~~~

It was supposed to be healing magic she possessed, so it struck Ryn as odd that the moments when she managed to make it manifest, it did anything but.

She fought off a wave of irritation as she rubbed her stinging fingers on her pants. She, Kota, and Kenelm were holed up in a tiny garden near his home, and he'd had her working to access her magic since dawn. It was a new skill, and one she was not yet adept at executing on demand. She was sweating, her head was pounding, and just now when she'd managed to call the magic forth, it had burned her fingertips something fierce.

"It hurts," she said through clenched teeth, her shieldenstone cutting into her palm.

"It is still new," Kenelm responded serenely. "Try again."

Ryn swiped at the sweat on her forehead and took two deep breaths to calm herself. Then she closed her eyes and reached for the magic again. The mental path to See her magic—the bright light that veined every living thing, so far as she could tell—had become more familiar, easier to duplicate each time she did it. From there, learning to find her own nexus of magic and bring it into physical being was a bit harder.

Biting her lip, she concentrated. Scarlet currents interspersed with onyx sparks danced around her, teasing, playful. She reached for them, only to have them bounce away, almost mocking in their joyful dance. She growled, and the bright tendrils began to move faster, nearly vibrating with energy. Ryn swiped at them, reached for the core of her being, frustrated and skating the very edge of angry...

There!

She had it! It wasn't a scarlet thread she held, but a blinding white rough sphere, from the very center of herself. It was hot, uncomfortably so, and *heavy*. She felt herself tiring quickly and bore down, refusing to give up when she had it now—

Without warning, she was thrown from her own head and jarred back into the physical by the sensation of her back hitting the dirt. There was a crash, and Ryn opened her eyes to find herself staring at a blue, blue sky ringed by gently-waving leaves. She blinked, trying to clear the stars from her vision as she sat up with a groan.

Ow.

"Ryn!" Kenelm's voice was laced with concern—the wild thought raced through her head that finally, something had cracked that irritating tranquility of his. "Ryn, are you well, young one?"

She grunted, a negative or an affirmative she wasn't even sure, and pressed her forehead to her knees. "That did not feel very nice."

Kenelm rubbed her back while Kota nosed her insistently until she raised her head and let him sniff her all over to ensure her well-being.

"Looks like it was a bit of a rough one," Kenelm agreed.

Brow furrowed, Ryn looked at her teacher. "What do you mean?"

The old man gestured around him, and only then did Ryn notice that every plant within thirty feet of her was dry and brittle. Even the old oak was cracked and smoking gently. Ryn's stomach dropped and her eyes widened.

"Did I do that?"

Kenelm nodded. "I am afraid so. This should be fun to explain to the groundskeeper."

Ryn felt her face flame. "Oh gods, no. Can't I fix it?"

"You can do a lot of things, Ryn-girl, but bring things back from the dead is not one of them."

Ryn groaned and hid her head in her palms again. "He's never going to forgive me."

Kenelm laughed at that. "The Eloni have talents of their own, my dear. Just you wait, he'll have this garden back and thriving in less than a season, don't you worry."

Still, apologizing to the gardener was no laughing matter. The old jade-skinned Eloni practically gaped at what she'd done, tutting mournfully at his plants—especially the oak.

"Fifty years old, that one," he commiserated. Ryn wanted to disappear.

On the slow, aching walk back to Kenelm's home, Ryn finally couldn't hold it in any longer.

"Kenelm, I don't get it," she began, throwing her arms out to the side in exasperation. "I have healing magic, or so you've said. *Healing magic*. Why is it every time I call it up it destroys something?"

Kenelm stopped walking, studying her for a moment. His face became very serious, not at all the jovial expression she had grown accustomed to.

"No, child," he explained, leaning on his walking stick. "You possess the ability to heal, and that is how the magic works best because that is what it was created to do. But the power itself is the power to infuse—and siphon—the very life essence of that which surrounds you." At Ryn's blank stare, he elaborated. "The power you see when you enter your mind? The lights?" She nodded, and he continued. "It's not just metaphysical manifestations of something inside your head, Ryn. Those are *real* veins of *real* life force, and you can see and control those veins. This is your power, and how it functions. Will you use it to steal the life of surrounding plants in order to save a life? Or will you use it to sap the vitality from your enemy as they stand before you?" He thumped her in the chest with his stick, gently. "You can use it to heal, yes; but it can also kill, as it did in the nagrat camp."

Ryn paused, then began walking again, silent as she tried to absorb this latest lesson. "I can kill with my magic deliberately." The thought terrified her.

Kenelm nodded. "Some Y'rai did it on purpose; they were the warrior-clan of Lareth, and they were generally regarded as slightly more dangerous than anyone—even their own people—were comfortable with."

Ryn gave her teacher a wan smile and buried suddenly-cold fingers in Kota's thick fur. Her lynx growled low in his throat at her death grip on him, and she loosened her fingers with some effort.

"I don't blame them."

~~~~~~~~~~

Brandt loved markets, he always had. As a child, Mother and Father had taken him often, believing it important that they—and he—interact with the people who supported the nation's economy, who grew the food and forged the tools and weapons, who depended on the Royal Family for protection and safety. They seldom attended the market for necessities, but his parents always bought something, chatted with as many as there was time for, and usually Brandt ended up going home with a treat of some kind. While his parents talked, he'd been permitted to run amok with the other children, playing tag amongst the shops and trees.

Those trips, along with most others not directly related to training or schooling, had stopped abruptly after his mother's kidnapping and his father's disappearance, but his love for the atmosphere of a marketplace had never truly abated. There was something exciting about the air here, rich with scents familiar and exotic, echoing with shouts of laughter and murmurs of haggling and folks sharing the latest gossip. If he ever felt like a regular man living a regular life, it was when he visited a market.

And so, in disguise and with plenty of spare time over the past week, Brandt had staked out an unofficial spot for himself near the north end of Thaliondris' trade district, under the shade of the magnificent Lelaenis tree, and had taken to simply enjoying the bustle as he did easy busy work—weapons cleaning or sharpening, sometimes recording their journey in his small travel journal or penning letters to his mother and uncle.

This particular day, he'd glanced up to notice a bedraggled-looking caravan limp to a fruit vendor nearby, the jolly tradesman calling out a cheerful greeting to the travelers. They had responded, tiredly, and the tradesman's eyes had widened then narrowed at the sight of them. They were dirty, dirtier than they should have been from simply traveling a well-worn road, and their clothes were torn. The crates were battered, scuffed and splintered, some of them broken outright, their wares spilling out every which way as the travelers tried to move them from the mangled wagon to the vendor's stall. Brandt stood and walked over quickly to help. The old woman who was bent over to pick up the errant red fist-sized fruits looked up at him, white hair falling in her face but doing nothing to conceal the livid black bruise blooming on her cheekbone. She straightened stiffly as he went to his knees and began gathering the fruits, a gnarled hand on her lower back, and gave him a wizened grin. Brandt marveled; he'd had a shiner like that before, he knew smiling hurt.

"Argh," she croaked good-naturedly. "Gettin' a bit ol' fer all this, lad." Brandt stayed kneeling, arms full of sweet-smelling pomes, staring up at her in something approaching awe. She noticed him gawking and winked, chuckling.

"Never seen an old hag before, boy?"

Brandt remembered his manners then, rising carefully and, unable to bow with his arms full, nodded once in respect. "My apologies, my lady, it is not your age that has bewildered me." He let his expression show his concern. "Are you well? Was your caravan struck by bandits?"

To his surprise, the lady laughed at that—not a bitter laugh, as he would have expected, but a genuinely amused one that crinkled her eyes nearly shut. She looked at his expression and it made her laugh again. "This? Oh laddie, it takes more than a bruise or—" she shifted uncomfortably, "—seven to knock me down. A few days and I'll be in perfect condition."

"What happened?" he asked again. This time, the old woman was deadly serious when she answered.

"Val'gren," she said, and he tried to ignore the way his skin crawled at the admission. "They attacked our caravan mere hours ago, two leagues outside of the city. Just a different sort of bandit, these days, it seems." She nodded, shoved a crooked finger at him. "Back when I was your age, they were a real threat, not glorified criminals. Ha!"

So close to the city? Brandt clenched his jaw, a sick feeling settling in his gut. "But they let you go free?" That was unusual, for Val'gren. They were always on the lookout for sacrifices to their god Skeðu.

The woman nodded, her expression mirroring the direction of his thoughts. "I'm not complaining, mind you, but I'm as confused as anyone. I thought sure we were done for. As it is, they knocked us around a bit and sent us on our way thoroughly lashed."

"With a message," a new voice said. The man who spoke was clearly in charge, for he carried himself with the air of one used to being obeyed. He glanced down at the pomes Brandt still held, and his face softened minutely.

"Aye," the old lady was saying. "But we'd be better served not passing such vile rubbish around. We may as well have given ourselves up as prisoners if we do exactly as they tell us!"

"The leadership of this city deserves to know—"

"Ach, laddie, they know already—"

"What message?" Brandt asked, a bit louder than was perhaps strictly necessary. Both the old lady and the stern man looked at him.

"It would seem the young Princes of Laendor are in residence in the city," the man started. The lady glared and tried to interrupt, but he spoke over her protests. "Râza, the leader of the Val'gren, requests that they be handed over to him."

Brandt's chest tightened and he focused hard on schooling his features into something vaguely interested instead of blatantly horrified. "Aren't the princes in Sannfold?"

"Aye, we all thought so, but evidently the Val'gren Hunt Chief has different information. And he won't stop attacking folks until he gets what he came for."

"Rubbish!" the old lady objected, rapping her knuckles hard against the man's head. "Think, boy, with the brain Aeos gave ye! He says he wants the princes, and I don' doubt it for a second, but if you think having 'em will stop him hurting everyone he can get his hands on, you're out of yer head." The man scowled at her, but said nothing, and it struck Brandt that perhaps she was his mother.

"Of course it won't stop him," the man agreed reluctantly. "But if he asked me to choose between me and mine and some bloody princes in some far off city, I know which hides I'd choose to save."

Brandt's blood ran cold at the confession, though he couldn't see any way to blame the man—in his position, he'd likely feel the same way. But the oldster was tutting, shaking her head.

"Don't know where I went wrong with you, boy, but I clearly fell short somewhere, if that's how you're thinkin' of our King and his family."

The man sighed. "Ma—"

"Don't 'ma', me," she snarled, motioning to the pile of red fruits on the display stand. "Git. I'll set these up, savin' your presence."

Summarily dismissed, the man left; the woman set to work, organizing the pomes on the table, turning them over and inspecting them as she went, muttering all the while. Brandt waited a moment, then reached for one and looked it over, watching for bruises or broken skin, placing the fruit gently down when he found none. He repeated this, and they worked in silence for several minutes.

"You disagree with him?" Brandt asked, quietly. The woman placed a withered hand on his forearm, and he turned to look at her, watery blue eyes meeting dark brown.

"My great-great grandpapa fought next to Brandt, Son of Veris, two hundred years ago," she said. "You know who he was, boy?"

Brandt nodded. "He was the first King of the Clan Vaeärne, Brandt the Compassionate, named for his generosity despite being a warrior all his days. I am named after him."

The old lady nodded. "Good. Then you know who he overthrew."

"Ferus Blackblade," Brandt answered. "He was known amongst his subjects to have a heart as dark as his famed sword. They say he kidnapped and bedded younglings, among other crimes."

"Exactly. The Clan Vaeärne lifted Laendor out of that era of horror and fear and brought us to one of prosperity and peace, even if it is tenuous at times." She shook her head. "Too many forget that. Some folks' loyalty is like the mist, visible when things are cool and peaceful, but dissipating under the heat of the day." She stood a little straighter, lifting her chin. "Still, some of us stand true."

The rush of gratitude Brandt felt set his knees weak, but he did his best not to show it. Instead, he nodded. "Aye, good lady. Some always stand true."

14

Ryn's progress was quick after that day in the garden. Within days she was able to call her power and hold it in her physical hands whenever she liked. Kenelm was beside himself with pride; he said her progress was excellent, especially for one who had no experience with the arcane.

Now she had a different problem, however.

"Steady, girl, settle." Kenelm's voice was low but urgent. "Don't force it. This is natural; let it come on its own, you need only manage the flow of it."

Ryn, who felt dizzy and hot and distinctly like she was about to lose what little she'd eaten for breakfast that morning, bit back a retort about just how natural this all was and tried to relax a bit. The magic, now that she'd learned to hold onto it, was like a raging river that had been dammed up far too long. It swamped her when she allowed it, and fought her when she didn't, resulting in a host of physical symptoms that ranged from merely uncomfortable to downright irksome. She hadn't had a good night's sleep in a week, and had been battling debilitating headaches at least that long. Worn down by exhaustion and pain, she was actually regressing in her training. She couldn't let the magic simply run ram shod, but the more she bore down, the more slipped through her grasp. It was disheartening work. Kenelm swore it would pass, that she would break through this hurdle, and she believed him—acquiring any skill worth having proceeded in much the same way—but she feared something catastrophic happening if she were to lose focus.

So the headaches got worse, she ate less and less, and her sleep continued to suffer. Now her hold on the magic was slipping during training, and it was only a matter of time before Kenelm called her on it. Redoubling her efforts, she furrowed her brow as she tried to stem the flow of power pulsing through her veins.

Ryn thought of the nagrat camp as she fought to stem the tide of her power. She could not afford to lose control like that again, not here, not so close to her teacher and Kota. The power did not seem to pay any mind, though. It sang through her veins, pounded in her ears, crawled through her bones. *Come on*, she thought, growing more frustrated by the minute. *I can do this.*

"Hold," Kenelm commanded, and she relaxed, letting go her grasp of the magic so it could trickle back inside her bones, where it would roil and fester, as it had since she first discovered it. But it took half a second to realize something was wrong. Goose flesh raced over Ryn's skin, hairs on her body standing straight up as though lightning was nearby, a roaring filling her ears.

The power wasn't retreating.

"Kenelm—" was all the warning she was able to give before the roaring reached a fever pitch and something hot broke through her skin entirely, a blinding blast that seared everything in a circle around her— again—and threw her to the ground. Her ears rang and all she could hear was her own ragged breathing as she forced the power back behind the dam and shored it up tightly as she could. She opened her eyes moments later to find herself sprawled half-sitting on blackened grass.

"Ow," she moaned as she moved slowly to get up. There was no response forthcoming from either of her companions, which prompted her to look up. Her heart stopped.

Kenelm slumped against a nearby stone wall, his face slack and eyes closed. Kota hadn't fared any better, lying too still beneath a large tree twenty feet away. The spot in which she had been standing looked like lightning had struck there; a blackened crater with cracks that spidered out from its epicenter, almost ten feet across. Every living plant in sight was dry and brittle, like it had been dead for months. Ryn sucked in a shaky breath as she forced herself to her feet, ignoring the screaming protestations of every nerve and muscle in her body, stumbling to Kota's side and struggling not to panic.

"*Kisa*," she murmured, not daring to touch him but wanting—*needing*— to be sure he was all right. He was breathing normally, the rise and fall of his flank told her that, and seemed to be coming around, twitching and whining as he woke. "Kota!" Ryn almost sobbed. "Come on, *kisa*, come back to me!" He did, with several low moans and a sudden snarl and swipe of his giant paw. Immediately, her lynx rolled over and stood, casting about, disoriented. He growled dangerously for a moment until his yellow eyes focused on her. He panted, then stepped closer, his trill a question she could not answer. Ryn drew back as though stung, but hurried to Kenelm's side now that she knew Kota would be all right. He, too, was coming around slowly, in obvious pain but not dying as far as she could tell. She called his name, shaking him firmly. He blinked blearily at her, pupils uneven, and gave her an intoxicated grin.

"You never mentioned you had such an explosive temper," he quipped.

"You're hilarious," she said, fingers searching gently for any damage to his skull. She studied him for a moment, then pushed him back against the wall when he tried to stand.

"Sit," she ordered. "I'm going to get the healers. You took a nasty rap to the head, I think."

"Wait, wait." Kenelm grabbed her hand and motioned for her to come closer. His dark eyes fixed on hers. "You're a healer. *You* heal me."

Ryn recoiled. "You're addled. I just nearly killed you simply attempting to hold my magic—"

"You broke it, you fix it," her teacher countered, grinning in a vague sort of way. "I'll talk you through it."

"You are out of your mind," Ryn muttered in answer, but knelt beside him anyway.

"Take your stone," Kenelm instructed, his eyes unfocused and bright. Ryn held it in a sweaty palm. Kenelm gestured vaguely. "Over the wound." She placed her shaking hand gently on his forehead, the rough stone between her skin and his, willing her stomach to quit roiling. "Good girl. Take energy from the plants."

"I killed them all," she croaked, voice cracking. Kenelm coughed a laugh.

"No, you didn't, not this time. They are only a bit charred. Try."

Ryn did as he said. She dug for her power, barely twitching this time when the clearing lit up with a myriad of glowing colors. Kenelm was right, she realized; she hadn't sucked the life out of anything. The mighty oak had barely noticed the fiery blast, and though the grass was blackened, its root system was unharmed.

Carefully, *carefully*, she drew out life force from the grass' communal center, from the oak's giant roots, and from the various small animals that lived beneath the ground. Minuscule amounts she drew, forcing her magic to comply; *only enough, no more*. It pooled around her free hand and arm, warm but not hot, bluish-bright. "I have it," she said through gritted teeth, blinking sweat from her eyes. She had no idea if she had enough, but it...felt right.

"Send it through the stone into my head," Kenelm's voice was weaker now, and Ryn wondered how long the process of drawing the life force from the garden had taken. She could tell her teacher was struggling to remain conscious. "Will it to...heal the damage...inside."

Taking a deep breath, Ryn closed her eyes and focused on Kenelm's aura. His purple-and-silver was fractured around the edges—a sure sign his body was in distress—and tangled, knotted around his head. A tiny dark spot rested in the center of the blinding mess, and that's where Ryn sent her magic. It flowed, scarlet mist working its way through Kenelm's skull to the injury, and there it swirled for several minutes, until the dark spot dissipated and the rough glass edges of his aura had smoothed out. Operating on instinct, Ryn released the rest of the energy as she opened her eyes. It danced back to its sources, disappearing into the earth and nearby trees.

She sighed, feeling better than she had in days. The magic flowed through her still, she could feel it, but it was...comfortable. It ebbed through her like blood through veins, pulsing gently in time with her heart; but it lacked the wild, fretful force of before. Her head didn't ache, her stomach had calmed, and when she looked to Kenelm and saw his brown eyes clear and smiling, she couldn't help but smile back.

"Well, that went better than I expected," Kenelm said, sitting up. "No pain at all, no lingering effects." He stretched experimentally, then probed his forehead with weathered fingers. "Well done, Healer Ryn."

Ryn flushed at the praise. Kota butted her affectionately with his head, and she rubbed his ears. "Magic can be unstable in the hands of younglings." Kenelm said. "There is no shame in an honest mistake made while learning, Y'ra." Ryn nodded, but the movement drew her attention to the Skyshifter's temple. She reached out and ran a finger over it before she could stop herself.

"There's a scar," she remarked, awed and a little confused.

"Aye," Kenelm answered. "Your magic speeds the process, but the body still does most of the healing itself. Scars will remain."

"Oh."

"Tomorrow you will rest again," Kenelm continued. "Soon we will work on healing something more substantial than a knock on the head."

Ryn nodded and let him speak, prattling on about his plans for her training, wishing she'd be here to see it through. But something in her bones told her it would not be. They would be leaving Thaliondris.

And soon.

~~~~~~~~~~~

Brandt looked over to Ryn, just out of earshot and leaning against the stone frame of one of the open arches the Eloni were fond of here. The garden outside was walled, to afford the guests privacy, but the arrangement was still far more open and vulnerable than he liked. Ryn was apparently of the same mind; she stood stiffly, alert. Kota lay in the corner, watching his mistress.

Both Brandt and Evin had, perhaps subconsciously, taken to spending a good deal of time inside and away from prying eyes. The Eloni had made no real attempt to locate the Princes that Râza was calling for, not that he could tell; but he and Evin had not hidden their brotherhood since arriving, and Brandt was sure someone would eventually make the connection.

Ryn, he suspected, was probably already wondering about it, but he hoped—foolishly—that she would write off their strange behavior as lingering exhaustion from their long journey here.

123

"What did the blacksmith say?" the woman asked, pushing off the stone arch and moving fully into the room.

Brandt made a face. "That we shouldn't even consider leaving until the roads are safe again."

Ryn snorted. Evin looked up.

Brandt went on. "I told him our mission would not wait for some upstart barbarian to lose interest in his prey." Evin laughed, and Brandt smiled. "He seemed confused enough not to berate me after that."

"How will we get out?" Ryn asked from beside the fireplace. She wasn't nearly as amused as Evin, but then that was fairly normal. Fear tickled in Brandt's spine; it was not the first time he'd considered that same...potential difficulty.

"They can't hold us here," Evin spoke up, serious now. "We are not Eloni citizens."

Ryn shook her head. "I mean Râza. He will surely recognize you both, will he not?"

Brandt looked to his brother, who appeared to be searching for an answer that would not confirm them to be the sought-after princes. He was as clueless as Evin evidently was.

Ryn sighed after the silence drew out to an uncomfortable length. "Let's all stop holding daggers up our sleeves," she said, pushing her fingers through her short dark hair and fixing troubled eyes on Brandt. "I know who you both are, Your Grace."

There was silence for a beat; Evin's mouth was opening and closing around the start of several different questions, but Brandt just wanted to know, "When did you realize?"

Ryn shrugged. "Neither of you gave it away, but I didn't get this far on my own by not paying attention." She smiled then, a little, though worry was sketched plainly on all her features. "The quality of your gear and your manner pointed to your nobility. Frequent and familiar references to the Royal Family made me realize you two were, if nothing else, close to the King. The way you've been hiding in this room since Râza's attacks started was the final puzzle piece."

Brandt sighed. "I suppose it was inevitable, though we rather hoped you wouldn't discover the truth."

Ryn raised an eyebrow. "Why is that, exactly?" she asked. "Surely your journey would be easier if you told everyone you were the Crown Prince?"

Evin huffed indignantly. "Really?"

Half of Ryn's mouth quirked up in a quick smile. "Well, present situation excepted, of course. I mean you could be staying at the best inns, eating the best food and enjoying the best entertainment, have an entourage and all the protection you need all the way to Retwood and beyond; and yet you choose to travel in disguise." She locked gazes with Brandt. "Why all the secrecy?"

Brandt considered before answering. He could tell her the entire truth, he doubted she would betray his trust, but having the Val'gren involved had changed things. He wasn't even sure of the entire truth himself, now. Perhaps a short, simple answer was best, at least for the time being. "Each Crown Prince is assigned a *jofurr aetla*, a quest that he must complete before he is deemed worthy to lead the kingdom." He looked to his brother. "Traditionally the mission is a secret to all but the King, the Prince, and one companion. The Prince must fulfil the quest on his own merits, not relying on his position or his fame to help him along. I was to be Gunnar's companion, but when he died, the quest itself became mine."

"And I wasn't about to be left behind," Evin interjected, quirking a grin.

Brandt's lips twitched. "Indeed." He turned back to Ryn. "We are to recover a family heirloom that was stolen many years ago by a creature that lives near Retwood."

Ryn studied him for a moment, then nodded. "Well then. You need not worry; your secret is safe with me and Kota."

"Neither of us would think poorly of you if..." Evin petered off, but then gathered himself. "Given your recently-discovered...abilities...and training with Kenelm, along with who we are, and the fact that none of us signed on to be hunted by the Warmaster of the Val'gren...you could not be blamed for leaving us to our own way." He looked to Brandt, as though a little unsure of this last. "We would even still pay you. One day in the Royal Archives, as agreed." Brandt nodded his own accord; it was only right.

Ryn's eyebrows furrowed and her face twisted into something resembling offense. "If you think I would leave you now, you have sorely misjudged my character, Evin." She used his name, not his title, and Brandt realized it was deliberate; she did not intend for things to change, regardless of their identity. He found himself relieved, and somewhat surprised by it.

Evin opened his mouth to reply when there was a knock at the door. Closest to it, Brandt turned and pulled the handle. Before him stood the youngster they'd seen running errands from time to time; he had been the one to deliver Ryn to them when she was released by the Menders nearly two weeks prior. Faelar, Brandt remembered. He favored the lad with a smile and a nod.

"Master Faelar, how may we assist?" The boy blushed to the roots of his white hair and bowed.

"My Lord, the Master of our city, Lord Áed, has requested your presence, and that of your brother and guide, in his council chamber at your earliest convenience. I'm, er—" he fidgeted, and Brandt gave him an encouraging smile. "I'm to accompany you there."

Brandt wanted to sigh, though he kept his features carefully neutral. *So it is to be this*, he thought. *They have discovered us*. He nodded to young Faelar. "We will come momentarily; only give me a moment to speak to my brother." Faelar hesitated, but agreed.

But the Crown Prince of Laendor turned first to his friend, the Guide he had hired, the Woman with the Lynx. Her eyes were hard, her face impassive. "This is your last chance," he said. "Remain here, with the Eloni. Tell anyone who asks that you knew not who we are. Disavow us, and you may escape our fate." He glanced to Evin, who was watching Ryn raptly, clearly torn between wanting her to accompany them and wanting her to stay here, be safe. Ryn spoke a soft word, and Kota rose to stand beside her. She tangled her fingers in his red spotted fur and planted her feet.

"Your fate will be ours," she said. Kota trilled, as though agreeing with her. Brandt nodded once, a gesture of respect as much as approval. He turned to Evin.

"Then let us go to meet it."

The trek to the city's center took far less time than Brandt would have liked, and in short order, they were brought before the Lord Áed in his receiving chambers. The Master of Thaliondris was every bit as stately as his title would suggest; he was tall and slender, almost willowy, after the fashion of his people; the swirling gold tattoos that bespoke his station covered so much of his skin that only hints of his milk-white complexion were visible. His flaxen hair and beard were near long enough to tuck into his sash, and he wore robes of scarlet-and-gold silk. There rested upon his brow a circlet of bone, cunningly wrought, carved and inlaid with gold runes. The Ossein Crown, legend called it, and it was said to have been crafted by Lord Áed's own father—for the Eloni were exceedingly long-lived—from the skull and teeth of the last dragon Ecalder a half-century past.

Lord Áed greeted them amiably enough, bowing his head briefly and twisting his hand over his heart after the way of his people. "Young Masters," he nodded to Brandt and Evin. "My Lady of the Y'ra, Friend Lynx," the Elon favored Ryn and Kota with a wide smile. "You are all welcome to me. Thank you for answering my summons so swiftly."

Brandt reminded himself not to be drawn in by the wood elf's good manners. Lord Áed of Thaliondris was an ally, true, but he was also an Elon, an elf of the Red Wood and fae of the Sapphire Lake, a creature older than Brandt's great-great-grandfather, wild and unpredictable as the mountain snows. This was no meeting over ale with his training fellows; rather a dangerous negotiation for the life of his brother and friends, however innocuous the trappings of it. He bowed deeply, the greeting of a Prince to a fellow Sovereign. "It is a pleasure, my Lord. You look well."

The Elon laughed at that, pointed teeth flashing white. "I look much the same as I have your entire life, young one. Come, let us dispense with

126

the pleasantries and move straight to the point of this meeting." With a word, he sent away the few servants who scurried about the room, though Jorlan remained at his post, right behind Lord Áed's right shoulder. The Master gestured an invitation; near the great fireplace on the East wall was a collection of the Eloni's strange wooden chairs, these covered in thick moss, around a small oaken table that also looked to be grown straight from the ground. "Please sit," Lord Áed was saying. "And be at ease, we shall not be overheard here."

Brandt sat, between the fierce wood elf and his brother. Ryn chose the seat nearest the edge of the semi-circle, and Kota stationed himself nearby, alert and straight-backed. He offered no threat, no growl or snarl, but his amber eyes never did leave the Master of the City. Jorlan took up a watchful stance behind Lord Áed's chair.

Once they were all situated, Lord Áed steepled his fingers and looked to each of them in turn. His bright green eyes fixed on Brandt's last. "You seem to have brought ill luck with you, Prince Brandt. It is long since Râza has been seen this close to my city."

Next to him, Brandt heard Evin mutter, "Does everyone know who we are?" Brandt ignored him, though Lord Áed laughed.

"Not everyone, Sir Prince; only a select few, among them myself."

"But...how?" Evin asked aloud, trying and failing to mask his frustration at their apparent inability to travel in disguise. Lord Áed's lips twitched and he sat back comfortably.

"I know a great many things I am not told, Evin." Lord Áed smiled again, somehow managing to make the expression genuine and non-threatening despite the pointed teeth and crown of bone.

"Like how to get us out of here without alerting every Val'gren within twenty leagues?" Ryn asked, only half-challenging. Brandt winced; this would be difficult enough without her offending their host before Brandt even had a chance to plead his case for their release.

But Lord Áed laughed again. "Indeed, my Lady, I know that too."

Ryn just looked at him. After a moment, the Eloni king nodded once and elaborated. "There is a spy in my city. A man, merchant by trade, who has been...*convinced*...to work for Râza and his ilk." Brandt felt his eyebrows climb toward his hairline. Râza had been recruiting?

"You mean extorted," Ryn cut in. Lord Áed's lips quirked in a smile.

"As you say. The Dark One does have his family in captivity and uses them to motivate the spy."

Brandt winced visibly, looking to Evin almost subconsciously. His brother's hazel eyes were very wide, and his face was slightly paler than normal. He looked vaguely horrified.

"Regardless of the spy's intentions," Lord Áed continued. "The fact remains that he is working for the Val'gren now, searching about and asking questions to try to find you two,—" he gestured to Brandt and Evin, "—and in the process, alarming both my citizens and honorable guests." The Eloni's eyes narrowed and his lips thinned. "This must end. And I have a plan to end it."

"What plan?" Evin asked, eyes still the size of tea saucers. Lord Áed sat back again, nearly reclining, and folded his hands together. The smile on his face was predatory.

"Râza wishes to have you, he shall have you."

15

The woods south of the Sapphire Lake were deathly silent and black as ebony. The moon was shadowed, and even the stars seemed dim, what he could see of them through the thick forest canopy. He ran, uncertain where he would find what—*who*—he was looking for, but knowing they were near at hand, likely watching him even now. The thought froze his heart in his chest, the breath in his lungs, and made his knees feel weak with fear. He hated himself for it, but there it was: he was terrified.

His stomach lodged itself in his throat as he stumbled, a tangled tree root holding tight to his foot, and fell. Branches whipped his face as he fell and his hands struck first, skidding painfully along the undergrowth. He found himself sprawled in the dirt and dead leaves.

Tanar sat up and ran a shaking hand down his face. It was wet; whether from blood or tears, he couldn't tell. His face and hands were both throbbing, and the foot that had gotten tangled in the root was screaming in agony. Still the forest remained stubbornly silent, aside from his own trembling breath, and still the stars remained faraway and dim. It was dark and cold and he was completely alone.

"Where are you?!" Tanar shouted, only half-expecting an answer. The silence seemed to swallow up his desperate call, like a living, insidious thing, and it became impossibly darker.

"I am here." The response was far closer to his right ear than he expected.

Tanar flinched away, scrambled back on sore hands and rump. He still could not see anything. His chest ached with the cold and his own fear.

The voice—Râza—chuckled darkly. "You are looking quite...out of sorts, my friend."

The designation made rage bloom hot in Tanar's chest. "I am no friend of yours," he growled. In an effort to restore his dignity in front of this, his enemy, he stood as smoothly as he could. It was not as smoothly as he'd have liked; his ribs screamed and his ankle collapsed, forcing him to do a sort of hop to stay upright. He straightened, the effort leaving him dizzy. "I have the information you...requested." He was careful to keep most of his disgust out of the word.

Râza stepped out from the heart of the shadow, gracefully and in no apparent hurry. He raised a single thin eyebrow, and the merchant was certain he had never seen such a simple expression look so threatening. The Val'gren Chief lifted his chin slightly. "Tell me."

Tanar took a deep, steadying breath.

Aeos, have mercy upon me.

"The Princes are in the city. I have seen them." He swallowed the fat lump in his throat that was making it hard to breathe. "I overheard the guards talking. The Eloni won't give them up." Râza didn't look surprised; indeed he barely reacted at all, which made Tanar even more nervous. He shifted his weight slightly, wincing at his still-screaming ankle. "They— they're going to try to spirit them out of the city, at midnight. With an armed guard of their very best."

~~~~~~~~~~~

Midnight came dark and cool that night; the summer was well and truly underway and the weather was mild even in the mid-northern mountains. The locusts had ceased their song hours prior, and the city was settled in for the night, so it was quiet when the princes met Jorlan and Nenna at the city's southern gates. Ryn and Kota arrived a few moments after them, emerging from the late night shadows like wraiths. Ryn was dressed to travel; a brand new cloak over leather and linen, quiver full of new arrows to match the new bow strung across her back opposite her echowood staff. The staff itself boasted a new feature, as well; the palm-sized gray stone he'd noticed her fiddling with lately wedged tightly inside the twisted dark wood at the head. He wondered about it, but figured it was neither the time nor place to ask.

Later, he resolved.

The commander acknowledged them with a nod then gestured for them to follow. He began to lead them along the wall, calling a quiet greeting to a watch guard as they passed. No one else spoke as they walked, not until they entered a nondescript, stone...well, *building* was a bit of an overstatement, Evin thought. 'Twas more like a hutch, he supposed, located between a cheery inn's personal garden and the ancient granite parapet, a small structure with one locked stone door. Jorlan pulled an iron key from his pocket and unlocked it, and Nenna helped him swing it open.

The inside was dark and still, but the wood elves lit two torches in stands beside the door and the light provided Evin with a look at the inside of the structure. There was a single room, no doors, no windows. Only a set of winding stairs set into the floor—old stone, but clean and sturdy. The elves didn't hesitate, leading their charges down and locking the doors behind them.

~~~~~~~~~~

Tanar bit back a yelp of pain as the chimaera beneath him lurched, jarring his aching head, his sprained ankle, and everything in between. He pulled at the rough ropes that bound him to the animal, wishing desperately they hadn't dragged him along for the massacre he was surely about to witness. Râza swore his family was nearby, but refused to tell him more until his information was verified and the Princes were dead.

As a citizen of Laendor, Tanar was fully aware of the consequences of his betrayal. He knew the kingdom's darling Crown Prince Gunnar was dead, knew King Eirik's nephew Brandt had been crowned soon after, and knew he and his younger brother were the last of their generation within the royal bloodline. The Queen was long-since dead, and neither the King nor his sister had exhibited any interest in remarrying; Tanar was acutely aware that he was not only robbing the Kingdom of its only Heirs, but also a widowed mother of her only sons.

Nevertheless, what choice had he?

Images of his lovely wife and his sweet daughter filled his mind; Brenna and Kesi, his heart and soul. He allowed himself memories of happy times, quiet nights in their village home, songs beside traveling fires, sightseeing in their many exotic destinations on journeys to sell his wares...it was a good life.

He'd had to choose between King and family, and Aeos help him, he chose his family. He would do it again, he decided, though he wondered how he'd feel in just a short while, looking down upon the bodies of the young princes.

The Val'gren mounted in front of him on the chimaera stayed the creature with a single gesture against its flank. It stopped with a huff, and Tanar tried to lean over to see what was happening. Râza had evidently called the halt, and was silently directing his dozen or so companions to strategic positions along both sides of the road just outside Thaliondris' Southern Gate. All was quiet, for now, and the dark was a thick velveteen blanket over their party.

Tanar squirmed, wincing at the pain and his own anxiety. He could barely even feel his ankle anymore, so cold and afraid was he.

"Still," the orange-eyed Val'gren against his front hissed. He wondered if this was the same monster who had so gleefully tortured his daughter with that strange pain-spell a few days ago. He swallowed his rage with some difficulty.

It's almost over, he told himself for the thirtieth time in as many minutes. *Almost done.*

The sound of thundering hooves came to them first, and then Tanar could see a small party of heavily-armed people riding toward them upon the road. There were five of them, accompanied by a large black shadow that loped along beside the white mare near the back. He squinted, trying to see what it was, and his heart leapt into his throat when he realized it was a lynx...a large wild cat beside a woman dressed in black.

Leyna, his mind supplied helpfully, and suddenly he was reconsidering everything. He hadn't realized the Guardian of Travelers was with the Princes, and while it was one thing to turn over a monarch you'd never met and who cared nothing for you, it was quite another to betray the folk hero your daughter—and every other young lass in the country—idolized. Especially when she'd saved *your* life not so long ago.

Brenna. Kesi.

Tanar bit back the warning that rose in his throat.

~~~~~~~~~~

The stairs wound down for what seemed like ages, narrow and spiraling, the light from Jorlan's torch casting shadows that danced along the ancient stone walls. Eventually they emerged into another small room, roughly circular like the one far above it, but far more wild. Here, moss grew along the cracked stones, and the floor was uneven and damp around a small pool about ten feet across. Evin raised a single eyebrow, nearly bursting with curiosity as to what the plan of escape was. He'd expected to be led to one of the city gates and spirited away, but this...was not something he had seen coming. He wasn't sure what they were doing.

"We have a spell that will suspend normal breathing long enough for us to get outside the city," Jorlan started to explain, and Evin understood all at once what they were doing here in this cold little room.

Their way out was *underwater*.

"Will the cat understand and follow?" Nenna asked shortly, fixing those odd lilac eyes on Ryn. Their guide nodded once.

"He will."

Nenna turned back to Jorlan, who grinned. "Very well then," he gestured to the pool. "I shall lead, Nenna will take up the rear."

Evin moved quietly behind Kota, instinctively placing Ryn and the lynx between him and Brandt, with the elves at fore and aft. When they'd arranged themselves, Jorlan nodded to Nenna, who moved to Evin first. She placed her two fingers at his temple and murmured a single phrase in their strange, flowery language. Evin jerked slightly as a sensation cool and smooth, like water, seemed to settle just under his skin, spreading over his body and then disappearing. He blinked, noticing Ryn shudder as she received the same treatment. After the initial shock of it, he rolled his shoulders, noting with some trepidation that he felt no different.

Kota and Brandt were much calmer in their reception of the spell, though Kota sneezed, and when Nenna finished casting it on herself and

Jorlan, she moved to the back of their makeshift line. The commander saluted then, and dived into the small pool; he disappeared beneath the surface and did not rise.

Brandt turned to look at him, and Evin flashed him a wholly insincere smile that communicated his thoughts without words.

Looks fun.

Brandt cocked an eyebrow—*you're a liar, little brother*—and splashed in after the lieutenant. He too, went under and stayed down.

Evin figured this was a bad time to mention how much he hated being submerged in water. As Kota's head slipped beneath the surface, right on Ryn's heels, he felt his stomach tighten and his palms begin to sweat. Shaking his head to clear it, Evin forced himself to step to the very edge of the water. He looked down.

It was mostly dark in the stone room—the only light came from the torches, which Jorlan and Nenna had placed in small brass braces near the door when they entered—but the water seemed to glow with a dim radiance coming from somewhere deeper. Perhaps there was a light below, or perhaps it was an effect of the spell, making it possible to see underwater, Evin wasn't sure.

Either way, he needed to move. Nenna was staring. He took two more steps before the hard stone suddenly disappeared and the water closed over his head.

~~~~~~~~~~

Tanar couldn't prevent the tear that slipped down his cheek as the first black arrow sailed through the air with a quiet hiss. It struck one of the princes—a golden-headed figure in the midst of the group who carried a pair of war axes slung over his back—and he fell without a sound. The rest of the group paused for a split second, then a howl of rage echoed across the wood at the same time the lead Elon shouted an order, and the entire group, save the dead prince's white stallion, tore off down the dirt road.

Right toward their ambush.

This time the merchant couldn't stop the cry of dismay that clawed its way free of his throat. Intent upon his prey, the Val'gren before him didn't even shush him, directing his mount into a collision course with the mare Tanar was certain carried the Guardian. The lynx kept pace with the mare, though it likely could have easily outstripped it, and as they drew closer, Tanar could see the white of its teeth bared in a snarl.

The chimaera pounced at the same time the Val'gren let loose a fearsome war cry, and Tanar squeezed his eyes shut entirely, unable to watch.

Chimaera met big cat with a crash of bone and teeth. It jarred him so badly he was thrown forward, smacking his forehead on his captor's hard leather armor. His bound hands afforded him no balance, but kept him astride the creature, and his entire leg seized in agony. Tanar screeched, equal parts pain and anguish, at the sound of steel meeting steel, but he refused to open his eyes. He heard a lynx's snarl, then a yelp, and then they were running full-out, the Val'gren hunter hissing rage-filled spells. Tanar dared a look.

They were chasing the group, the famed Eloni mounts showing the speed for which they were so renowned. The lynx was not beside the Guardian; dead or injured, he presumed, but left behind either way. The woman was turned in her saddle, firing arrows steadily that bounced harmlessly to either side. Tanar found himself urging her on silently, hoping beyond hope one of those long arrows would strike the orange-eyed monstrosity mounted in front of him.

The horses pulled further ahead, and Tanar could see there were three left now—a dark-haired man with a bow, an Eloni with a bear-paw standing out white against her face, and the Guardian—but Râza called an order, and the chimaeras somehow gathered yet more speed, slowly closing the distance between Val'gren and their targets.

As they ran, Tanar prayed like he'd never prayed before.

~~~~~~~~~~~

The water was neither dark nor cold, which helped keep Evin's fear at a much more manageable level. *I can do this*, he decided, and dived to meet the figures he could see moving below him. As he drew closer, he could make out the forms of Jorlan, Ryn, Kota, and his brother; the latter gave him a thumb up to confirm his welfare. Evin nodded to Brandt, startling when Nenna appeared behind him; he hadn't heard her enter the pool. She gestured to Jorlan, who turned and began to swim. Everyone followed.

They moved through the water at a good clip—the elves were obviously more acclimated to such exercise, because they showed no signs of slowing even when his muscles were screaming in protest—but the journey took long enough for Evin to get a look around. All around, spindly plants swayed to and fro in the currents, black against the dim glow of the water. It didn't take long for Evin to realize the light wasn't coming from the water itself, but from the figures inside it; that is to say, they themselves were glowing, from the spell Nenna had cast. It was a brilliant use of magic, Evin thought; it kept the swimmer warm, calm, and able to see, while allowing the caster to only bewitch one person, rather than the entire body of water.

It wasn't much longer before Jorlan turned them upward, and their heads broke the surface with a splash. Evin sucked air into his lungs, the spell broken as soon as his face met cool night air. He shook the water from his eyes and moved toward the edge of the pool, examining his surroundings as he did so.

They'd emerged from a natural pool inside a large cavern. Unlike the stone building back in Thaliondris, this one was left completely alone by the Eloni, dark and damp and full of natural mineral formations. Jorlan led them through a dizzying maze of tunnels before they finally reached the entrance, a tiny opening mostly obscured by vines from the outside. Evin had to marvel at its success as a secret passageway: even if one managed to find the entrance to the cavern, the tunnels would prevent them finding the pool—and even if they found the pool, which might be only one of several, there was no indication of any underground tunnel or entrance into the city.

It was brilliant in its simplicity. He smiled as he wrung out his shirt. They were lucky it was summer. Brandt was saying goodbye to Jorlan and Nenna, and Ryn was checking her gear one more time—he saw her compulsively examine the gray stone at the head of her staff. Her long fingers lingered there, thoughtfully, and Evin found himself wondering what she was thinking about.

He would ask her tomorrow, he thought, as the wind shifted and he shivered. Brandt gestured, and with a heartfelt gesture of respect and thanks to the elves, Evin followed his brother into the long night.

~~~~~~~~~~~

Tanar had no idea how either the horses or the chimaeras were managing such speed with no rest. They had been running for what had to be hours by now; the sky to the east was just beginning to lighten, the smallest amount, when they finally caught the lagging Eloni warrioress. A chimaera near the front of their group pounced with a final burst of speed, and Tanar shouted hoarsely, a useless, helpless "no!" but it was lost in the victorious war-cries of the dozen Val'gren hunters watching.

Cries that went silent in half a heartbeat.

Just as the first rays of dawn sprang over the horizon, and the chimaera's outstretched claw struck the snow-white horse, all three of their targets winked out of existence with a burst of bright light and the unmistakable chime of magic. Tanar's heart thumped painfully in his chest as the Val'gren pulled their mounts up short and simply stared at the spot their quarry had been. The only sound that could be heard was that of the morning birds beginning to sing around them, and the chimaeras breathing heavily below them, tired out from their run.

Tanar couldn't pinpoint the emotions that coursed through his chest; confusion melted into joy as he realized his information had been wrong, thank all the Astra he'd been *wrong*...and then joy cooled and hardened into terror as he realized:

His information had been wrong.

Brenna. Kesi.

By the Light.

Suddenly more afraid than he'd ever been in his life, Tanar chanced a look at Râza. The Val'gren Warmaster was looking straight at him, rage obvious in the way darkness gathered round him like a living thing. It swirled about his form until he was invisible, save for that pair of menacing scarlet eyes, still fixed on Tanar's now-bloodless face. Pressure built in the air around them, Tanar could feel it, like the buzz in the air before a lightning storm; he squirmed on the back of the chimaera as all the hair on his body rose to stand on end.

"Please—" he managed.

The power exploded, black cloud dissipating around Râza, and there were a multitude of small *plunks!* around him as everything went deathly silent. Confused, Tanar looked about, stomach dropping as he realized the sound was that of every bird in the vicinity falling dead from blackened trees. His eyes widened and moved back to Râza, who had dismounted and was walking toward him slowly, eyes never leaving his.

He suddenly knew what was about to happen, like he knew the sun would rise fully within the hour. There was no question, it was simply inexorable fact.

"It appears our friend's information was…faulty," Râza spoke, and his voice turned the blood in Tanar's veins to ice. He shivered, pulling at his bonds instinctively, though some part of him knew it was useless. "Nevertheless, I am, above all, a man of my word. It's time to reunite him with his family."

Tanar froze. His chest hurt. He wasn't breathing, he couldn't remember how.

It didn't matter anyway.

Râza stepped up close, white lips curling into a smile.

"*Aufero.*"

It was the last word Tanar ever heard.

16

In spite of everything that had changed in Thaliondris, Brandt noticed that he, his brother, and their guide fell easily back into the habits they had established on the road before reaching the wood elves. Chore assignments did not change; Ryn still foraged and scouted, Evin still hunted and cooked, and Brandt still washed and mended. They still sparred before dinner and told stories after while Kota gnawed at the remains of their meal. Night watches remained, and though both of them thought he didn't notice, Ryn and Evin watched the sun rise together every morning.

That last bit was new, a practice Brandt thought must have been established in the city. Evin had always been the most chipper of them in the mornings, it was true, but he did not fall asleep easily, so he tended to guard his sleeping hours fiercely. Usually he took the first watch, preferring to go to bed a little later but sleep through the night. Apparently, Brandt reflected, he had found something in his and Ryn's early morning discussions that was worth losing an hour of sleep over.

Watching them sit together before the lightening sky, huddled warm in his bedroll and barely awake, Brandt thought he knew what it was.

His brother's unrelenting charm and happy-go-lucky attitude aside, Evin had surprisingly few true companions. Most everyone knew him for his wit, and his talent for tracking, his unbeatable speed borne of that lithe form so unusual among their people, or his propensity to say too much too loudly. Evin was certainly more suited to fighting than diplomacy, and it was no secret to anyone.

But, Brandt reflected, very few people actually knew Evin for his generous heart, or his unique insights, or the way he seemed to remember everything. Evin was not famous for the way his eyebrows knitted momentarily when he was trying to hide an amused reaction, or how he sniffed when he lied, or the faith he had in the Old Tales. Very few really *knew* his brother, and those who did had been a part of his life for nearly as many years as he'd been living it.

Ryn seemed to be the exception to that. Why, Brandt barely knew, but she responded to Evin in a way that made him think she had known him for years, when she'd known him for weeks. And Evin had been good for her too; she was far more relaxed and open now than she'd been even at the river crossing, and in spite of the whole upheaval discovering her Y'rai heritage must have caused, she seemed to be handling the new abilities—and responsibilities—fairly well.

Evin said something just then that made Ryn snort, the sound loud enough and rude enough to jolt Brandt from his comfortable, in-between space and wake him fully. He sat up with a sigh, garnering their attention. Ryn had the grace to look slightly ashamed, and Evin pulled away from her slightly. Brandt wanted to laugh; did they think he was blind? Instead, he scowled.

"Sun's up. Let's move."

~~~~~~~~~~~

Ryn shivered slightly in the mountain air; the evenings and mornings had become colder since they'd left Thaliondris almost a week prior, picking their way carefully through the secret mountain pass Lord Áed had spoken of. It was the only passable way through the Dragonback Mountains east of the great elven city, marked by a series of carved runes that glowed at the presence of the amulet the Wood Elf had given Brandt. The way was not easy, but it was manageable, and each day they gained a bit more elevation as the leagues passed slowly beneath their feet.

But it was growing colder the higher they went, which was why she was out here right now, in the orange-pink light of the sunset, stark naked. Submerged bathing would soon become dangerous—a wet body meant a cool body—so after this there would be little chance to wash thoroughly until they reached the plains again. She intended to take full advantage.

She had taken Kota and ordered him to stand guard at the path, then sequestered herself in a smallish pool formed by several boulders in the shallow mountain stream. A willow lent its branches to the little pond, making it just about as private as was humanly possible out here.

It was almost pleasant.

Ryn hurried into the water; it was bracing, but the rocks retained some heat from the day's sun, so it was not unbearable. She washed quickly, taking special care to scrub the dirtier areas of her body—under her nails and arms and the bottoms of her feet—and washed her hair twice, relishing the scent of the lapis flower oil she'd bought in Thaliondris. The oil smelled wonderful, a little sharp and spicy with a hint of floral sweetness, but not so sweet as to attract unwanted insects during her travels. It was one of the few things she splurged on as often as she could manage.

She hummed a little to herself as she scrubbed the oil from her hair, fingers still unused to the shorter length. Despite the rigors of traveling, she found herself glad to be on the road again, just her and Kota and the two men she'd come to regard as friends. Lately Ryn had found the brother-princes to be much more relaxed; and now that he wasn't preoccupied with hiding his identity, Evin's evening tales had grown richer with detail. Brandt seemed less tense since they'd left Râza far behind, though Ryn herself couldn't help but wonder what had happened to the Eloni city in the aftermath of their trickery. Had the sorcerer attacked the city outright? Disappeared entirely now that his quarry had moved on? Or was he still there, terrorizing travelers entering the Eloni's domain and slowly suffocating their trade routes?

She wondered, too, about that spy to whom Lord Áed had fed incorrect information, in order to lead Râza off in the wrong direction at the wrong time. She couldn't imagine things had turned out well for him.

Râza must have been so angry.

The spy was probably dead.

Honestly, she hoped never to find out. The fate of the spy had been a bitter point of contention in their party; Brandt had been merciless in his focus on his brother's safety and the completion of the quest, but Evin had argued passionately for Lord Áed to spare the man's life somehow. Eventually, the Lord of the Eloni had agreed to send two of his best to scout the Val'gren party after their decoy was dispatched, to see if it were possible to save the spy. Evin had grudgingly acknowledged that was the best anyone could do and thanked Lord Áed sincerely.

While Ryn herself quietly shared Brandt's opinion—the spy had brought this on himself, extortion or no—the force of Evin's compassion had moved her unexpectedly. She found herself growing more fond of the man by the day.

Shivering, Ryn jumped out of the pool and dried herself quickly, slipping into her clean clothes and kneeling to scrub the dirty ones to dry overnight. The Warmaster of the Val'gren was not easily fooled, she thought, though if anyone could do it it'd be the Lord of the Eloni; still, she wondered if she oughtn't start scouting a bit when they made camp at night. Maybe climb a tall tree and see if there was anyone on their tails before they settled to sleep.

Tomorrow, she decided, she would begin doing that. Just to be safe.

Nodding to herself as she wrung out her now-clean breeches, she stood and turned to go, arms full of damp clothes and her Y'rai knife. Her stomach lurched into her throat as she tried to move and her right foot caught in something—the willow root, she knew instinctively—throwing her forward and toward the ground. She barely had time to realize she was going down before brown filled her vision and she thumped headfirst into something soft, but firm.

"Oof!" she heard Evin grunt as his arms went round her in an attempt to keep them both on their feet. She felt the wet clothes pressed against her front, cold, but everywhere else there was nothing but warmth.

She should have stood immediately on her own two feet and laughed it off. She should have pulled away and maintained her distance. She should have punched him in the shoulder playfully.

She should have done *anything* else.

Surprised by the feel of warm, strong arms around her, Ryn did not laugh, punch, or pull away; instead she stayed where she was for a moment, trying to register what was happening, before her body betrayed her and she burrowed into Evin's heat, gooseflesh erupting all over her chilly bare arms. It was all quite pleasant, despite the distant alarm bells going off in her head that were drowned out completely by a woodsy, masculine scent.

"You smell good," She muttered into his shoulder. She felt a shudder wrack his frame, and wondered momentarily if he was getting ready to push her away. Before she could panic, however, she felt his face press against her damp hair and his breath brush her ear as he whispered back,

"So do you."

Ryn knew what the heat that bloomed in her stomach meant, even though her experience with it was admittedly sparse. She had heard people speak of this—in tavern corners, in giggles in dark alcoves as she passed by—this swooping sensation in her belly, this tingle in her fingertips where she felt the texture of his leather jerkin, this thrill that ran up and down her spine as his breath ghosted against her skin.

Desire.

Fear tightened in a heavy knot in her chest that overrode even the effects of his dozy warmth as she jumped back suddenly. She struggled to regain her equilibrium at the sight of her friend in the failing light and stuttered, "Yes well, that would be the...the bathing—the lapis oil. Yes. Here."

She dumped her wet things in his arms unceremoniously and stumbled back to camp, Kota picking his delicate way behind her, sniffing at whatever struck his fancy. Evin was a minute behind, looking a bit shell-shocked as he hung her wet things on the thin wooden rods near the fire.

And though they sat in their customary positions by the fire—Ryn next to Evin on one side and Kota on the other—she carefully avoided touching him, and slept further from both brothers that night than she had since they had begun traveling together.

Because absolutely no good at all could come of any situation that included her, Evin, and *desire.*

17

Three days later, Ryn knew the idea to scout before bed had been a wise one. "They've found our trail," she reported, still breathless from her run down the ridge. They had set up camp under a slight overhang, boxed in by evergreens that blocked most of the incessant wind. The late evening sun shone bright on Ryn's face, making her squint to see her friends. "We're being tracked. I wasn't sure before, but now it's unmistakable."

Both men stopped what they were doing to look up at her. There was silence for a moment, broken only by the crackling of their supper fire and the soothing noise of evening songbirds.

"How far are they?" Brandt finally asked, rising from his perch on a log to bank the fire.

"Not far enough," she answered. Evin moved now too, packing up his cooking utensils and stuffing them in his pack. "Only about a league, and they haven't stopped for the night."

"Neither then shall we," Brandt said, and nobody argued the point.

Ryn followed suit, re-packing her own bedroll and tying it quickly into its proper place beneath her leather pack. She swung the whole thing onto her back and picked up her staff as she rose, half-subconsciously confirming the grey shieldenstone still sat in its carved head. She ruffled Kota's fur and Brandt turned to her, gesturing for her to take a small strip of the hot meat he'd been cooking. She acquiesced gratefully, holding the sizzling venison gingerly between her fingers as she blew on it.

"Thank the Light the food had time to roast first," Evin grinned. "Aeos forbid we go hungry, Val'gren or no!"

Ryn allowed herself a smile at his attempt to lighten the mood, but it didn't last long. Whatever luck Lord Áed had been able to grant them with his rumors and his secrets had run out. Râza was on the hunt.

They traveled through the night, and while Ryn wasn't exactly unfamiliar with all-night runs, she remembered near dawn why she hated them so. Just as the sun began to turn the black velvet sky a quiet blue, Brandt called a halt in a small clearing. Evin bent to rest his hands on his knees to catch his breath. Brandt's face was grey in the wan light. Kota huffed and nudged Ryn's leg before lying down right where he stood. She knelt to confirm he was well, only tired, then met Brandt's gaze. His normally-vibrant eyes were dull with exhaustion, and the set of his face registered a measure of desperation under the stony determination. He blinked at her.

"I'll check," she said, in answer to his silent question.

Have we gained enough of a lead to rest safely for an hour or two? She hoped so. She shimmied up the tallest tree she could see on the ridge, blinking as the sun came into view at last. When Ryn reached highest bough that would hold her weight, she turned carefully to squint toward the west.

There.

Flocks of birds, screaming as they took to the sky in fear, far too near for comfort. And beneath that, there was…something. Ryn couldn't quite put her finger on it. It made her heart race in her chest and her upper lip bead sweat. It felt sinister and dark, so unlike what she had grown used to seeing in the forests and mountains and lakes around her. Something in that direction made her jumpy, itchy, like that prickly feeling when one is being watched. It was when she found she thought of it as Black, though all she could see was green and blue and purple, that she realized it wasn't her physical eyes telling her, it was her Sight.

Now that was an interesting development. Kenelm had mentioned nothing about Seeing without intending to.

Ryn shook herself—no time for this now—and cursed. If her eyes and her Sight were correct, the Val'gren were close; closer than they'd been the night before. Not only had she and her friends *not* widened the gap at all, it had in fact closed slightly.

How? Ryn wondered desperately. *Even Val'gren must rest sometimes.*

Swallowing her disappointment, she left the tree and ran back to the princes and her lynx. They looked up at her arrival; she shook her head in response to the unasked question of whether rest was an option, and Evin groaned softly. Brandt smacked him on the shoulder encouragingly, and Ryn forced a smirk onto her face, hoping it looked genuine.

"Come now, oh mighty Sir Evin," she teased. "Are you to be outrun by some capering halfwits wielding glorified toothpicks?" Golden eyes sparkled at the description, and Evin's lips quirked.

"Hardly, my Lady."

She didn't hesitate to offer her signature rejoinder. "Still not a lady."

"Unless my eyes deceive me—"

"Less flirting," Brandt ordered, hoisting his pack. "More running."

Evin winked as he checked his sword and stood, but Ryn took a moment to kneel and speak to Kota. She held his head and looked into his yellow eyes. "Are you well, *kisa?*" she asked softly. He gave her a small, strange little mewl and batted her face lightly with one massive paw. "We've got to keep running," she rubbed his tufted ears. "They'll catch us if we don't."

Kota huffed and hopped back, crouching almost playfully, as if to say, *well, come on then.*

She went.

~~~~~~~~~~~

The sun was nearing the western horizon and the terrain had turned truly treacherous when next Brandt called for a break. As they went deeper into the mountains, the hills had become steeper, the stone underfoot more unstable, the woods darker. Evin leaned against a tough old evergreen, trying to breathe normally. Never before had he been forced to make this sort of speed for this long without rest. Looking around at his companions, he thought it safe to assume they had not, either. Ryn had collapsed where she stood, on her hands and knees gasping for breath. He could see the small tremors wrack her frame on every exhale and knew it was sheer willpower holding her upright at all. Brandt was in no better shape, legs shaking visibly as he leaned heavily against a boulder jutting out from the ground like an over-large thumb. Kota had fared best of them all, though he sat beside Ryn and huffed as he nuzzled her red face.

"We're going to have to make a stand," Evin ventured, knowing he'd receive backlash from at least Brandt on the issue. They were Heirs to the Throne, now more than ever before, his brother would say. They could not be so reckless, nor engage in battle with anyone who might recognize them as the Sons of Signy, anyone who might understand their importance. And, as always, his older brother was right—they could not do those things. But they could not run forever, either, and all of them were nearing the end of their reserves too quickly. If it came to a fight right this moment, none of them would last a minute; but if they waited for their pursuers to catch up, prepared for an assault...

"We cannot." Brandt's reply was expectedly grumpy. "They are Val'gren, Evin, not mere bandits. They would destroy us, or worse, take us hostage—"

"What if we hide?" Ryn asked, voice raspy from disuse and exhaustion. "I know many shadowing techniques we could use. They could stand mere inches away and not see us."

"We'll not hide!" Brandt was looking at her as though she'd suggested he dress up as a peasant girl and hop on one foot while singing a love song backward. Evin, giddy with fatigue, tried not to laugh aloud at the mental image. "We are Signy's sons, princes of Laendor, and warriors of the Keep—"

But Ryn was rolling her eyes. "Yes, yes, I know all that, and please excuse me if I don't take a proper moment to be impressed by it; but I'm not talking about honor, or pride, or whatever it is you men so enjoy tossing around as your reasoning for stupidity. I'm talking about *survival*, and the certainty that we cannot outrun this hunting party, nor can we beat them in a full-on fight. We need to disguise ourselves."

"They will find us," Evin supplied, before the two could start fighting. And fight they would, for her slight against a warrior's honor would not sit well with Brandt, but they had more pressing problems and Evin had no desire to play mediator at the moment. Their surrounding terrain had given him an idea. "When the trail stops, they will search under every leaf and rock until they uncover our position." Both of them looked ready to argue, so Evin held up a forestalling finger. "But I may have an idea."

The plan took almost an hour to set up properly. Ryn first confirmed that the Val'gren were far enough behind them to give them a few hours' respite, and then they set to work. None of the preparation was nearly as exhausting as constant running, nor as demoralizing as fleeing like a hunted animal, so when they at last settled into their places to wait, Evin found himself inexplicably wide awake.

From where he hid, sequestered among the branches of a thick bush, he could see both Ryn and Brandt's positions, though he could only see his brother's face because he knew exactly where to look. He resisted the urge to scratch at the drying mud on his face, inwardly amused that he and his Royal Brother, the Heir to the Oaken Throne, were sitting in the middle of the woods covered in dirt and leaves awaiting an enemy. He knew Brandt found it considerably less amusing and more humiliating, but Evin couldn't help but laugh. It was just too odd.

It turned out Ryn's shadowing techniques had been quite impressive and relatively involved. She had erased their original trail and forged a new one leading through a narrow, booby-trapped schism onto a small plateau. Here, where they currently lay in wait, was perfect for an ambush—Evin's idea, and a decent one, if he did say so himself. One side of the clearing was backed up against a sheer rock face, blunt and gray save for a few hardy little plants pushing their way out of cracks in the rock. To the south, the clearing dropped precariously off into a near-bottomless chasm; Ryn's hiding place was on that side, between a couple of large boulders at the edge of the cliff. Evin hadn't liked that idea much, thinking it rather dangerous should she fall asleep while they waited, but she assured him that both she and Kota had excellent balance and even better self control; they would not sleep or fall.

The eastern edge of the plateau sheltered both him and Brandt, inside an impossibly dense thicket that would easily block any escape from that direction.

Their enemy would track them here, bottled through the tiny opening and trapped where Evin, Brandt, Kota, and Ryn could take them out easily.

Like fish in a barrel, he'd said to them, grinning as he saw Brandt come to agree and Ryn begin thinking which traps would work best in the space they had. Once the traps were laid, she had insisted they cover their faces in dirt to hide their light skin. Pale, he believed she'd called them, eyeing him specifically, though he'd easily flustered her with a coy wink before turning to find some loose dirt on the barren plateau.

Evin yawned as he grinned at the memory. He'd never before met a lass so easily turned around by his gentle teasing, but far from annoying him, it rather endeared him to his friend. It was the only way he ever saw her lose some measure of the rigid control she kept over her reactions and her expressions; even when she was in danger, she always seemed perfectly at ease, confident and self-assured. He knew a good portion of that came from living on the road, where having a thick skin was a necessity, but he did like to see beneath her careful façade now and then, and a bit of flirting seemed to accomplish that easier than most anything.

He felt his lips thin slightly and his heart skip in his chest when thoughts of harmless banter turned to the memory of the riverbank a few nights ago. Evin had gone looking for Ryn, after she'd been away from camp longer than usual, but he hadn't really expected to find her by her nearly knocking him over. He definitely hadn't expected her to freeze and then practically burrow into him, making a soft noise that had left him weak in the knees and warmed to the core.

He'd needed a moment before following her back to camp.

Evin was no idiot; he knew what these feelings meant, knew what he wanted from her, and he also knew he'd never really get it. She was far too galvanized against anyone invading her heart, far too much a traveler and a loner, far too used to being alone.

Still. He *wanted.*

It was his last conscious thought before he drifted into a light doze.

He was awakened not long after, feeling as though he had not slept at all but instantly and severely awake. Something was happening. A few yards away, Brandt was stock still, his eyes wide in the wan light. Evin did not move, for their painted disguise helped blend them in with their surroundings, true, but it also depended heavily upon complete stillness.

One of their traps had been tripped. Firelight bathed the clearing nearby, and he could make out a couple of dim silhouettes; three of the impossibly-tall and slender Val'gren he could see, as well as their chimaera mounts. He knew there were more behind them, unable to pass through the narrow opening just yet. They were speaking quietly to one another, examining what appeared to be the body of one of their comrades lying still and quiet on the ground. Evin strove to make out the words.

"...are nearby?" A deadly-cool voice asked. It was answered by one deeper, languorous in a way that made Evin's blood run cold.

145

"I know this trap," it said. "This is the work of that bitch you all fear so much, the girl with the pet wild cat."

"*Leyna?*" the first voice asked again, only a slight catch at the end betraying any fear at all. The other snarled.

"The same. Strap him to one of the beasts; we will burn him after we catch our prey." The voice strengthened to carry to the whole group. "And beware. They've snared the path, the cowards."

General bustle followed the order, and the voice belonging to the one in charge spoke again, something Evin could not hear. He turned his head slowly, minutely, to get a better look. Figures robed entirely in black lifted the hunter their trap had managed to kill, bound him to the flank of a dirty-brown chimaera. The tallest of the lot stood a little off from the others, studying the dark around them.

Evin's stomach dropped when the sparse clouds moved and moonlight shone against the man's white face. His eyes were blood red.

Râza.

He held his breath against the sucking gasp that instinct pressed upon him. He looked toward Brandt—his own self-soothing behavior, and a shamefully juvenile one at that—and had to swallow a small sound of confusion. His older brother's face was a cacophony of expressions ranging from hate to rage to desperation to fear and back again. Brandt couldn't seem to decide on one particular emotion, and it made Evin dizzy. He looked toward Ryn's hiding place instead, uselessly, for he couldn't see her at all. He shifted, managing a slow, deep breath to soothe his jangled nerves.

For now, his part of the plan was to wait in readiness. Painfully slowly, he pushed himself off his stomach and nocked an arrow silently. He focused on breathing, kept watching the Val'gren, who had finished with their dead companion and now awaited further orders from their leader.

Râza strode into the clearing, somehow avoiding all the rest of their traps easily, and studied the dirt at his feet. He cursed vividly and stood, turned back to his men, expression fierce. "The trail dies here. Our quarry is hidden; they think to make a stand. Find them—all four of them—and do not even think to let your fear of the little huntress stop you—"

He was interrupted by the whiz of an arrow from the boulders to his left, but the Val'gren Warmaster twitched, moved back just enough that the sharp stone arrowhead missed his face by a hair's breadth, and the hunting party sprang into action at the strike. Ryn's traps took down two more as they rushed into the clearing, and Evin took the opportunity to let his own arrow fly. He finished off one of the trapped ones, then drew and aimed again, this time at Râza himself. Still recovering from the last shot, the Warmaster didn't quite move fast enough to avoid this one, and Evin's goose-fletched arrow buried itself deep in his shoulder. The Val'gren leader roared his fury even as Evin cursed his aim; half the hunting party broke off their search of the cliff's edge from whence Ryn's arrow had come to head his way. He tossed a galvanizing wink at Brandt, who was standing now and readying to charge, then shot again—this time at one of the other Val'gren, the nearest one, who was poking his way closer to Evin than the others.

This one was perhaps not so experienced as Râza, and Evin's aim was more true; the arrow found a home between the man's eyes, and he dropped like a stone. Evin moved now, keeping low to the ground like he did on hunts, balancing on the balls of his feet to lessen the noise of his step, moving close to the edge of the thicket. He shot again, this time hitting a sword-wielding hunter in the ribs as he raised his rapier high. Shouts alerted him to the fact that one of them had been found, and the location of the bustle told him it was his brother. His chest tightened and he moved toward the disturbance, hoping to pick some of them off, but he was interrupted by the cry of battle that took him by surprise from his right. He turned, dodging instinctively, and barely managed to avoid the lightning-fast blow intended for him. Unthinking, he let fly, shooting the Val'gren in the eye. This one screamed when he shot it, and the sound was as horrifying as any he'd ever heard—and he was no stranger to screams.

His position compromised, Evin shouldered his bow and drew his long sword. He spun to meet his next attacker, a young Val'gren with orange eyes and deliberate, swirling scars covering half his face. They traded blows, his opponent impossibly strong and quick. Evin had not been this challenged by a spar in a good long time, and far from being appropriately frightened, he found himself instead exhilarated. He laughed when his next block met steel and shoved his way into the other man's defenses.

The Val'gren seemed surprised at this reaction and tried to backpedal, but Evin was in his element now. The swordsmasters at home had always said he was quick and light on his feet, but that was not typical of his people. Most of them were thicker, stronger; so he was always at a sort of disadvantage in those departments. Speed often helped him avoid situations where strength would fail him; but at last he had an opponent as fast—or nearly as fast—as he. It was a real challenge, in an area in which he excelled, and it made him smile. Nimbly, he spun his sword in a complex move that smacked the weapon clean out of the Val'gren's hand, and its bright eyes widened as he drove his sword deep into its belly.

"Surprise," he taunted, and drew out his sword. The dying Val'gren's expression twisted into something resembling rage, and Evin yelped at the line of fire that spread down his calf where the man had dealt a final blow with its dagger. *Sloppy work, not seeing that coming,* he chided himself. Luckily it was a painful but shallow laceration, and he had other worries. Not wasting any time, Evin started in the direction he knew Brandt to be, noting with some satisfaction that of the twelve hunters Ryn had counted as the

Val'gren drew near, about half lay dead. Snarls told him some others were engaged with Kota, the thump of a staff against flesh nearby belying Ryn's location. Steel struck steel to his left—*Brandt*—and he headed that way at a run. What he saw as he drew closer sent his heart racing and moved his feet impossibly faster.

Brandt's double axes gleamed in the moonlight, flashing against the massive shadow that stood before him. Râza, somehow unhindered by Evin's previous arrow in his shoulder, had a blade that was blackened steel, nearly impossible to see; Evin's heart skipped a beat when he realized that meant Brandt was basically fighting blind. The Val'gren Warmaster knew it, too, and smiled; a feral, vicious expression that Evin never wanted to see directed at his brother. He scowled and in one smooth motion, un-shouldered his bow and nocked an arrow. Normally, he'd have just shot and readied himself for another strike, but in an instant, he caught a glimpse of Râza's sword raised high above his head, aiming to descend and cleave Brandt in two. That, in itself, would hardly have shaken him—there were a dozen ways to block such a blow.

But Brandt wasn't using any of them. Unable to properly see the weapon in the dark, his brother was readying to block a blow from the side, not above. He hadn't a chance...

"Hey!" Evin bellowed, letting his arrow fly and praying his aim was good. Aeos smiled upon him, for the arrow buried itself neatly in Râza's thigh, and before the man even had a chance to react, Evin shot him again. This one pierced the Val'gren's side—a slowly fatal shot, Evin thought wildly, if untreated—at the exact same moment Ryn appeared out of the shadows and drove her Y'rai blade deep into Râza's chest. He was a warrior, he knew enough about anatomy to know her blow had landed too far to the left to kill the Val'gren quickly—

He never got to finish the thought, as something slammed hard into him from the left. He hit the ground with brutal force but didn't have time to move before a horrible growling filled his ears and pain lanced through his left shoulder. He cried out as the pieces slotted together enough for him to realize he'd been bowled over and bitten by a chimaera—one of the Val'gren's mounts, probably—and the creature was dragging him along, shaking him in its jaws like some sort of mouse.

He heard shouting—Ryn and Brandt, trying to help, he guessed—though it was Kota who reached the creature first. A lynx's scream joined the monstrous growls, and Evin yelped as he was jostled about by the teeth dug into his shoulder.

The skirmish lasted mere seconds. Evin clawed desperately at the skull of the thing holding him, unable to get his bearings but hoping to reach its eyes and motivate it to let him go. Suddenly, the chimaera lurched backward, whined, and there was a sickening feeling in his stomach as Evin fell.

Oh this won't end well.

He was conscious long enough to realize the giant catlike creature had finally let go of his shoulder before he hit the sturdy ledge. His head smacked something hard, there was a ringing sound, and then everything went dark.

~~~~~~~~~~

The second-worst experience of Brandt's entire life had been the night his cousin and friend and future king, Gunnar, had died on that Astra-forsaken patrol. The Val'gren were never supposed to be anywhere near their location, and no one knew how they'd been found, but the barbarian hunting party had been sizable and had struck hard and mercilessly. Gunnar had been heroic to the last, fending off four of them while standing over a wounded comrade, bellowing for reinforcements.

The reinforcements had come, but not before a javelin pierced the Crown Prince's heart, shredding Brandt's world before his very eyes.

But the worst experience of his life was happening right now, watching Evin disappear over the edge of a precipice so steep it may as well have been a cliff. He heard a shout, hoarse and painful-sounding, and as he stumbled to the edge, he realized it was his own. He arrived just in time to see his little brother and the monstrous chimaera crash into a ledge perhaps twenty feet below. The thick shale held for a moment but then buckled beneath the force, sending the creature into the depths with a scream, while a clearly-unconscious Evin rolled perilously close to the edge. Ryn appeared at his side and cursed in a tight voice, spoke quick words that Brandt couldn't understand. His attention was completely taken up by Evin, bleeding and broken below, and barely avoiding the fate the chimaera had suffered.

Please don't move, brother, don't wake up.

"Brandt!" Ryn's voice was high, cracking as she punched his shoulder hard. "Come on, we have to get him off there!"

Shaking himself, the Prince stared at her and somehow managed to push back the shock that threatened to render him paralyzed. Some part of him knew he couldn't afford that, that Evin couldn't afford that, so he grabbed the rope Ryn held out to him. "I'm lighter than you," she said, talking fast as she fashioned a series of knots in the rope. "I'll go down, harness him, you pull him back up. There are handholds down there that I can hang onto until you send the rope back down." She added, as she leaned back and tested the tension on the rope he held tightly, "Just don't forget to send it back for me." She was only half-kidding, he knew. She kissed a panting, bloody Kota on the head and tied herself into the makeshift harness.

He lowered her slowly until she shouted for him to stop, and then he waited, trying to be patient as the rope jostled and pulled—Ryn harnessing his brother for the ride back up. When at last she yanked the rope and called for him to pull, Brandt pulled the rope taut and then began hauling his brother up the steep slope, praying he wouldn't accidentally injure him further. He shuddered to think of the damage done to Evin's body by such an attack.

When at last Evin flopped over the ledge in a manner so undignified Brandt would have teased him about it if he hadn't been so horrified, the elder pulled him fully to safety before kneeling beside him, gingerly cataloging his injuries. Bruising on the side of his face, including his temple, seemed to indicate a concussion at the very least; Evin also sported that horrific bite wound beneath the shredded leather armor of his left shoulder, lacerations and bruising over every bit of exposed skin, as well as abrasions from being dragged over the rough ground...

"You promised not to forget me!" Ryn chided gently, climbing over the ledge.

Brandt jumped, blinking at her. "How did you—?" His first words since Evin fell.

"It's not quite a vertical face," she smiled thinly. "And there were handholds all the way up here, so I came on up." He nodded, turning his attention back to his brother. "How is he?" Ryn asked, softly.

"This could be bad," Brandt answered, trying not to choke on the words.

~~~~~~~~~~

Ryn sighed as she pulled herself to her feet, patting Kota once as she went. The lynx stayed where he was, curled around Evin's sleeping form, carefully avoiding his bandaged head. She stretched, muscles sore from her long vigil, and moved slowly to where Brandt sat watching guard across the small plateau. Her friend looked up at her approach, his expression bleak and his skin gray with stress. Ryn sat down beside him.

"He will recover," she said, eager to put Brandt's mind at ease.

But the man scoffed, quietly. "He was thrown by a rampaging chimaera off a cliff," he protested. "It's a wonder he isn't—"

"Hush," Ryn interrupted. "Do not say it." She shuddered, playing again the horrifying image of her friend careening off the cliff, held tight in the massive jaws of a slavering chimaera. She continued a moment later. "He skidded along the face and a few ledges broke up the fall on the way down; but his injuries are extensive. Brandt, he...should not be doing as well as he is."

"Did you use your magic?" Brandt asked, almost suspicious.

Ryn shook her head. "Only to check his physical wellbeing. I do not trust the healing magic yet and would not use it on anyone I cared for."

Brandt stared hard at her for a moment, then grunted and turned back to his watch.

Ryn took a breath and continued. "He is healing too quickly. Already his bruises fade." She hesitated, uncertain how the next question would be received. "Brandt, he heals as I do. Is there Y'rai blood in the royal ancestry as well?" The hypothesis fit; it would account for the Prince's string of good luck, his ability to be reckless and not end up dead, would account for some of his height and grace, perhaps.

But Brandt rounded on her. "He is no such thing! Evin is Laendorian, a human through and through!"

"Brandt, I did not say—"

"Bite your tongue, before you speak more malicious lies!" Brandt ordered, and Ryn did; not because she was afraid of him, but because he was far too upset about this for it not to be true. "He is my brother, and *I* certainly have no such abilities. You are wrong."

Ryn sighed. "Two people with the same parentage can have differing levels of Y'rai blood, based upon how much resides in the mother or father—"

"I told you not to speak of it again."

"Unfortunately for you, I don't take orders!" Ryn snapped. "You act as though inheriting the ability to heal oneself or others is a curse, something to be feared rather than embraced!"

"Is it not?" Brandt asked acidly.

Stung, Ryn quieted and turned away. She stood to go, then faced Brandt. "Say what you will, but your brother is not precisely what you claim he is. To me, it is no matter, I care not; but whatever his story, it may come out eventually if you keep denying it so vehemently."

She turned and limped away, every nerve screaming from the day's excitement. She'd barely made it three steps when Brandt called her softly.

"Ryn, wait."

She stopped, sighing, and turned back to him. To her shock, she saw wetness on his dirty cheeks, and his blue eyes were downcast. Brandt struggled visibly with something before beckoning her jerkily to come back and sit. With a glance to confirm Evin slept still, Ryn complied.

When she sat, Brandt let out a long breath. "What I am about to tell you goes no further than the two of us, do you understand?"

Ryn cocked a brow—a noble of Laendor possessing Y'rai blood was hardly reason for such shame-ridden secrecy, unless she was missing something—but nodded. Brandt turned to look over the rugged mountains; a defense mechanism, as if the truth were easier to tell not looking anyone in the eye.

She knew the feeling.

"Evin is my... *half*-brother," Brandt confessed, choking a little on the last. Ryn swallowed her reaction to this, ignoring the way her stomach dropped. A bastard child among the court was a scandal Evin would have trouble recovering from. "We do not share the same father, although mine loved him as a son without ever even meeting him."

Brandt coughed past a sob, a tight, pained sound that made Ryn wince in sympathy. "What happened?" she asked. It came out a hoarse whisper.

"My mother was kidnapped by the Val'gren when I was barely out of nappies," Brandt said. "Not the nagrat, but the Val'gren themselves; taken, likely to be used as a sacrifice. My father and my Uncle Eirik would abide no such thing, and rode with the hunters to recover her." Ryn tried very hard not to wince visibly; *of course.*

She knew the tale of Signy's Abduction—everyone did. It was something of an epic love poem among the minstrels. The pieces slotted into place, and Ryn realized with a punch of dread where this story was headed.

Brandt went on. "Even with all their might and ability, it was many days before they found where Mother was being held, and the rescue was...difficult." He pinched the bridge of his nose in an attempt to compose himself, and Ryn couldn't resist the urge to place a supporting hand on his shoulder. Rather than calm him, the gesture seemed to undo what composure Brandt possessed, as he choked out a near-silent sob and rubbed his eyes fiercely. Ryn said nothing; words seemed useless here anyway. Nothing she could say could fix this.

"Only five of them returned, including Mother, and I remember they were all brutally injured," Brandt continued. "But Mother remained ill for a long time, even after her injuries healed. I was too young to understand, but my father was not. When she confirmed what he suspected the Val'gren had done to her, he swore vengeance on the lot of them and left to exact it. We never saw him again. Mother was barely starting to show."

"By the Light," escaped Ryn's lips without her permission. That was *not* part of the story the minstrels told. Brandt shuddered.

"When word got out, everyone assumed Mother had conceived shortly after she returned, and she never corrected any of them. I don't know if Uncle even knows."

Ryn stared dumbly at him, at a loss for words. Evin was not only a bastard child, he was fathered by a Val'gren, a *monster*, one of the enemies of the entire human race....now she understood Brandt's uncharacteristic rage at the mere suggestion his brother could be anything other than entirely Laendorian. If his parentage were to come to light, Evin would be cast out of the kingdom, forced to live as she did and acknowledged as dead to his family, and that would be the best case scenario. He would be shattered beyond repair, and Brandt would never see him again.

"Does he know?" she finally croaked, already knowing the answer. Brandt shook his head.

"Mother and I are the only ones, as far as I am aware. He must never find out," the Heir was adamant. "Ryn, it would kill him. You cannot tell him."

She considered. She trusted Evin, a phenomenon she was unfamiliar with but was quickly becoming attached to. It was comforting to have someone to share your experiences with, someone you could believe when they said things, someone who would come to your aid when you needed it, whether you asked or not. This trust was a new, fledgling thing, and she hesitated to betray it.

Still, Brandt was not wrong. Such a revelation would only ruin Evin. She shuddered to imagine the way his face would fall, the spark leave his golden eyes and the pain embitter his too-soft heart. Everything that made him *Evin* would shatter, be crushed beneath the despair and shame such news would bring, and for what? It would save no one, benefit no one, help in no way.

Still.

She shook her head. "No, I will not tell him. But Brandt, someone must. He has a right to know." She held up a hand when he started to protest. "And it should be you."

Brandt's face, already bloodless, paled further. "I know," he whispered, and those two words were so broken, Ryn felt her heart spasm in response.

She moved, pulling him to her by her arm around his shoulder, and cradling his head when it crashed into her collarbone. Brandt's back shuddered beneath her palms and pinpricks of wet heat soaked through her leathers. Ryn stroked his tangled hair and said nothing, wishing she could comfort her friend with promises that all would be well, that Evin would be all right and that everything would go back to the way it had been—but knowing he would find no peace in sweet lies. Instead she pressed her forehead to his damp hair and let her own tears fall too.

She didn't even think of it until much later, that Brandt's story hadn't really answered her question.

~~~~~~~~~~

Evin woke to quiet humming coming from somewhere to his left. He wondered fuzzily if his Mother had caught up to them, for the voice was feminine and sweet, if a bit low. His first instinct was to open his eyes and look, but that thought got no further before the agony registered.

His head was *pounding*, an angry counterpoint to various and sundry other pains that were not exactly insubstantial. His shoulder, in particular, was on fire, and his muscles protested even the slightest hint of movement on his part. He lay still for a moment longer, putting off the eventual necessity of moving as he tried to get his bearings.

He remembered...something. Vague impressions of wan moonlight and shouts of battle, quickly sharpening to real memories—the stretch of muscle as he drew his bow and let fly, killing a Val'gren hunter, gutting another who was stupid enough to challenge him up close, another of his arrows buried in Râza's thigh and one in his side...Ryn's blade in the Warmaster's chest...then a lot of noise, a lot of pain, and nothing.

He let the moan loose now, rolling his head and forcing his eyes open despite the pain, and the humming stopped. He was sorry; it had been soothing. He blinked hard against the bright light that assaulted his stinging eyes. After a moment he could see that Ryn sat nearby, one hand in Kota's fur as always, the other on her staff, sitting guard. The sun was not yet peeking over the mountainous horizon, though morning had well and truly broken, the sky pale blue and untouched by clouds. They were in a forest of thin-trunked asley trees, their spindly branches and large leaves dappling the light that played over Ryn's face. She was looking at him, and her expression held such relief it was almost pained. It made his chest ache with the desire to hold her and soothe it away.

"Good morning," she greeted quietly. "I'm glad you're awake. How do you feel?"

Evin opened his mouth to answer and all that emerged was a croak. Ryn smiled and reached for a water skin, tutting at him to stay still when he tried to sit up. Dizzy with the effort, he acquiesced and laid back, let her bring the water to his lips and help him drink. After he'd had a few sips—but not nearly enough—she drew the skin away, to his groaned protest. She smiled.

"Too much too quickly and you'll get sick," she provided. "You can have more in a few minutes. Now, tell me how you're feeling."

"Like I got run over by a troll," he rasped, trying to soften the pitiful sound of his voice with a smirk.

Ryn laughed. "That was weeks ago, my friend. Here," she put the skin to his lips again and he drank greedily, though he didn't protest when she took it away this time. "Let me look you over."

"Look all you like," he answered cheekily, and she pinched his bicep—probably the only part of him that didn't hurt, he thought—before moving very close and looking directly into his eyes. He blinked, startled by the proximity of her face, and tried not to study the freckles dusting her nose or the pale scar across her cheek. She said nothing, just watched his eyes for what seemed like an inordinate amount of time, and Evin finally snorted and blinked. "Usually I buy a lass dinner first."

Ryn's face took on an extraordinary expression, and she jerked back, pushing him down in the process. Evin coughed as his back hit the dirt, seeing stars. "Ow."

Ryn sat there for a moment, saying nothing, then nodded once. "You seem better. We might be able to leave tomorrow." Then she stood, quickly, and walked away, leaving a grinning Brandt behind as she stalked out of the camp. Evin moaned and looked back up at the sky.

"Finally met a lass who doesn't swoon at the sight of you," his brother teased.

Evin scowled. "I don't want her to swoon," he confessed, then shut his eyes again. Brandt left it alone and came to sit nearby. The silence stretched for a moment, then his brother spoke.

"She's right. We'll see about getting you up later and then try to move on tomorrow."

"What happened?"

Brandt sighed at that. "A chimaera ran you down, dragged you over a ledge. You hit a shale outcropping, the chimaera kept falling." Evin didn't open his eyes, but he didn't have to in order to sense his older brother's distress. "You're lucky to be alive."

He hummed his agreement, thinking he should say something to ease Brandt's mind, but he couldn't think of anything. After the initial excitement of waking up, his head now felt like it had been used as a battering ram, thoughts slow and muddy. His shoulder hurt too.

"Râza is gone," Brandt continued after a moment, and Evin was conscious enough to feel grateful for that, at least. "It's difficult to believe he could survive his injuries, but Ryn and I have both scouted the area pretty thoroughly in the last couple of days, and there's no sign of him. We burned the others."

"Least he's not here," Evin mumbled, the words heavy in his mouth. Brandt seemed to notice, laid a gently hand on his forehead. His brother's fingers were cool, it felt good.

"Rest, Evin."

So he did.

~~~~~~~~~~

They did end up leaving the next day, after all, despite Evin's weakness. All three of them knew the longer they stayed, the higher the chances Râza or his cohorts would come back. So even though the younger prince was barely on his feet, Ryn took his pack and Brandt slung his brother's arm over his shoulder, and they left the campsite near the cliff that Evin had nearly died upon. They took more frequent breaks, and the pace was agonizingly slow, but they were moving, at least.

The mountain pass loomed nearer with each halting step, and Ryn wondered how they would ever make it through. She'd never been through this particular pass, but she'd seen plenty in her day, and they were never easy going. Steep, rocky terrain; narrow, sometimes-nonexistent paths; and truly treacherous weather, especially near the summits, made traveling mountain passes a dangerous undertaking even in the best of circumstances. With one member of their party far from recovered, it was likely to prove particularly troublesome.

Yet on they pushed, for four days, each one seeing Evin a little stronger and taking a little more of his own weight. Ryn was at first astonished at his progress, but each time the thought crossed her mind, so did the conversation she'd had with Brandt about it—along with many other confusing and unpleasant emotions, not the least of which were grief and a fierce protectiveness that made her itchy. She would see every Val'gren she met for the rest of her life destroyed for this, she promised herself. Still, she said nothing, just caught Evin when he nearly fell, took over his evening duties, and played dumb when he waxed flirtatious, same as she had since the day they met.

It was the night before they would reach the pass itself—starting tomorrow, the way would be even harder—and they were camped beneath a large outcropping about halfway up a ridge. The location was inconvenient for pitching camp, hard and cold, but it was also the safest spot around. The fire was bright and cheery against the chill darkness, and the stars winked above them, a brilliant backdrop for the bright yellow full moon. Evin had insisted he could sit the first watch, despite his obvious exhaustion—"I'm injured, Brandt, not broken"—and had his bow out, back to the stone as he looked out over the steep ledge, the other mountains close around them. Ryn was packing up the remnants of their dinner and readying herself for sleep. Brandt had left the campsite to relieve himself, and Kota was lying near the wall gnawing on the remains of a mountain hare.

"You fixed me, didn't you?" Evin asked, out of the blue. His face was unreadable when Ryn turned to look at him, his tone even and carefully blank. She moved over to him and sat.

"Brandt and I both patched you up after we got you back," she answered quietly, playing for time while silently cursing herself for not seeing this coming. She had no idea what she was going to tell him, and hadn't discussed it with Brandt at all.

"That's not what I mean, and you know it," Evin answered, leveling her with a dead-serious look she had never seen on his face before. She wasn't even convinced, until this moment, that the younger prince knew *how* to be completely serious. It was an intimidating expression, those gold eyes hard and the lines of his mouth all turned down, eyebrows furrowed. She shivered at the subconscious comparison to Râza's deadly expression when she prevented him slicing Brandt in two. Ryn sighed and nodded, figuring it best not to insult Evin's intelligence by pretending not to know what he was talking about.

"I do know, but I didn't heal you," she said, looking him straight in the face. There was a lightning-quick myriad of emotions that played over his pale face—fear, skepticism, pain—but the one that eventually settled into place was not the one she expected. His eyes chilled and narrowed, and she wondered fleetingly if she was about to witness something else she hadn't previously been convinced Evin was capable of—anger. He said nothing for several seconds—long enough for the silence to become distinctly uncomfortable—then turned away from her.

"I did not expect my given trust to be worth so little, I must confess." There was something off about his tone, even more so than his words, which made a truly unpleasant emotion clench in her stomach.

"What?"

"Do not lie to me," he said, turning back to her, and this time she felt her own face betray her—wide-eyed and guilty—before she could school it into something less incriminating. Evin saw it, lips thinning as his glare sharpened.

"I would not," she answered, now cursing Brandt for staying away so long. How long did it take to piss?

"Then why am I healing so quickly?"

"If I had healed you, you would have been completely well instantly," she tried to reason with him. "Evin, I used my magic only to check your progress, to see things my natural eyes would not tell me. I am not skilled enough to heal on my own yet, you know that."

Evin rubbed his chest defensively. "I know that is what you told us."

"I have never lied to you."

"Perhaps not directly, but you do like to leave things out, don't you?" Ryn looked at him incredulously; that was hardly fair, given the rather large secret he and his brother had thought they were keeping from her for a good portion of their journey.

"You know who I am. I have never hidden that, which is more than can be said for you," she responded, aware her tone was growing colder by the second.

Evin didn't seem to care. "What of this deal of ours? Why do you need a day in the Archives? What could you possibly learn that would be helpful to a *meylika?*"

Ryn tried not to let the hurt cross her face, she really did. It wasn't the first time she'd been called a homeless hag, but it was the first time in years it had come from someone she cared about, and the pain, while familiar, surprised her a little. She growled, though Evin looked a little shocked at himself for using such a derogatory term.

Probably against his courtly manners, isn't it?

"That is really none of your concern, sir prince. I fail to see why you would care, I being such a nameless nobody and all."

Evin looked stricken. "Ryn, I—"

But she was already gone, stalked to her bedroll and crawled in, calling Kota to her. She hated to behave so childishly, but she needed to get away before he saw the tears on her cheeks. She swiped at them surreptitiously, silently half-daring him to notice.

Stupid ass. She was as angry at herself as she was the prince—well, both of them really. Brandt, for wresting a promise of silence from her. Evin, for being such a hard-nosed, intelligent idiot. And herself, for caring in the first place.

Brandt came back soon after, huffing at the climb to their large ledge and stomping around as he readied for sleep. *Stupid, loud lug.* Ryn cursed herself as she closed stinging eyes, determined to ignore the pit in her stomach and sleep. Angry and hurt though she was, she was also exhausted, and she was nearly unconscious when she heard Evin's voice entirely too close to her ear.

"I am sorry, *nileth*," he whispered, and pressed a kiss to her hair.

18

If Ryn had heard his apology that night, she gave Evin no indication in the days that followed. She was not rude, for living and traveling with someone didn't lend itself to cat-fighting, but she was distant in a way that made his heart sink. He wondered if he had been wrong. Perhaps he had just not been injured as badly as they originally thought. Perhaps his daily progress was normal given his body's own strength and Ryn's herbal salves.

Even if something *was* different about how he was healing, it had been unkind of him to accuse her; a slip-up brought on by too much pain, stress, and exhaustion, and too much pride to admit it.

It took them three days to get over the pass and begin the long descent out of the Dragonbacks. The weather and terrain were unrelenting; and each day, Evin grew more exhausted. His head had stopped aching constantly, but the long cut on his leg throbbed and he was fairly certain the chimaera bite was infected. He had woken that morning feeling feverish and shooting pains kept lancing down his arm and into his chest. Knowing how quickly a battle wound could turn, he called Ryn to him where he sat by the morning fire with Kota. The lynx had assumed the role of comforter since his accident; lying close to him at night and in the chill mornings, walking pressed up against his thigh all day unless his mistress had need of him, and bringing the prince gifts—often dead hares. It was more soothing than Evin cared to admit. He patted the big cat's flank affectionately. Ryn hesitated, but came as requested. She sat gingerly across from him, looking wary.

"What is it?" she asked.

Evin took a deep breath, shocked at his own gall. "I...need you to heal me." He said it as calmly as he could, as though he were asking for nothing more than a spare pouch or a tin of water, in a probably-futile attempt to head off the reaction he suspected he'd get from such a request.

She did not disappoint him. Her eyes widened before narrowing to green slits, her face flushing. "No."

"Please," he said, though he'd expected this. "Ryn, I am sorry for being an ass before, and I realize it's dangerous, but I will not make it to Retwood like this."

She blinked. "You are improving, getting well. Too quickly, remember? We will manage." Then she stood to get up, hesitating only when he began to unlace his leather jerkin. She raised both eyebrows when he removed it, pulling the linen shirt beneath out from his waistband and wrestling the loose garment over his head one-armed. Her confusion turned to concern in an instant when she saw the red staining the bandages wrapped tightly around his shoulder wound.

"Evin," she started, going to her knees at his side and looking him over carefully. She pulled her small knife and cut the bandages loose with a practiced hand. Her eyes widened and she swallowed convulsively.

The deep lacerations had taken on an unhealthy angry red color, standing in stark contrast to Evin's light skin. Clear liquid and blood oozed sluggishly from the wounds, staining the bandages red and yellow. The smell was horrific, and Evin shuddered, though Ryn barely reacted—it was clearly not the first time she'd dealt with injuries that looked like this. But the most worrisome thing was the streaks of unhealthy red that followed the paths of his veins beneath the skin—blood sickness was the demise of many a soldier or traveler whose wounds became infected. Ryn touched his chest gingerly, her face paling as she traced the infection crossing his left pectoral muscle. She swallowed.

"It's headed for your heart." Her voice was quiet, tight with dread. "Evin, how long...why didn't you say anything?"

"Overnight," he responded, eager to absolve himself of the impression he was stupid or stubborn enough to put his own life in danger. "It's felt tender and warm for a while, but it didn't look like this last night when Brandt changed the bandages."

Brandt chose that moment to come stomping back into camp, his arms full of spare clothes they'd washed and set out to dry in the morning sun. Evin had noticed his brother grow more and more serious the closer they limped to their destination, and he wondered if it was the seriousness of the quest itself or something else entirely that was weighing on his older brother. The other opened his mouth to say something, probably a morning greeting, saw Evin's shoulder, and dropped the clothes he was holding in the dirt. He strode over to his brother in two steps and bent over to look at his shoulder. Brandt's six-foot-something frame was nothing to joke about, and with him looming like this, Evin felt like a child who'd gotten his good clothes dirty.

"Infection?" Brandt asked quietly, and moved so Evin could see his face properly. The younger was almost shocked at the fear in his brother's eyes.

Ryn nodded, answering for him as she studied the rest of the wound. "This must hurt."

Evin gave her a confirming grimace, but said nothing.

She looked only a moment longer, then sighed. "And you want me to try to heal this." It was more a question of confirmation, with Brandt there to hear and contribute. She wanted approval from both of them before she continued, something Evin could understand, even if the idea of his brother trying to veto something he had asked for was just a little galling.

It wouldn't be a problem, apparently. Brandt said, "I see no other choice." Ryn jerked her head in a gesture of reluctant agreement.

"Me neither. I have no herbs that can tackle an infection this severe." She looked at Evin. "I can try to heal you, but I am not confident in this skill yet." Her frame shook slightly beneath a nervous shiver. "I don't know what will happen. I could hurt you worse, and none of us would forgive me for that."

But Evin shook his head. "It has to be done. It's that or nothing worth doing, and you and I both know what will happen if we do *nothing* about this." He motioned to the streak headed for his heart for emphasis. Ryn winced visibly at the implication. Blood sickness was a horrific and messy way to die. She nodded once, decided.

"Lie back and hold onto something. I have no idea if this hurts," she ordered. Evin did as he was told—noting with an odd mix of annoyance and gratitude that Brandt rolled back to sit fully before scooting closer, offering his hand for Evin to squeeze. Grown man or not, Evin took it. His brother smacked him affectionately on his good shoulder and motioned to Ryn, who looked instead to Evin.

He gave her a smirk. "At your convenience, my Lady."

The fact that she didn't comment on the title indicated how nervous, perhaps even frightened, Ryn was about this; but she took a deep breath and placed a slightly-shaking hand over his injured shoulder. In her other hand she held her staff across her lap, the rapidly-warming gray stone in its head mere inches from Evin's side. She didn't touch him, but he could feel the heat from her palm on his injured shoulder. It prickled uncomfortably. Ryn closed her eyes and concentrated, and after a few seconds, the prickling became an outright itch, making him jerk in surprise. Evin looked down, his eyes widening.

Silver light was coalescing between Ryn's hand and the ruined skin of his shoulder, bleeding into the wound and lighting it up from within. The ugly red of the infection looked almost black next to it, but only for a moment. The light pulsed through his veins, leaving nothing but the clean white of his skin behind; it itched like mad, though, and Evin gasped in discomfort. Ryn did not stop, the light moving through the rest of his body, from the top of his head to the tips of his toes, tingling wildly as it went. The cut on his leg—the only other substantial injury he still carried— screamed in protest, then quieted instantly. Finally, the light sparked out of his capillaries and the silver sphere above his shoulder dissipated. Ryn fell back with a gasp, dropping her head in exhaustion. Evin sat up quickly, scratching thoughtlessly as he moved his shoulder, laughing outright when he realized there was no pain. He could feel three thick scars where the chimaera's claws had savaged him, but he was too relieved to pay them any mind.

Evin sat up, swaying as the blood rushed from his head, and stretched luxuriously. He laughed again, and this time, Brandt laughed with him.

"Ryn!" he said jubilantly. "This is incredible! I feel fantastic! It was sort of itchy, but..." He trailed off as he looked down at her. She was still sitting on the forest floor, breathing shallowly as she leaned heavily back on her hands. Kota came to her, sniffing and rubbing against her shoulder, refusing to take his eyes off his mistress. She was looking at him, trying to smile, but her face was drawn and gray, like she was in pain.

Evin moved to kneel beside her quickly, aware his brother was standing just behind him. "Ryn?"

She shook her head. "I'm not sure," she murmured, knowing what he wanted to ask. "I got dizzy and exhausted after healing Kenelm, but it was nothing like this." Kota nudged her with his head, trilling his concern deep in his throat. Evin understood the feeling.

"Does using your magic hurt you?" Brandt asked, incredulous. "None of the legends say anything about Y'rai power being detrimental to the user, do they, Evin?"

He shook his head. "Not that I'm aware of, but it's been so long since anyone has manifested that magic that very few, if any, scholars on the subject remain." He turned his attention back to their friend. "Ryn, I'm sorry. If I had known—"

"You'd have done no differently," she answered, more firmly now. She forced her head up and looked him directly in the eye. Her face was the color of weak porridge. "You were dying. The trade is a wise one."

Somehow that did not make him feel better.

~~~~~~~~~~~

It wasn't long before Ryn began to wonder how accurate her assessment of the situation had been. They had only been moving for an hour and already she had thrown up twice, her legs were weak and shaking, struggling to hold her weight plus that of her pack; she had stumbled more than once—though she'd managed, thus far, to hide her weakness from the brothers. Her head was pounding fit to burst, her eyes pulsing beneath the lids; her skin felt hot and tight, achy as though she had contracted a flu; and everything—the sounds of the forest, the bright sun shining down, the wind on her skin—felt like *too damn much*. It was like the time her dinner had been drugged in that one tavern in Elyshall, the one she never went back to.

She wiped her sweating face on her sleeve, righting herself as the movement caused her to trip over her own feet. This was ridiculous; what was happening to her? Had she done something wrong? Pushed too hard? She wished Kenelm were here to advise her, though he'd probably just shout at her for healing Evin in the first place.

Not that there'd been any other choice. She'd tried so hard to head off infection in that shoulder, all while knowing bites from animals nearly always turned toxic. You never knew what had been in their mouths before your body part was.

She took a deep breath—a mistake, as it triggered another wave of dizzy nausea, and she croaked a halt before stumbling into the trees to throw up once again.

The next few days were much the same, Ryn never feeling particularly better or worse, just overwrought and exhausted and nauseated all the time. She stopped trying to keep food down after the first night, instead taking to water lightly spiced with ginger and herbs, when they could find them. It wasn't nearly enough, not for the amount of walking she was doing, but at least throwing up was easier if it was all water already. The princes were concerned, she could see it in their faces, hear it in the strain of their voices, but she barely cared. She could hardly summon the energy to push forward with a smile.

She slept through her watch the second night, and after that, neither of them woke her for one at all. She was too grateful for it to give thought to her stung pride.

They made it to the river that marked the halfway point from the pass to the valley on the fifth day since Evin's healing, and that was the day Ryn noticed she was beginning to feel a little better. Hopeful and in good spirits, they made camp a little early that evening and relaxed. Evin shot two rabbits, and Ryn found some wild onion and parsley, so they dumped the whole mess in a pot with water and salt and cooked up a stew for dinner. Both men began caring for weapons—Brandt took her bow as well and began to oil it—while Ryn lay her head against Kota's flank and closed her eyes, let the sun bathe her face, relishing the warmth of it against her skin; it was no longer an intensely hot or bright sensation, but comforting, as it ought to be.

So they passed a few hours this way. Evin stirred the stew now and then. The smell of it made Ryn's stomach rumble pleasantly. The sun dipped down beneath the mountain peaks to the west, casting long shadows over the forest. Kota sighed beneath her head, and slowly, Ryn fell asleep.

She woke abruptly, confused, to someone shaking her. Before she even opened her eyes all the way, she knew something wasn't right. The air smelled wrong, sharp and smoky, and the hairs on her neck stood up at the tang of magic in the air. She sat up blindly, forcing sore eyes open. "What's happening?" she croaked, noticing the men were packing their things hastily.

"That," Brandt answered tightly, gesturing behind her. Ryn turned and gasped.

The entire mountainside behind them was lit up by fire. It was nearly a league away now, but moving fast—moving their direction—and devouring everything in its path. Ryn didn't hesitate, rolling to her feet and stumbling a little. The swiftness of the move brought the nausea back full force, and she took half a moment to breathe slowly and calm her stomach. But only that, and then she began packing as quickly as she could. Konn and Tarya Darksbane had heaped the rock and dirt that made up the mountain range over the ancient dragons and abandoned them—and the stories said unquenchable firestorms in the Dragonbacks were Skyslayer's revenge, such as it was.

Shouldering her pack and using her staff to stand, Ryn decided it didn't much matter now where the fire came from. What mattered was getting out of these accursed mountains and to Retwood. Perhaps there, they could refit and rest up. Kota nosed her thigh gently, pushing her toward the princes, who were tossing things hurriedly into their own packs and standing quickly. Together, they fled.

19

The three travelers who stumbled into The Blue Flagon three days after the baelfire were haggard and exhausted as any ever seen in the town of Retwood. Dripping rainwater from every piece of tattered clothing they wore, they stumbled into the inn and asked for two rooms before shutting themselves in for several hours.

Brandt emerged first, in time for dinner, and moved to the main room of the lodge where he asked for three tankards of ale and chose a spot near the blazing hearth. It was still summer, but even the plains on this side the Dragonbacks were higher than his home in Sannfold, and the air was a bit chill. He sipped his ale quietly, enjoying the rich heady taste as he awaited his brother and their friend.

Friend.

He pondered the title his mind had assigned to the Lady with the Lynx. It fit, he supposed; she had saved his life multiple times, restored his brother to him, and he and Evin had both returned the favor on this journey, but that was to be expected when one traveled with another. It was no remarkable thing. Her bloodline, and the magic within it, clearly made her someone of import; but the idea of befriending someone simply because of their usefulness was repulsive to Brandt. No, their friendship had begun earlier than that, before Thaliondris. He remembered how difficult it had been to make the decision to leave her and strike for the city, in the hopes of finding help for both himself and Kota, and decided that must have been his first inkling that the lass had become more than a simple guide to him.

He suspected she was much more than that to Evin, and probably had been for much longer.

Sighing deeply, Brandt took another swig of ale. She was right about Evin, too, and he was going to have to tell his brother about Ràza. Before the monster found him and told him himself, in whatever twisted, evil way such a creature would. How had the Val'gren found them? Discovered their identity? Hunted them down like animals for slaughter? Eirik, Brandt, and Evin had been the only ones who knew of their quest—even their mother had been kept in the dark, though Brandt suspected she had known more than they told her. She was a princess, after all, had been through the process of crowning a new King before with her own brother. Eirik's quest, thirty years prior, had been similar to theirs—find the Sword of Laresh, one of their ancestors whose weapon had been stolen centuries before. The quest, while not easy, had been possible at least; there had been a lead on the sword long before Eirik came of age. His final test as Crown Prince had been to follow the lead til it ended—and either bring the sword home, or tell of its final loss. For his son Gunnar, the King had crafted such a quest: reports had trickled in when the Crown Prince was still a stripling, of the First Crest of the Vaeärne, an amulet of untold value and, if the stories were to be believed, magical power. Further, more recent, investigation had tracked it to the Lair of the Beast, north of Retwood, and Gunnar's *jofurr aetla*, his Crown Quest, had been thus assigned: he was to retrieve the amulet. He had been allowed to choose one companion, but no one else was to know of the quest, as was tradition. Gunnar had chosen Brandt.

When he had died, both the crown and the quest had fallen to Brandt instead, who'd had little choice but to bring Evin, for the younger knew of the quest without being told and had threatened to follow him from afar if Brandt did not bring him along. He didn't normally respond well to threats of that nature, especially from someone he'd *taught* how to track the way Evin did, but Brandt wasn't convinced all was well in the Court of the King. Someone had given Gunnar's position away that fateful day, there was no other explanation for it, and it stood to reason all the male heirs to the Throne were likely in grave danger, if there were a spy among the court. Of course, taking Evin meant leaving no one behind to protect Eirik, but Brandt had many secrets, and one of the weightier ones was the knowledge that between Eirik and Evin, his loyalties lay entirely with his younger brother.

Given Evin's parentage, that may have made him a traitor in some eyes. Perhaps even in Uncle Eirik's. He did not care.

"What have you ordered us, Brother?" Evin smiled as he flopped down in the chair to Brandt's left, reaching for his foamy mug.
Brandt allowed a small grin to form as his brother tasted the ale, groaning at the taste of something other than water or tea. It really was very good ale. "Nothing, yet. I did not know what you wanted to eat."

"I could eat anything," the younger man responded with a good-natured laugh. "I'm hungry enough to eat a moose."

Ryn joined them then, a hand reaching down automatically to tangle in Kota's fur, but the lynx wasn't with them. To no one's pleasure at all, Ryn had sent him to skirt the town gates and find somewhere warm to hunker down. Both men had protested, until she explained that no one liked a large wild cat hanging around their inn, and it was hardly the first time they had utilized this arrangement, she and Kota.

That did not mean she was happy about it. Flexing her hand, the girl sighed and moved to grab her own tankard. "Ale?" she asked, and Brandt nodded. "Good." She sucked down half the tankard in one go, then met both their eyes, practically daring either of them to say a word about it.

Neither did.

"I have been doing some thinking," Ryn said, eyes tired and face drawn. She looked much better than she'd been immediately after healing Evin, but still not fully well.

Brandt felt his stomach flip with uncertainty—what was swirling behind those green eyes? Would she betray his trust? Ryn took a deep breath to gather herself, then said very quickly, "There is something neither of you know about me. My mother was Laendorian, as I've told you, and I grew up in Bren Valley. But my father..." She swallowed, studied her tankard for a moment. "He was from Southdale, and it was no secret." She studied their reactions for a moment—but this was nothing terribly surprising to either man, socially unacceptable though it was, and now Brandt realized perhaps part of the reason she'd been on her own for so long.

Not exactly enemies, Southdale and Laendor weren't precisely allies, either, and neither country would want to claim one so obviously half-bred. When neither of them said anything, Ryn continued earnestly, as though she needed to convince them. "Papa was a good man. He'd been cast out of his home in the south, why exactly I never learned, but he and Mama loved each other more than any couple I've ever seen. They were excellent parents. Papa showed me how to hunt and track and gather, how to survive anywhere, and what plants will heal instead of kill." She blinked rapidly, hard, took a slightly shaky breath. "He could make anything grow anywhere, and served our town faithfully as a healer for years, but no one there liked him because he was a foreigner. I took more after him than Mama." She shifted uncomfortably, looking down at her cup again.

So folk hadn't liked her much there, either, if she took after her foreign father.

"Talos was like Mama, though," she smiled. Brandt didn't know who Talos was, though he suspected he must be the long-lost brother Ryn mentioned from time to time. "He was the pride and joy of Arodar. My uncle had even named him his heir to be lord of our lands."

Arodar. He knew the town. It had been destroyed a decade or so ago by a vicious Val'gren attack. Lord Rayleng and his entire family had died. Pieces slotted into place, and Brandt's eyes widened.

"He deserved better," Evin murmured from his side, reaching across the table to put a hand on Ryn's where she fiddled with her tankard. She stilled and sighed.

"They all did."

Brandt felt for Ryn, he did. He'd suspected she had some tragic history, but he hadn't known how extensive it was or how closely their stories resembled one another. His life, too, had been shattered by the Val'gren, more than once, though he'd been lucky enough to get to keep his mother and brother, at least. He felt a kinship with his wandering friend that was entirely new.

"I'm sorry about your family," Brandt said gently. "Thank you for telling us." Ryn managed a small smile for him, then leaned back and sighed softly.

"Why bring this up now?" Evin asked suddenly from beside him. He took another sip of ale before continuing. "Obviously you've fulfilled your contract; we made it to Retwood in one piece." He laughed a little, a brittle sound. "Stars, I'd say you went above and beyond to make sure that happened. You must really need that access to the Archives. But why tell us this now, at the end of the job? Did you think it would matter to us that you're half Southdaler?"

Ryn shook her head. "Because I—" she started, then paused. A second later, she huffed in annoyance and emptied her tankard. She set the tin pint down deliberately and looked Evin in the eyes, then Brandt.
He waited, intrigued to hear her answer. Ryn set her jaw visibly. "Because somewhere along the road, this became more than a job. I trust you both to see past my parentage and remember all the times I've proven my worth. Our contract may be fulfilled, but Kota and I wish to accompany you to the end of your quest and see you safely home."

Brandt forcibly schooled his features so she didn't see his surprise. He knew Evin held Ryn in high regard, and he himself trusted her implicitly; but he'd never been convinced she was the type to let a job get too personal.

Then again, this job had been extremely personal for all of them since Thaliondris. Frankly, he found himself relieved she didn't want to cut and run, for the journey back was to be nearly as dangerous as the journey here.

"Well, you have to come to Sannfold anyway to obtain...payment...for your services," he said, smiling kindly. "Perhaps we should all just go together."

Evin grinned, and Brandt knew it was the right choice. She and Kota would be invaluable on the way back, even though that hadn't been their original commitment. "Do you wish to agree on another contract?"

Ryn looked affronted, and both he and Evin laughed outright. "I thought not." As the serving girl passed, Brandt asked her for three more ales. She nodded once and moved to retrieve them.

"Brandt and I feel the same way, you know," Evin added, once the laughter quieted and they were all properly stocked with more ale. "You're more than just a guide now, you're a friend. Frankly, we both owe you a blood debt several times over—"

Ryn held up a forestalling hand. "If you truly count me a friend, do not keep account, Evin. I'll hear none of it."

"Well then," Brandt answered, raising his freshly refilled tankard. Evin followed suit, then Ryn. "I'll drink to that."

And they did.

All three ate a quick meal of roast lamb and hearty bread, full of the companionable silence that comes from complete exhaustion and total unity of purpose, finished their drinks, and retired to bed. The next day would be one of resting and refitting, the last they would see on this side of the quest. The Beast's Lair awaited.

It was a wet night, the darkness near complete as the clouds covered the moon and stars. As the Watchman called the hour past midnight, a lone figure picked its way through the muddy streets. Well-armed and dressed for traveling far and fast, no one challenged him as he slipped out of the town gates uncontested.

20

Ryn woke hard with a knot in her stomach, a few hours after falling asleep. She sat up quickly, examining the darkness of her room in an attempt to locate anything amiss, scratching her head distractedly. Her brain itched. Nothing seemed to be wrong; the room was warm and quiet, the embers of her dying fire still glowing dimly in the fireplace. There was no sense of immediate danger, nothing that gave her pause inside these four walls.

Still something, *something* wasn't right. She scratched her head again and threw off the covers. Dressing quickly and pulling back her sleep-mussed mop of hair, she grabbed her staff and left her room, navigating the inn's few corridors until she stepped out into the fresh night air. All seemed well; the homes and buildings around her were dark and quiet, the wind rustling through the nearby trees. She sucked in a deep breath, letting the bracing breeze chase away any remaining sleepiness, trying to hone in on what was bothering her. But even out here, all seemed quiet—

The punch of adrenaline hit her just before the ear-piercing scream did. She was running before she quite knew what she was doing, headed toward the city walls. She knew that sound—unfortunately, so did the guards, and a wild animal—a lynx—that close to town was as likely as not to get shot just for being there.

The fuss caught her eye as the walls came into view; several guards above her and to the left were talking in low, urgent tones, and an archer was running toward them across the rampart. It didn't take a scholar to realize what was happening, and Ryn shouted her alarm even as she took the steps up to the wall by twos.

"Wait!" she bellowed, reaching the top and not stopping. The guards had seen her now, and were gathered in a knot with their weapons out. Their expressions ranged from wary to outright dangerous, and Ryn slowed as she neared, noting that the archer's attention was on her as well. "Wait, please, don't shoot!"

The highest-ranking guard's eyes narrowed. "Shoot what, lass? The crier hasn't given news of what the threat is yet."

She cocked an eyebrow. "I heard the sound." The archer moved, as though he'd just remembered why he was there, and Ryn dashed in front of him—a near-suicidal move at the best of times, and this man had an arrow nocked already, but she barely cared. "Don't!"

The archer glared and made to shove past her, while the one who'd spoken before asked, "Ain' no other way, lady. We don' like killin' them neither, but this un's too close to town. We gotta keep 'em scared of us, or they'll—"

"He's mine!" she shouted, standing her ground. Blanket silence met her words, looks of pity and wariness transforming into suspicion instantly. Lynxes were rarely even seen, much less tamed; in their eyes, she was either a liar or a sorceress.

"Your'n, is he?" the commander's eyes narrowed severely.

Ryn swallowed. "Just...let me go to him. I'll take him away from here and you won't have to deal with him again." She patted the air in a conciliatory gesture. They appeared unmoved, so she let some of her fear show on her face. "Please, we mean you no harm, we are just passing through town and I left him outside the walls to avoid any alarm."

"Then why is he here now?" the archer asked, voice low and threatening.

"Something must have gone wrong." Ryn looked back to the leader. Large he may be, but the man obviously wasn't a bad sort. Just doing his job, he was. "Please let me go."

After a moment of consideration, the big man lowered his sword and nodded. His guards did the same, and Ryn shot off toward the side. She vaulted over it, managing to catch a couple of handholds on the way down so that the impact, though jarring, didn't leave her broken and gasping at the bottom. She hit the ground running, and barely saw his large shadow before Kota was there before her. He nudged her face with his nose and mewled in his throat, pawing at her and rearing backward any time she tried to soothe him.

"*Kisa*," she murmured, reaching for him, but he dodged her again, clearly wanting her to follow him. "Kota, settle. What are you doing here? What's wrong?"

"Ryn?" The shout came from atop the city gate, not far from where she knelt, and she recognized the voice.

"Down here, Evin," she called back, moving out of the trees and into the light, keeping Kota behind her in case the guards decided to change their mind about the lynx's safety. "Something's wrong with Kota."

"Perhaps the same thing that is wrong with my brother," Evin responded, worry clear on his face even from this distance. Ryn felt a ball of anxiety coalesce in her stomach. "He's gone."

She took a deep breath, trying to figure out Brandt's angle here. It would make sense that if Kota had seen the elder Prince, he would come fetch Ryn as quickly as possible—but she didn't like what that implied. Did Brandt really intend to take on the Beast by himself? How?

Better yet, why?

"Settle our account at the inn and get our things," Ryn called up to Evin. "Kota and I will wait down the road a half-span or so." Here, she looked to the big guard. "Will that satisfy you, sir?"

He nodded, and she turned, clicking her tongue at Kota. The lynx, apparently glad to be moving in the right direction, bounded ahead of her, down the road. Evin disappeared from the wall, presumably to do as she had said, so Ryn went to the spot she said she'd be and waited.

~~~~~~~~~~

Brandt moved as quickly as he dared through the pitch-black night. The moon was new, the sky clouded, so there was no light at all from the heavens, and he traveled in near-complete darkness.

How appropriate, he thought. Appropriate that he be in the dark figuratively as well as literally, for he really had no idea what he was doing now. He knew only three things. The first, that the quest must be completed: the amulet must be recovered from the Beast in his lair—or he must wrench from the creature an account of its whereabouts and then go somewhere else to retrieve it. The second, that Evin must be left behind: this entire journey had been a mess, and his brother was closer than ever to finding out about his own identity in all the wrong ways. Brandt could not stomach the thought of Evin being told by a monster, or worse, taken by Râza or one of his brutes. The lad would be safe in Retwood.

He won't stay there, a voice whispered in Brandt's mind, one that sounded suspiciously like his common sense. *You know your brother, he'll come after you.*

He ignored it and kept moving. The third thing he knew, beyond all doubt and with all certainty, was that Râza knew what Evin was to him. He had hoped otherwise, tried to convince himself they were being hunted by the Val'gren simply because they were the last two remaining Princes of Laendor, and their ransom would be substantial indeed, tried to deny the truth that stared Evin in the eyes that night they had stood against Râza's hunting party.

Those blood-red eyes had sparked with recognition upon seeing his younger brother, and nothing had ever scared Brandt so badly.

Râza knew Evin was his son, and suddenly, the quest itself had become secondary; a nuisance, a chore to be completed before Brandt could get back to the real business of protecting his brother.

The implications of Râza knowing Evin were immense and terrifying. How long had the monster known? Had Evin been observed before they even left Sannfold? Had Râza's agents ever been close to him, seen him, *touched* him?

Had this entire quest been a giant trap to lure in his brother?

He did not know, and frankly thought it rather far-fetched—it had been Gunnar's quest originally, after all—but that did not matter; it was possible, and so he intended to keep Evin as far from the jaws of the trap as he could. The Beast's Lair was an eight hour walk north of Retwood. He would travel there and arrive by morning, perhaps just as his companions were waking. While they went about their business and began suspecting his absence, and then worrying and searching for him, he would be completing his task, recovering the amulet. By the time they mounted a search, he would be on his way back and perhaps run into them on the way.

Evin would be furious, and Ryn would quietly seethe, but the task would be done and they could make for the hunting lodge in Wellys at all speed. Brandt would get Evin back into the safety of their most isolated and well-protected family home, and then he would tell him the truth, with Mother by his side. They could tell him carefully, gently as possible, and give him time to absorb and process it before going back to Sannfold and presenting the amulet to Uncle Eirik.

He nodded to himself. Yes, that was a good plan. It was definitely the best he could hope for at this point.

On he walked, navigating by the sparse light of the stars and keeping his goal in mind. The sky began to lighten as he drew closer to the entrance of the Beast's lair, and he hoped that this day would see the end of a creature that had terrorized Retwood for years. Once upon a time, the townspeople had thought to do something about it, but the war party consisting of every able-bodied male and some of the females had been decimated entirely. It had nearly destroyed the town. So now, they kept watch, but did not make any particular challenge to the Beast, for the creature was formidable beyond telling.

Brandt was going to take him on single-handedly.

Son of Signy, he congratulated himself. *This is either the bravest or the most dimwitted thing you've ever done.*

The entrance arrived almost as suddenly as the dawn did, a yawning cave mouth that was unnaturally dark just beyond its rough stone arch. The contrast was so great between the inside of the cavern, dark and cold that seeped into his bones, and the warmth of the sun rousing the birds to sing cheerily in its dappled light, that Brandt just had to stand and wonder at it for several full minutes.

What am I doing?

At last, he pulled himself from his reverie, gathered his courage, and moved from the light into the dark.

21

Evin was angrier than he could ever remember being. The night air was cool on his face, but still he felt warm, and he knew if the light were better, his ears would be visibly red. His heart pounded in his chest and his breath felt short, but very little of it was because of the grueling pace he and Ryn had silently agreed upon. Pine needles crunched under his feet, the stars shone brightly overhead, and the air smelled sweet and fresh, but none of it held any appeal for him, not now.

His giant oaf of an idiotic, chivalrous, stupid brother had left to take on the worst of the quest alone. The Beast was no trifle; Evin had fallen asleep reviewing everything known about the creature in an attempt to manage some sort of attack plan—an entire army had once tried to kill the thing and failed, but sometimes numbers would lose where cunning could win out. He'd drifted off with the seedlings of a plan dancing around his skull, the very beginning of an idea that could have caught the thing off guard and seen them all home safely, Crest in hand.

But Brandt had other ideas, apparently. Ideas he felt no need to share, and battle lust he felt no need to temper with wisdom.

No, Evin thought, that was not like his brother. Brandt was the eldest in every way; far more steady and intense than Evin himself, more like to think a decision to death than make it too quickly. Brandt wasn't being rash. He had a good reason and a strategy for what he was doing.

Really, that hurt Evin worse than if Brandt had just rushed off half-cocked. The man wasn't being hotheaded; he was deliberately excluding Evin, probably because of some motherly, misplaced desire to protect him, and in the process he was going to get himself killed. Evin wondered if his noble, hard-nosed simpleton of a brother had considered where that would leave him. Evin without Brandt was…was…

Well, it was not an idea to be borne, for one thing.

"You're quiet," Ryn remarked, falling back to walk beside him. Kota moved silently ahead, barely a whisper in the still night, a dark shadow moving amongst pine and asley—and his mistress was nearly as invisible. Evin couldn't even hear her breathing right next to him. Not for the first time, he understood how she'd survived all these years in the wilderness. He scowled, not that she could see it.

"Brandt is an idiot," he answered. *A dead idiot, if we can't reach him in time.* He ignored how his chest constricted at the thought.

"Your brother wishes only to keep you safe," Ryn said quietly. He almost retorted to that, but she didn't give him time before continuing. "Though I happen to agree this is a foolish way to do it. His place is at your side, as yours is at his."

"We are stronger together," Evin insisted, echoing the mantra their war masters had pounded into their skulls since they were but lads. "Fire and ice, they call us at home. He's the steady lion, I the unpredictable fox."

Ryn chuckled. "I can see it," she agreed. "But a lion may take on many beasts alone."

Evin's eyes narrowed and his face felt hotter. "Not as many as he can with the fox by his side."

Ryn stopped so quietly he wasn't even aware of her absence until her hand closed round his arm. He turned to face her, a wraith in the dark, moonlight dappling her dark hair as she lowered her hood. Now he could see her face, sort of. She looked immeasurably sad.

"I am only saying don't be too angry with him," Ryn said. "Brandt loves you and wants to keep you from harm."

Evin clenched his jaw. "I'm no child, Ryn. That's not his call to make. There is a reason a prince is assigned a companion for his *jofurr aetla*! Brandt needs me as I need him—we're safest at one another's sides!" His breath came out in a great shaky rush. "And he knows it too. Something else is going on, something not right. He's been acting strangely since the fight with the Val'gren."

Ryn reached for him, squeezed his good shoulder. "Evin, we almost lost you that night. It shook him."

A feline growl interrupted them, and Evin turned to see Kota's yellow eyes glowing nearby. The lynx pawed at the ground impatiently. Ryn smiled.

"Let's go get him," she said quietly, bumping Evin's shoulder with her own as she passed.

He followed, still annoyed but at least heartened by her camaraderie. The lynx turned and bounded ahead, clearly in a hurry, stopping often to sniff this or that. Evin and Ryn followed, Evin's resolve renewed. He would save Brandt from whatever mess the man had gotten himself into, take his rightful place at his brother's back.

And then, when this was over, he intended to punch him square in the face.

~~~~~~~~~~

It didn't take long for it to become clear that this was more a stupid decision than a brave one. Brandt had snuck in as quietly as he could, but there was only one way in or out that he'd been able to scout. The cavern was huge, with a long winding entrance that was as dangerous as it was dark. It opened into a cave so massive he could not see the borders of it. He stuck to the edge wherever possible, a hand on the walls to help navigate. Sickly-blue orbs provided weak light in the long, rough-hewn corridor, but Brandt stayed in the shadows.

Idiot he may be, but he had no intention of offering himself up on a platter for the Beast.

Still, intentions are often for naught, and entering the Beast's manse— what would have been, he supposed, a great room or parlor—he was greeted by the sight of the Crest of the Vaeärne, displayed upon a pedestal in the very center of the room. He'd never seen it before, but he knew immediately what it was from artists' renderings, though the likenesses had been rather...embellished, it seemed.

The amulet was a rough-hewn stone, about the size and shape of Brandt's thumb, deep cobalt shot through with leaf green and set in a delicate gold wire that wrapped around the bottom and top in a graceful arc. At the top of the setting was a phoenix wrought in fiery gold, beak wide open in a cry, about to take flight—the family crest. The entire thing was mounted on a slender gold chain. All in all, it was small enough to fit in the palm of his hand. Brandt could just hear Evin's reaction to it.

We came all this way for that?

But he knew better. The house of Vaeärne, for all their royal status, had never stood too much on ceremony or gaudy rings and heavy furs and luxurious silks. He knew other royals did, and the Blackblade clan that had reigned for much of Laendor's rocky history did; but Brandt's ancestors had risen from poverty a mere five generations ago, and they never forgot it. Not even Evin, though he could be youthfully oblivious at times. Brandt thought the amulet—for all its simplicity that belied its value—perfectly symbolized their family and the understated potential within it.

Brandt wondered for a mere second why the amulet would be sitting out in the open like it was, but then nearly laughed at himself. Who would be stupid enough to walk in and take it?

Other than him, of course.

Not wasting a moment, he snatched the heirloom, stuffed it in a pocket, and turned to go.

"Rather too easy, do you not think?" came a mocking, raspy voice from the shadows to his left. Brandt spun, raising his sword, but there was nothing there. Instead, a laugh came next; a languid, lazy sound that seemed to come from everywhere rather than any one particular direction. He turned in a slow circle, straining his eyes against the shadows in an attempt to see something, anything.

One of the blue orbs went out.

Brandt moved fast, rolling to the edge of the room and placing the wall at his back, sword held before him in a defensive position, but still he could see nothing threatening. Another light blinked out of existence, dimming the room further and making it impossible to see much of anything anyway, but Brandt still tried.

"I've been expecting you, eldest Son of Signy," the voice came again, right next to his ear. Brandt flinched away in spite of himself, swinging his sword blindly and meeting nothing but air. The laugh sounded again, raising gooseflesh on the prince's arms. He said nothing.

"You followed our trail perfectly," the voice continued, this time right beside his other ear. "And you brought your dear little brother with you. How...*splendid*," the word sent chills down Brandt's spine. "Especially since he's the one we wanted all along."

With a roar of impotent rage, Brandt slashed in the direction he thought he heard the Voice, prompting another of those languorous laughs. The sound set his teeth on edge.

"How unfortunate for you that I left my brother behind," he growled, holding his sword in one hand and feeling along the wall for the exit with the other. He needed to get out of here, get Evin as far away from here as humanly possible. Intelligence on the Beast had been spotty at best, with only a few stories of the creature's horrors, but little useful information about its actual abilities or how to kill it; and Brandt wasn't very keen on Evin trying to find out.

"Ahh," the Voice tutted. "So you did. How unfortunate for *you* that he is coming anyway. My spies see all. But fear not." A laugh. "Young Evin is in no danger. Râza wants him not only alive, but well. You, on the other hand..."

Before Brandt could respond to that, the dimmed orbs came back on, and brighter than before, lighting up the entire room in an instant. Brandt squinted and blinked at the stabbing light, struggling to adjust. When he did, he felt all the blood leave his face.

The Beast had assumed a form.

~~~~~~~~~~

They came upon the Beast's Lair at last, shortly after the sun had risen. Ryn sucked sweet morning air into her starving lungs—they had run the last few miles, some horrible sense of dread driving Evin on. He'd given her nothing by way of explanation, simply begun running and expected her to follow.

She had.

The air around the place smelled rotted, decayed. The darkness was so complete, Ryn felt the first stirrings of actual fear. Kota trilled, a gentle sound intended to comfort, and pressed his nose into her palm. Ryn smiled and stroked his furry ears.

"You have done so well, my *kisa*," she whispered to him. "I am proud of you." The lynx pushed up into her caress, bunting her with his head, and she laughed despite her budding terror. "Now comes the hard part."

Evin had not taken his eyes off the entrance to the cave since they arrived. Now he looked to her, his eyes hard and cold as amber, his face set.

"Are you ready?" he asked.

Ryn would have followed him to any one of the seven hells at that moment.

"I am."

They plunged into the dark together.

The corridor was long and serpentine, with plenty of uneven knots to trip upon, but they made it through with no incident. When they reached the end of it, Ryn sucked in a quiet, surprised breath at the vista that opened up before her, burying her fingers in Kota's fur and twisting just hard enough to stop the lynx in his tracks. He didn't take much convincing, baring his teeth silently as he stood beside her. She sensed rather than saw Evin halt on her other side, a short chuff of air his only sound.

"By the Astra," she whispered.

The Beast clearly wasn't a simple animal; the stalagmites in the cavern had been filed to a smooth black shine with deadly sharp points, eerie blue light shone from floating orbs placed strategically throughout the main cavern, and crowning it all was a well-built stone home almost large enough to be called a castle. The blue light created shadows in strange places, shifting as they floated, giving the entire scene a surreal, flat quality.

A shout of distress reached them from inside the manse, and Evin started forward with a growl of his brother's name. Ryn caught the crook of his elbow, but he twisted away.

"Don't ask me to wait outside," he warned.

Ryn shook her head. "I would never. But if you storm in there without thinking, you'll get yourself killed." Evin did not argue the point, so she continued. "Let Kota and I sneak in first, get the lay of the land. Give us sixty seconds and then come."

Evin didn't look happy about it, but he nodded. "Just do it quickly." Ryn hugged him tightly then motioned to Kota, who melted into the shadows at her left, while she moved to the right and crept inside.

A massive arched foyer met them just the other side of the entrance, and at least one of the Astra was smiling upon them: they had to go no further to find Brandt. The Beast, Ryn could not yet see, but Brandt was on his knees in the very center of the room, face bloodied. Strange runes were etched into the stone surrounding him, and they glowed black and purple, sending tendrils of wicked-looking light through the man in their midst. Ignoring the way rage bloomed in her chest at the sight, Ryn snuck behind one of the mighty mineral pillars that decorated the place, trying to stay hidden but get a better look.

She could learn nothing here, so she ducked forward a few pillars and tried again.

What she saw froze the blood in her veins to ice.

Brandt was standing over the kneeling figure, a look on his face she never thought she'd see; it was cruel triumph, all arrogance and brutality. Confused, Ryn looked back to the man on his knees and had to bite back a full-on gasp.

Her eyes had not deceived her. It was Brandt, golden head bowed and shoulders bent.

Brandt was standing over.... *Brandt?*...gloating. Laughing, now.

"You are forsaken, as you always knew you would be. It was our intention to draw your brother here, but I think my Master will not mind destroying what of the Royal House I manage to get my hands on—"

"You'll not touch him!" Evin stepped into the weak light. His face was washed white as a ghost, and it contrasted frighteningly with his dark hair and eyes that looked black in the flat light. Ryn felt her heart skip a beat in fear at the look on his face.

It was nothing short of deadly.

But the impostor Brandt merely smiled blandly. "Oh, I'll definitely touch him, and you will more than allow it once you hear what I have to say."

22

"Evin!" Brandt shouted from the floor, lurching to his feet. Ryn nocked an arrow as the Beast kicked the back of his knees out from under him and followed it with a blow to the back of the head that had the Prince curling forward, resting his head on his forearms as he struggled to remain conscious with a moan.

That was all it took for the younger of Signy's sons. Evin leapt, covering the distance between his writhing brother and the monster that wore his face in a single bound, sword raised high. At that exact moment, a snarl sounded from the shadows, just behind the blur of lynx that pounced at the Beast, and Ryn held her arrow at bay to avoid hitting an ally. The Beast simply waved his hand, and both man and wild cat went flying in the opposite direction they'd intended. Kota skidded across the rough stone floor back into the darkness, making Ryn shudder, while Evin smacked hard enough into one of the pillars that it cracked beneath the force. The Prince's head thumped into the mineral stone, and Ryn swallowed bile as she made her move. Her arrow flew straight and true, only to be plucked from thin air by the monster that wasn't Brandt. He turned and grinned in her direction.

But Evin had pulled himself upright already, swaying a little from the blow to his head, shuddering against what Ryn knew was a horrifying headache.

"You will *not* touch him," the prince repeated, just as dangerously as before.

"And you, clearly, will not touch me," Not-Brandt laughed. "Sit down, Evin," he waved a hand and Evin fell back against the pillar, his legs folding and rump hitting the ground none too gently. Ryn began to move, knowing it was important not to stay still long enough for the Beast to get a lock on her location. A quick glance into her magic told her Kota was fine; up and moving silently too, in the shadows across the circular room.

The Beast was still talking. "And let me tell you something your dear sweet brother has kept from you."

"Stop," Brandt murmured weakly from his place inside the circle, raising his head slowly. It clearly took a lot of effort, and Ryn winced in sympathy. Not-Brandt grinned at the bloodied prince before fixing his gaze on Evin, who stared back stubbornly.

"Did you know you were fathered by a monster, little brother?" Not-Brandt asked conversationally. Ryn shot again, this time from directly behind the creature, but he caught the arrow again, mere centimeters from the back of his skull.

He turned, that terrifying smile etched on his face although carven from stone. "Come now, pretty archer, come out to play." Ryn found herself yanked forward by some invisible force, thrown through the air until she landed, skidding hard on her knees and looking up at Brandt's face leering down at her. The Beast paused, lifted her with his magic so he could look her in the eye. Ryn thrashed in midair, struggling to get free and hoping to keep the creature's attention on her, not Evin.

He could not find out like this.

"Let me go, you motherless swine," she commanded, teeth bared. Not-Brandt laughed out loud, the sound very much like the Crown Prince's own laugh, only less joyful and more cruel.

"Shall I?" he taunted, then stepped closer, moving his face to her neck and inhaling long and slow. Ryn choked on something like a whimper, refusing to give him the satisfaction. Instead, she snarled and kicked toward the creature's shin only to find her leg completely unresponsive. She nearly panicked at that, squirming against the intrusion of the Beast's nose near her vulnerable neck. After a long minute, Not-Brandt drew back, and the look on his face was neither teasing nor amused.

"Well," he said thoughtfully, "you really are something else entirely, aren't you, little one?"

"Let us go, or you'll wish you never laid eyes on me," Ryn threatened. She didn't dare glance down at Evin, who she knew was struggling to rise, lest she direct the Beast's attention to him. If he could just reach his sword...

Suddenly, Kota came out of nowhere, teeth and claws both bared, aiming for the creature's throat. He never made it the whole way, but his claws raked the Beast's shoulder, leaving deep gouges that bled black, and the attack drew enough of the creature's attention that Ryn fell to the floor, knees buckling. Not stopping to think, she released her staff from its back sheath and struck Not-Brandt upside the head even as he threw Kota off entirely. Her lynx landed in the shadows with a thump and a whine, but Ryn knew he'd be back up again in mere moments. The Beast had barely been knocked off balance by her blow, but now he was angry. With a growl of rage, he raised a hand, slamming Ryn against a nearby pillar and holding her there. She snarled, squirming.

"I'll come back to you in a moment," he promised, turning his attention back to Evin, who'd managed to get his hands on his sword and came up swinging. Almost bored, the Beast sighed and threw him back with his magic again. From the corner, Brandt moaned in distress at the treatment of his little brother.

"As I was *saying*," the Beast continued. "Pay attention, Evin. Your whore of a mother was kidnapped by the Val'gren just before you were conceived, did you know that?"

Evin just glared.

The creature sighed and waved a hand lazily. One of the blackest runes in the stone circle glowed bright for just a moment, and Brandt began choking in the center, bent over and spitting up blood. "There," he smiled. "Answer."

"Yes!" Evin shouted. "Stop it! Yes, I know that!"

Ryn pulled at her invisible bonds, knowing Brandt was going to need more than bandages if they hoped to get out of here alive.

Not-Brandt smiled. "Do you know what they did to her while they had her?"

"Quiet!" Ryn shouted. She didn't even want to hear this, and it wasn't her mother they were speaking of. All she knew was that if she had been made to suffer such a humiliating, horrifying torture, she'd not want it bandied about like a bad joke. Not-Brandt's smile was making her stomach churn. She needed to stop this, and now...

There. Kota was nearby, and up. She willed him to attack the Beast, just once more, so she could get to him. She had her Y'rai knife; she would not miss this time.

As if he read her mind, Kota leapt out from the shadows, this time on the creature's left, right beside Ryn. She gasped as the bonds holding her loosened, and in one smooth motion surged forward even as she drew the dagger. The blow made it home, the mountain-forged steel burying itself neatly in the Beast's chest. The monster screamed his rage as his chosen form winked in and out of existence a couple of times, tossing Ryn aside like a leaf in the wind. She flew backward and hit the stone, then blackness descended.

~~~~~~~~~~

"Ryn!" Evin shouted, though he didn't slow his course. Taking advantage of the Beast's injury, he drew his own hunting knife and threw it, aiming for the creature's chest. The wild toss went low, and instead sunk hilt-deep in its belly. Evin didn't stop to watch the result, just lurched toward his hurt brother, barely hesitating at the border of the rune circle until Brandt choked a warning.

"Don't, Evin, no!" The elder's eyes were fluttering as he tried to stay conscious, and he began fumbling for something in his left pocket. Evin went to his knees on the very edge of a purplish rune, hating desperately that he couldn't reach Brandt. He was so *close*, if he could just touch him, pull him out of there…

"Brandt!" Evin called urgently. "Come toward me, brother, I can't do this on my own. Come on!" Brandt's breathing was all funny, shallow and too quick and wheezy, and Evin didn't want to think about what that meant. His brother shook his head, his hair lank and sweaty, his hands shaking.

"I cannot," Brandt confessed, heavy and pained like it hurt him to even breathe. "The runes…something holds me here. It's like being stabbed with a thousand blades, Evin, I don't know how to…" Shaking himself, Brandt seemed to gather his strength and whipped his right hand out. He shrieked in agony as he brought it back to his chest, but his goal was accomplished—a small stone on a golden chain bounced to the floor at Evin's left knee. He looked down to see that Brandt had given him the Crest of the Vaeärne. The blue crystal was glowing as brightly as those evil runes, making the gold phoenix seem almost alive.

"Put it on," Brandt coughed, spitting more blood. It speckled his white lips, and Evin stifled a sob. He couldn't lose Brandt, it wasn't an option. Still, he did as he was told, and his brother smiled for a moment, before his wide gaze fixed on something over Evin's shoulder and he gasped. Evin turned, sword at the ready, but his blood froze in his veins and he doubted he'd have been able to use it anyway.

A tall figure loomed over them, strong and slender and red-eyed, Y'rai knife and his own hunting knife still buried in its torso, blood blooming black as night around the wounds, too slowly. But the face…it was *Evin's*. Cruelly contorted, expression one of triumphant malice, but his own face nevertheless. Evin's heart dropped into his stomach as he tried to stand. The Beast grabbed him by the collar and yanked him close, grinning.

"You are Râza's son, Prince Evin, and it's time for you to come into your own as his Heir."

No.

~~~~~~~~~~

Ryn woke to Kota pawing at her insistently, using a bit more claw than was strictly necessary, nipping her fingers and pushing at her. She sat up as quickly as she could, noticing two things immediately after confirming that her lynx was all right. First, Evin and the Beast—who now looked like *him*, which was just all kinds of strange—were locked in a strange sort of silent battle, staring each other down. Second, Brandt was about two minutes from dying. Her Sight told her he had suffered massive internal damage and was bleeding out into his own body.

By all that's good and holy, no, please.

She grabbed her staff, which had fallen nearby, and threw herself toward the Crown Prince, yelping as the light from the runes touched her for only a moment. Ryn didn't know how to fight the magic, so she did the only thing she could; she looped her elbows under the Prince's armpits and pulled him toward the edge of the runes. It was like pulling him through sucking mud. The magic didn't seem to want to let him go, and lances of agony kept stabbing through her nerves, but Ryn kept pulling. Finally, *finally*, she broke him free and laid him flat, ignoring the discomfiting fact that Evin and the Beast were still staring one another down, something around Evin's neck glowing bright blue. Ryn shook the distraction out of her mind, readjusted her grip on her staff, and placed her free hand at the nape of Brandt's neck. Kota trilled and nudged the Prince's shoulder before assuming a guard stance. Reaching for her magic, Ryn kissed his head and got to work.

~~~~~~~~~~

Râza's son? Was such a thing possible? Mother had been kidnapped, he knew that much, but he had always assumed—since he was old enough to understand how these things worked—that she had conceived shortly after her return, probably as a celebratory reunion of his parents. It was in his name, even; Valevin, as it was in it's completion, meant child of joy. Why would his mother call him so if he were the result of a...of a...

He could not name the crime, not even in his mind. It was too heinous, too terrifying to think about.

It could not be true. It could *not*.

He was his father's son, Torin's son, and Brandt's brother. Where would he go, what would he do, who would he be without those?

No.

Evin's denial, the pain and rage and fear, all swirled together into one massive emotion that made his head swim; it coalesced from an emotion into an intention, and Evin barely noticed the bright bluish light that began to emanate from outside the circle of runes, so focused was he on those red eyes before him. The amulet began to heat, searing the skin of his chest and lending its golden light to the Beast's borrowed features.

~~~~~~~~~~

Ryn was locked in a battle of her own, fighting for the life of Laendor's Crown Prince, against time itself. At first she fought with her magic, trying to bring it under her control, but within seconds had given that up and simply let it flow. She found herself merely a vessel for the

184

healing magic, drawing energy from the sparse underground life and giving to Brandt, coaxing his broken body back to wholeness. The strange plants in the room died within moments, and Ryn began stealing from the Beast, siphoning his nasty, dirty life force into his victim. Vaguely, she registered a sense of revulsion at that.

~~~~~~~~~~

"Râza is coming for you, young one," The Beast smiled.

Suddenly filled with a power Evin had never experienced before, he drove his sword mercilessly into the creature's belly, then tilted the blade up and pierced its heart. Gold fire ran along the edge of his blade, and this time, the Beast choked, red eyes rolling back and then disappearing entirely as the monster reverted to its true form—an old man—before expiring on the stone floor.

"Let him come," Evin spat.

~~~~~~~~~~

The creature thumped to the cold stone, dead. Ryn gasped when his life magic, evil as it had been, winked out of existence.

And suddenly, there was death all around. The Beast was gone, dead, and the only life left in this barren place was that of the brothers, Kota, and her. Stealing from either of them was out of the question. A memory blasted its way to the forefront of her mind, as clear as the day she'd sat in the garden with Kenelm and learned to See.

"Can I give of my own energy to heal?"

Kenelm frowned. "You're capable of that, yes, but it is not advisable. You could die."

Without hesitation, Ryn gathered the magic, then pulled from her own red-and-silver aura, pouring her life force into Brandt; she could hear her own cry of agony, far away, primal fear taking over her brain, trying to make her stop stealing from the source of her own life, but she shoved it back.

Brandt. Brandt was what mattered.

She gasped; breathing was becoming difficult, and she couldn't even tell if it was going to be enough, by the Astra it *hurt....*

Her heart thumped painfully in her chest, once, something cracked in her ears like thunder, and everything went black.

23

She was held captive by icy chains, shivering in a cutting wind.

The Beast stood before her, wearing Evin's face with those hideous red eyes, grinning maniacally. The expression made her howl with rage and despair when written on her friend's handsome features. "You thought you could cheat death for the Son of Signy, did you, pretty thing?" Not-Evin laughed. "It matters not. He is dead now, and Kota too. Evin has taken his place at his father's side. I have won."

Images assaulted her; she could not close her eyes:

Brandt, gasping for breath through a lung punctured by three arrows...

Kota's body, broken on the rocks of a dead valley, ugly gray-skinned nagrat stabbing into his flesh with their crude knives, preparing him for butchering...she stopped breathing, a second scream ripping itself from her throat at the sight...

Evin kneeling before her, blood streaming down his chest from a severed throat as he begged her, "Ryn, help me....please help me...."

And above it all, the Beast's arrogant, lazy laugh echoed.

Faintly, someone called her name. Was it her name? She couldn't remember anymore. But the voice was warm, forcing a throb from her frozen solid heart and melting the ice around her wrists and ankles...

"Ryn, I'm here. I'm here and I'm not going to leave you."

Who...?

It didn't really matter, anything was better than the monster's laugh.

She welcomed the blackness that descended, exhausted and grieving.

Ryn first became aware she was fighting to regain consciousness on the frayed edge of a horrible vision.

Mama, Papa, Talos, their home...so much death, everywhere.

You're dreaming.

Evin, Brandt, Kota...they lay before her, blood pooling beneath them; but Evin was stirring weakly....

She had to heal him! But she could not; her power failed him, her grasp on the magic slipping at the wrong moment, a victorious Râza crowing his triumph over her friend's broken body.

Wake up!

She sat bolt upright, gasping, surrounded by darkness. There was a tiny lamp in the dark room, giving off a bit of light, and she was swathed in

186

blankets on a bed. Kota was awake beside her, blinking slowly as he lay at her side, and her eyes filled with tears at the sight of him whole and hale.

He's alive, he's not broken and dead at the bottom of a ravine, nagrat crowing in delight at their victory, at their kill...

She shoved the thought away, throwing her arms around the warm lynx and letting loose a cry of sheer joy. Kota purred loudly, licking her shoulder and nuzzling her head as she held him close. He crawled into her lap, almost knocking her over but she refused to let go, tears wetting his fur.

"Gods, Ryn, you're alive!" someone croaked, voice breaking. Ryn looked up to see Evin's—*thank Aeos, golden*—eyes blazing before he folded her in a hard hug that stole her breath away. She let him, too happy he was alive and well to protest. Besides, he was warmer even than Kota, and she was *freezing*. After several long seconds, he pulled back and held her at arm's length, choking on something she wasn't sure wasn't a sob. "You're all right!"

She nodded, heart still pounding as the nightmares of the last days dissipated slowly. The movement made her dizzy and she swayed. "Brandt?"

Evin shushed her gently as he supported her neck, pressing her to lie back down. "Brandt is fine," he answered. "We feared you might not be, though. You were completely unconscious for seven days, Ryn. What did you *do?*"

She swallowed and moaned, pain making itself known now that she was awake. "He was dying. I couldn't...let...I...healed him."

Evin nodded, absently stroking her cheek. It felt soothing, so Ryn didn't slap his hand away like she might have normally. "You did, but at what cost to yourself?"

"Does it matter?" she asked, fixing him with a piercing glare—as piercing a glare as she could manage, anyway. Evin shifted uncomfortably. She narrowed her eyes when he didn't answer immediately. "What's going on, Evin?"

Her friend didn't say anything for a long time, staring hard at the rough wood floor beneath his feet. After a few moments he took a shaking breath. "Brandt lied to me," he said quietly, and when he looked up, his eyes were hard. "For years, he lied to me. He knew...that...about me and he never said a damned thing!" A muscle in his jaw clenched and unclenched quickly as the prince tried to control his rampaging emotions. Ryn felt her heart sink—she'd expected this, and it couldn't have happened in a worse way.

"He was trying to protect you—"

"Don't defend him!" Evin nearly shouted. He stood and paced the floor furiously. "I can't, Ryn, don't you see? I can't go back there now. I can't ever...face them, not after knowing...and he never even said!" She was stunned into silence, and he sat again with a sigh a moment later. "I'm sorry, I shouldn't burden you with all this immediately after you wake. Are you thirsty?"

She was incredibly thirsty, but she wanted to address this. She took a breath to say something more, but when he turned back with her cup of water, his eyes were so sad she couldn't bring herself to mention it again. She set the offered cup aside when he sat down on the edge of her pallet and laid a hand on his stubbled face. Tears ran over his cheeks and her fingers, and she whispered his name but could think of no other comforts. Words seemed cheap, so she let him hold her and weep for his lost innocence, for the horrific crime against his mother, for the pain of betrayal by a brother.

She hoped beyond hope he could someday find it in his heart to understand Brandt's impossible situation and forgive him. These two were far too close to consider the alternative. It would break them both.

Ryn squeezed Evin a little closer at the thought, suppressing a shiver—of cold or despair, she could not say.

~~~~~~~~~~~

Ryn's recovery was long and painful. It turned out giving one's own life force to heal another was rather a trauma, she thought wryly. At first, she could barely sit up for more than a few minutes at a time. Her temperature ran blistering hot to terribly cold and she suffered severe dizzy spells as her body struggled to regain its equilibrium.

Five days after waking, she was able to stand, for a moment. Three days after that she took her first, halting steps in the middle of the night when she refused to wake Evin to get her a cup of water. She got the water, though she spilled it all over herself and ended up having to wake him anyway to help her back to bed.

It was two and a half weeks before she was able to travel; their party moved slowly as they left Retwood amongst much pomp and circumstance—the townsfolk were overjoyed at the defeat of The Beast and shocked to discover they had sheltered their princes unawares.

Evin and Brandt followed the great road back to Sannfold—no need for secrecy now. The princes were returning triumphant, with the Beast dead and the Crest of the Vaeärne in hand, and word spread quickly. They were treated with respect and decency the entire way back, given free accommodations and meals, paraded through the streets of small towns as they worked their way back west. Both men made sure Ryn and Kota received the same treatment they did at every stop.

But all was not well within their little party. Evin was still painfully distant from Brandt, who seemed to have slipped into something of a depression after the wreckage the Beast had inflicted. His head pained him often, and Ryn, thinking she had done a shoddy job healing him back in the Beast's manse, insisted upon examining him the moment she was strong enough. She was shocked to find his aura fractured and sharp, the colors of his life force subdued in a way that bothered her, though she could find no evidence of physical injury; she didn't say anything to him, but she realized she was looking at a literally broken man. She snuck a look at Evin's aura that night as she tucked herself into her bedroll and wasn't surprised to find his looked much the same, except with more sharp edges. Evin was angry, deeply angry, and his moments with Brandt were filled with awkward silences and pained undercurrents, nothing like the journey east had been, even at its worst moments.

The night before they were to reach Sannfold, Evin came to Ryn outside the inn as she watched the sun set and let the last of its warmth soak into her skin. She'd had trouble getting truly, pleasantly warm since her near death, and she relished every bit of heat she could get. She ran her fingers mournfully over her shieldenstone, feeling her skin catch over the new ragged edges where red-purple crystals peeked through. Evin sat beside her on the grass, pressing his leather-clad shoulder to hers. Ryn tensed for a moment, but when he didn't move, she relaxed. They sat like that for several minutes. Evin placed a hand over Ryn's on the head of her staff.

"Your stone?" he asked. Ryn swallowed the lump in her throat.

"It cracked when I…in the Beast's lair," she answered, carefully glossing over the details of Brandt's healing. She hadn't told her friends about stealing from her own life force; she didn't expect Evin—or Brandt, for that matter—would respond to news like that very well. She was sure the broken stone and pouring her own life into someone else were related.

Kenelm would *kill* her.

"Does it still work?" Evin's question took her by surprise a little; she wasn't used to someone…caring. She nodded.

"I think so. I checked on Brandt's health with my Sight the other day and it worked just fine."

Evin nodded and squeezed her hand, letting go with a sigh. They sat in silence for a few moments, letting the birdsong fill the quiet. After a while, Evin stirred.

"I'm not going home," he confessed softly. Ryn sat up and twisted to look at him.

"What?"

"I'm not going back to Sannfold," he confirmed. "I cannot do it, not yet. I need time."

She thought for a moment, then asked, "Where will you go?"

He looked lost.

"Come with me," she offered. "We make a good team, you and me and Kota." And Brandt, she wanted to add, but thought that might not help the situation. Evin nodded.

"I would like that."

"I have to stop in Sannfold first," she said. "Meet me by the big oak south of the city, at the foot of Mount Aldnast, in three days. We will go south together."

He was gone in the morning, Kota with him. Ryn had sent the lynx to guard him until they met again. She and Brandt continued at daybreak, joining the foot traffic that led into the largest city in Laendor. It wasn't long before Brandt was recognized, and an impromptu parade led them to the castle, where he was greeted by his Uncle Eirik warmly.

Ryn studied the King while he embraced his nephew. He was young still, not yet in his fiftieth year, though his auburn hair was already streaked with a few light grays. His blue eyes were stern, though his lips wore a ready smile at the sight of his Heir, and his words to Brandt were warm and kind. He looked about, behind Brandt, a moment later and his brow furrowed when he did not see Evin. He looked to Brandt, question on his tongue, and the elder just shook his head.

Eirik asked no more questions, only led them all inside and ordered a great feast be prepared to celebrate the Crown Prince's triumphant return. Ryn begged Brandt not to make her stay for that, so he escorted her to the archives and introduced her to the old, severe-looking Tomeskeeper, giving the man instruction to help her with whatever she needed. She told him the record she wished to view, and he disappeared with a swift bow.

When the man left, Brandt caught her hands in both of his own. "I will not see you again, will I?"

She forced a smile, surprised how the thought of leaving him behind made her heart ache. "You will," she assured him, believing it. "I cannot say when, but you will."

Brandt swallowed, eyes moving to his feet before coming back up to meet her steady gaze. She recognized his behavior as similar to the night he'd told her of Evin's parentage, and knew he was fighting tears. His face showed nothing but naked pain as he implored her, "Guard my brother, Ryn. Guard him with your life."

On impulse, Ryn pulled him to her with all her strength. "You know I will." She kissed his cheek, then turned as the Tomeskeeper arrived again.

When she looked back, Brandt was gone.

ABOUT THE AUTHOR

Megan Graham is a Colorado native who loves reading, music, and movies. Her hobbies include hiking, camping, and anything that involves stomping around in the back country of the Colorado Rockies. Adopted at an early age, she grew up the eldest of four. She and her siblings were highly encouraged to read as children, and she became a voracious fan of the printed word. Her parents also taught their children that creativity was a vital part of the human experience, and the four of them became successful vocalists. The Graham Family Singers sang over 300 times in 13 states during Megan's childhood, and she continues to sing today, releasing covers on platforms such as iTunes and Spotify. She is in the process of writing her very first original album, along with a sequel to this novel. Megan lives in Denver, with her best friend, parents, three cats, and two dogs.

Made in the USA
San Bernardino, CA
14 April 2018